Eloise had almo̶st̶ ̶[...] when she spied [...]

He came out of the Old Towne Books and Coffee shop with a pastry box in one hand. After a full-body stretch and yawn, he adjusted his straw cowboy hat on his head. He looked every inch the cowboy. A giant bear of a cowboy, maybe. His black T-shirt clung just enough to emphasize his broad shoulders.

Not that I care about his shoulders.

She didn't. And she didn't want him to see her there—not caring—so she needed to get a move on...

But he turned and saw her. Even from here, she saw him hesitate. Then he smiled. And it was infuriating. He might not know it, but last night he'd poked at her biggest insecurity: that she was a bad mom.

He lifted a hand in acknowledgment and took a step in her direction.

No. No way. Her morning had gone from sunny and hopeful to hot and tense, and it was all thanks to him. She spun on her heel and headed, double-time, around the corner and as far away from Mike Woodard as possible.

Dear Reader,

It's been a while since our last visit to Garrison, Texas—and I'm so happy to be back. We've had engagements and babies and weddings and festivals, and we're just getting started.

Mike Woodard has his hands full. One of the only EMTs in the county, Mike balances his time between work, volunteering as a rodeo pickup rider and caring for his father.

Eloise Green is still trying to find her footing in Garrison, and she worries over her children. Her daughter, Kirby, is an upbeat, precocious five-year-old, while seven-year-old Archie is often tense and anxious.

When she's reunited with the boy—now a ridiculously handsome cowboy—who betrayed her trust and shattered her heart, she's surprised by how raw those wounds still are. She can be neighborly, as is expected in a small town, but she won't befriend him. No matter how many times they're thrown together, how much the kids love his dog, or how kind and loving he is with his father, she'll keep her guard up. At least she'll try.

Until our next Garrison adventure, stay well and read happy!

Sasha Summers

HEARTWARMING

Home to Her Cowboy

—

Sasha Summers

HARLEQUIN®
HEARTWARMING™

ISBN-13: 978-1-335-47580-0

Recycling programs for this product may not exist in your area.

Home to Her Cowboy

Copyright © 2024 by Sasha Best

All rights reserved. No part of this book may be used or reproduced in any manner whatsoever without written permission except in the case of brief quotations embodied in critical articles and reviews.

This is a work of fiction. Names, characters, places and incidents are either the product of the author's imagination or are used fictitiously. Any resemblance to actual persons, living or dead, businesses, companies, events or locales is entirely coincidental.

For questions and comments about the quality of this book, please contact us at CustomerService@Harlequin.com.

TM and ® are trademarks of Harlequin Enterprises ULC.

Harlequin Enterprises ULC
22 Adelaide St. West, 41st Floor
Toronto, Ontario M5H 4E3, Canada
www.Harlequin.com

Printed in U.S.A.

Sasha Summers grew up surrounded by books. Her passions have always been storytelling, romance and travel—passions she's used to write more than twenty romance novels and novellas. Now a bestselling and award-winning author, Sasha continues to fall a little in love with each hero she writes. From easy-on-the-eyes cowboys to sexy alpha-male werewolves to heroes of truly mythic proportions, she believes that everyone should have their happily-ever-after—in fiction and real life.

Sasha lives in the suburbs of the Texas Hill Country with her amazing family. She looks forward to hearing from fans and hopes you'll visit her online: on Facebook at sashasummersauthor, on Twitter @sashawrites or email her at sashasummersauthor@gmail.com.

Books by Sasha Summers

Harlequin Heartwarming

The Cowboys of Garrison, Texas

The Rebel Cowboy's Baby
The Wrong Cowboy
To Trust a Cowboy

Harlequin Special Edition

Texas Cowboys & K-9s

The Rancher's Forever Family
Their Rancher Protector
The Rancher's Baby Surprise
The Rancher's Full House
A Snowbound Christmas Cowboy

Visit the Author Profile page
at Harlequin.com for more titles.

Dedicated to my precious mother, Jeannie,
who supports everything I do (and write)!
I love you so!

CHAPTER ONE

ELOISE TUCKED A strand of wavy brown hair behind her ear and offered the blue-and-white stoneware bowl to her five-year-old daughter, Kirby—and held her breath. Her daughter's resistance to eating anything green had become a nightly battle. "One spoonful."

"Peas." Kirby wrinkled up her little freckled nose and leaned back in her chair, crossing her arms over her chest. "Peas are icky. And squishy. And gross."

"They *are* mushy, Mom." Archie, her seven-year-old son, nodded. "They also look like rabbit poop." He announced this lovely tidbit of information without breaking a grin.

Really? Where did he come up with this stuff? Eloise stifled a smile and ignored her grandfather's muffled laugh. Archie was hysterical—which made it hard to stand her ground on important things like eating vegetables, bedtimes, and not harassing Grandpa Quincy's sweet cat, Dandelion.

"Rabbit poop?" Kirby squeaked and pushed her

plate away. *"Ew."* This word was drawn out—for full effect.

"Yep. A spoonful of peas is like a little pile of poop," Archie went on. "But rabbit poop isn't green." He paused, pushing his glasses up on his nose. "Is it?"

"Archie." Eloise tried to sound stern. "Let's not talk about rabbit poop at the dinner table."

Archie nodded, scooping mashed potatoes onto his fork then pausing to ask, "What about whale poop?"

Grandpa Quincy didn't cover his laugh this time. He had a big, booming laugh that was impossible to resist. Archie started to giggle. Then Kirby. Even though she wasn't thrilled over why they were laughing, she loved the sound of it.

When they'd quieted down, Eloise said, "No." She eyed the peas and set the bowl aside. "No poop talk, of any kind, at the dinner table."

"It's okay if you don't like 'em, Freckles. I do." Grandpa Quincy reached for the bowl. "I'll take a big ol' helping of peas."

Eloise smiled and handed over the bowl. "There's plenty."

Kirby sat, slouched in her chair, staring at her plate. Her big mossy green eyes—the same color as Eloise's—narrowed as her frown grew.

"Come on, Freckles." Grandpa Quincy used his most encouraging tone. "Eat up those yummy mashed taters and your momma's crispy fried chicken. If you do, I might have a pink cupcake for dessert."

As much as she appreciated her grandfather's support, offering them sugar this close to bedtime guaranteed chaos.

Kirby perked up, her brown ponytails swinging. "With sprinkles?"

"Yup." Grandpa Quincy winked. "Pink *and* white ones."

Kirby clapped her hands.

"All you have to do is eat up your dinner first." He pointed at her plate with his fork.

Kirby's nose wrinkled again but she picked up her fork, scooped up some potatoes, then let them fall—splat—back onto her plate.

"She doesn't like mashed potatoes." Archie took a big bite of mashed potatoes.

Surprise. Since they'd moved in with Grandpa Quincy, her daughter's list of food she would eat continued to shrink. Kirby had always been on the slight side. Her lack of caloric intake was something Eloise worried over—on top of all the other things she worried over. She wouldn't push the mashed potatoes, but Kirby had to eat *something*. Other than cupcakes, that is.

"Your fried chicken is like one big chicken nugget." Eloise hoped Kirby would buy her sales pitch. Chicken nuggets were still one of the things Kirby would always eat. "Here." She pulled Kirby's plate closer, cut the fried chicken breast into small pieces, and slid the plate back in front of her daughter. "See? Now it's just like home-made chicken nuggets."

Kirby's eyes narrowed and she sucked in her cheeks as she leaned forward to inspect her mother's handiwork.

Eloise—Grandpa Quincy and Archie, too—waited to see what happened next.

"'Kay." Kirby speared a piece of chicken and ate it. Then another piece. "Yum. This is so good, Momma." She chewed with enthusiasm. "Yum-yum-yum." She murmured around her mouthful of food.

"Right? It is good chicken." Unlike his sister, Archie would eat almost anything.

Grandpa Quincy nodded. "Your momma is a good cook. If she cooks it, I'm going to eat it."

Eloise had always enjoyed cooking. Growing up, she'd spent some holidays and one week every summer here with her grandparents. She'd helped out with countless meals in Gramma Beryl's kitchen. Cooking had been her gramma's love language and she'd had a lot of love to give. When Eloise had been too young to cook, Gramma Beryl sat her on a stool to snap beans or shuck corn and watch and learn. When she was a little older, she'd been allowed to peel potatoes or pound the steak until it was the perfect thickness to batter and fry. Later, she'd mastered perfect cream gravy, smooth-as-silk mashed potatoes, flaky and sweet pie crust, and iced tea.

"We've got a big wedding coming up this weekend. Your momma gets to work her magic and make beautiful flower arrangements for the ceremony and the bride." Grandpa Quincy owned Garrison Gardens, the only flower shop in Garrison. "Warden Hattie Carmichael is marrying Forrest Briscoe. I remember when she was a little thing, all braces and red hair and freckles—"

"Freckles like Kirby?" Archie asked.

Kirby was very proud of her freckles.

"Only Kirby doesn't have red hair. She has brown hair. Like me and mom."

"No one has freckles like our Kirby." Grandpa Quincy grinned. "They're good people. The both of them. Truth be told, I can't imagine a better matched pair. It's nice when good things happen to good people."

Grandpa Quincy, a lifelong Garrison resident, knew everyone and everything about his hometown. She was still learning the names and faces of Garrison, but she'd managed to piece together some things from her childhood visits. She knew the Briscoe and Crawley families owned the two largest cattle ranches in these parts—and had a lot of influence in town. The Schneiders owned Garrison Family Grocer's and were, in Grandpa Quincy's words, good folk. Garrison even had its own celebrity in retired country singer Buck Williams—now owner of Buck's Bar and Honky-Tonk.

Grandpa Quincy had warned her about one group in particular. According to him, the Garrison Ladies Guild were a bunch of gossipy do-gooders "with too much time on their hands." He'd gone on to say their leader, Miss Martha Zeigler, was apparently prickly, opinionated, and "entirely too much."

Eloise had yet to do much exploring for herself. Between the kids, sorting through the mess of paperwork her ex-husband had left for her to deal with, and working at Garrison Gardens with her grandfather, it was hard to carve out an hour for herself beyond her early morning walk.

"Will the bride wear a big white dress?" Kirby asked, looking hopeful.

"Hattie?" Grandpa Quincy chuckled. "She's not one for dress wearing but…maybe. I guess we'll see, won't we?"

Fortunately—or unfortunately—their family had received an invitation to the event. Which meant she'd have to keep an eye on the kids while she and her grandfather set up the flowers for the ceremony *and* she'd have to hope they'd behave through the ceremony and reception.

The good news was the ceremony was outdoors. Both the wedding and the reception were to be held under Garrison's beloved legendary tree, erste Baum. The tree, sometimes called the First

Tree, was purported to be the oldest in Texas. Seeing it firsthand, Eloise could believe it. The tree's canopy was massive, providing shade for a large gathering—like the wedding that would be taking place this weekend.

"Need help, Momma?" Kirby loved flowers. "I can help."

"Of course you can, Freckles." Grandpa Quincy nodded.

Kirby smiled broadly, then ate the last bite of chicken.

Grandpa Quincy pointed at her plate. "You did good, Freckles. Ate all your chicken up."

"Can I have more, Momma?" Kirby asked, holding out her plate.

More? "Of course." Eloise slid another chicken breast onto her daughter's plate, cut it into small pieces, then slid the plate back to Kirby.

"Momma... I need you to sign a paper from Miss Ramirez." Archie pushed his glasses up and glanced her way.

She knew that expression. It was his I'm-in-trouble-please-don't-be-too-mad face. "Oh?" Miss Ramirez was Archie's second-grade teacher. Since kindergarten, Archie's talkative and inquisitive nature had him sitting right next to his teacher's desk. By the end of the year, Eloise knew his teachers well. He wasn't a bad kid; it was the opposite. He was charming and well-liked—just like his father—but he was a talker. "What about?"

"Well…you know." He shrugged, shoving an extra-large forkful of mashed potatoes into his mouth.

Eloise exchanged a look with her grandfather.

"He was talking," Kirby said, devouring her chicken. "Again. Lots and lots."

"Archie." Eloise set her fork down. "We've covered this, hon. There's a time and a place for talking, right?"

He nodded.

"I know it's hard and you're still making friends, but you have to listen to your teacher. It's disrespectful to talk over her—or interrupt during lessons. When it's free time or you're on the playground, talk all you want." Eloise stopped then. The kids, like her, were still adjusting to their surroundings. And, so far, they were doing well. Archie was talking too much, but it could be worse. At least he was being himself—not clamming up or acting out in a destructive way. It was, in a weird way, a relief that he was his chatty self. "Bring me the paper after dinner and I'll sign it, okay?"

"Yes, ma'am." Archie had lost one of his front teeth, giving him a jack-o'-lantern grin. "It's so hard. Words just sort of…come out. But I'll try harder, Momma, I promise."

"Thank you." She couldn't resist that grin of

his. "Everyone done?" She waited for them to nod. "Archie, go on and pick out your clothes for tomorrow. Kirby, get your nightie and I'll be in the bathroom to get your bath started in a sec."

The kids scurried from the room, and Eloise started to clear the table.

"You look tired, El." Grandpa Quincy stood, helping her carry the plates and cups into the kitchen. "You worry too much. Kirby and Archie are happy little things. You're doing real good with them, you hear? Just breathe."

Grandpa Quincy always saw the bright side of things. She tended to be a realist. "Thanks, Grandpa."

"I swear, little Kirby looks so much like you did at that age." He kissed her temple. "And I like peas—even if they do look like rabbit poop." He chuckled, stacking the plates by the sink. "I got this. You go on and get them tucked in and we can watch the news together. Maybe some of that game show, too."

She smiled up at her grandfather. Grandpa Quincy's evening routine meant watching the nightly news and the latest episode of *Wheel of Fortune* that he recorded daily. Now that was her nightly routine, too. "You're sure?"

He nodded.

"Okay, thanks." She headed down the hallway to the bathroom. The door was closed but she heard Kirby's squeal, Archie mumble something, and a cabinet door slam. The two of them were up to something, she just knew it. She took a deep breath and pushed the door wide.

There, on the bathroom floor, was a towel and an empty bottle of Benadryl. A bottle that had been mostly full and should have been locked in the medicine cabinet... Kirby and Archie both spun to face her, their hands behind their backs.

She eyed the empty bottle. "Guys. What happened to the medicine?"

Archie and Kirby exchanged looks. *Guilty* looks.

Her lungs went tight. "Archie?" she repeated, panic welling.

"I...I drank it." Kirby spoke quickly. "I did it."

"You what?" Eloise's heart slammed to a stop, then kicked into overdrive. This was bad. This was really bad. Kirby was so tiny... "Grandpa," she called out, crossing to her daughter. "Grandpa, call 911. Tell them to hurry. Kirby drank an entire bottle of Benadryl." She squatted on the floor, terrified, and tugged her daughter into her arms. *Please, hurry. Please.*

There was nothing Mike Woodard dreaded more than a call concerning children. Nothing. Now he had pulled up in front of Quincy Green's garden-like front yard, preparing for the worst. He grabbed his bag, jumped from the ambulance, and ran to the open front door.

"I'm right behind you." Terri, Mike's partner, called after him.

Mike nodded, the protocol for an overdose scrolling through his mind. Luckily, it didn't happen all that often around these parts. But this, a little kid, didn't always have a happy ending. Adrenaline was coursing through his veins, preparing him for what was to come.

"Mikey." Quincy Green stood in the open front door. "Bathroom." He pointed down the hall, his expression taut and his pallor gray.

He nodded and ran in the direction Quincy indicated. "EMT." He pulled on a pair of gloves as he scanned the room.

A young boy sat on the bathroom floor, his face covered with his hands. A young girl was quietly crying while a woman—mom, most likely—wiped the girl's face with a washcloth.

"She drank a bottle of Benadryl." The woman didn't look at him as she held out the bottle. From the rigid posture to the waver in her voice, it was clear the woman was barely holding on. "It was almost full."

A *whole* bottle? "How long ago?" Mike moved closer, taking the little girl's pulse and flashing a penlight in her eyes. So far, all the girl's vitals were normal.

"Maybe seven minutes?" The woman eased her hold on the little girl. "Her name is Kirby."

"Kirby." Mike offered up a smile. "Hey there. I'm here to help you."

Kirby wasn't buying it. She leaned into her mother and shook her head. "Momma."

"It's okay, Kirby." The woman patted her back. "We need to do whatever he says, okay? That medicine could make you really sick."

If this little girl had ingested an entire bottle of Benadryl, things were more dire than that. There was no time to waste.

"But medicine is supposed to make you better." Kirby's lower lip wobbled.

"It does." Mike nodded. "But only when you're sick. And only a little bit." He pulled open his bag.

"What do we do?" the woman asked. "What do I do?"

Now wasn't the time to assign blame to the woman. *But* he couldn't help wondering how the kids had access to the medicine. A parent's top priority should be keeping their children safe. "We need to go for a ride in the ambulance." He glanced behind him to find his partner, Terri, waiting outside the bathroom with the gurney.

"Of course." The woman stood, lifting Kirby. "And then?"

Terri headed into the room. "We'll pump her stomach—"

"Pump my stomach?" Kirby squeaked. "Pump?" The little girl stared at her brother, panicking. "Archie!"

"I did it." The boy jumped up. "Not Kirby."

"You did what? *You* drank the medicine?" Their mother turned, her forehead creasing. "Archie." Her voice broke. "You have to tell the truth." She looked back and forth between them. "Both of you. *Now.*"

Mike frowned. "Kids, this is serious. We need to know exactly what happened. We can't afford to waste time." He and Terri exchanged looks.

"I thought it was shampoo." Archie pointed at the bottle on the counter. "And Grandpa Quincy said he needed to give Dandelion a bath with his special cat medicine shampoo." He looked over at his sister. "So, me and Kirby wanted to be nice and give Dandelion a bath for Grandpa and we used the medicine to give him a bath."

Mike was lost.

"We need to get her to the hospital." Terri was right.

"Let's go." Mike gestured to the gurney.

"Wait." Archie, the boy, grabbed his arm. "Kirby didn't drink it. Really. Me, neither." He ran across the room and opened a bathroom cabinet. "See. She doesn't need to get pumped. She doesn't."

"I don't," Kirby wailed. "I really don't."

Inside the cabinet was the most pathetic-looking cat he'd ever seen. The poor thing was shivering, it's gray-and-white fur covered in goopy, purple liquid.

Mike frowned, processing the boy's words.

"You washed the cat in Benadryl?" He scratched the back of his neck. This was a first.

The cat let out a pitiful meow.

"It's medicine." Kirby sniffled. "Dandelion needs medicine shampoo."

"Poor Dandelion," Quincy Green said, peering around the doorframe.

It might have been Mike's imagination but it sounded like Quincy Green was trying not to laugh.

"You didn't drink any of it? You're sure?" Terri asked, hesitant.

"No." Archie shook his head. "I didn't. My sister didn't. We didn't. Really. We're sure, aren't we, Kirby?"

"No way. It tastes nasty." Kirby stuck out her tongue.

From the puddle of purple-stickiness the cat was sitting in and how saturated the feline was, Mike believed them.

The kids' mother slumped against the bathroom counter, looking stunned, as tears started streaming down her cheeks. "You two…" All the color drained from her face as she let Kirby go.

"I'm sorry, Momma." Archie did *look* sorry.

"Me, too." Kirby sniffed. "Do I have to have my tummy pumped?"

"Not if you didn't drink it?" Mike had to be sure.

"Not one drop." Kirby nodded.

"This isn't funny. It's serious business," the kids' mom added, her voice breaking.

Both children nodded.

"Promise we didn't do it, Momma." Kirby hugged the woman's leg. "I'm sorry."

"I'd say they're telling the truth." Terri squatted by the open cabinet and was studying the cat. "Might want to give your veterinarian a call, Quincy. Make sure the cat's going to be okay."

"Will do. Best see what we can do for Dandelion." Quincy came into the bathroom. "Come here, sweet girl." He reached into the cabinet and lifted the cat. Strands of the congealed medicine dripped from the cat to the interior of the cabinet. "You definitely need a bath now."

Dandelion offered up another pathetic meow.

"We're sorry, Grandpa," Archie mumbled.

"You two are going to help Grandpa." Archie's mom said. "And clean this up."

"Yes, Momma." Archie followed his grandfather from the bathroom.

"Me, too. Me, too. Poor, poor Dandelion." Kirby ran after them.

"Well…" Mike wasn't sure what to say. To say he was relieved was an understatement. But it was more than that. Times like this challenged his professionalism. What could have happened tightened his stomach… Snatches of his own childhood surfaced and made things ten times worse. Which didn't help. He took a deep breath.

Tonight had a happy ending. That was a win. That's what he needed to focus on.

"I'll put the gurney up and start the paperwork." Terri was smiling as she pushed the wheeled bed back down the hall.

"I'm sorry to have caused a fuss over nothing." The woman ran a shaking hand over her face. "I...I panicked."

"Calling was the right thing to do." It was. But none of this should have happened to begin with. "I've got some papers for you to sign. And...a few pamphlets on how to safely store medicine and poisons in the house so your children won't have access to it." He pulled off his gloves.

For the first time, her gaze focused. "Excuse me?"

There was something familiar about the woman—something he couldn't quite pinpoint. "Well, ma'am." He paused, trying to keep his voice even and calm. "The best thing to do is take steps to stop these sorts of things from happening." He chose his words with care. If he started laying blame at her feet, she'd get defensive and stop listening. But his job wasn't just to provide life-saving measures, it was also to educate folk. As much as he'd like to think tonight's scare was lesson enough, he wasn't going to count on that.

"These sorts of things?" She blinked, her words tight. "You have a pamphlet that prevents kids from washing a cat with Benadryl?"

"No." He was amused, in spite of himself. "Mostly, it's about prevention. Accidents can happen, of course, but there are things we can do to reduce the chances."

There was a moment of strained silence before she said, "I can assure you this has never happened before and it won't happen again, Mr..."

He'd give her the benefit of the doubt—this time. But he was still leaving the brochures. "Woodard." He held his hand out. "Mike Woodard."

Her gaze widened, fixed on his face, before she blinked, drew a deep breath, then shook his hand. "Eloise... Green." It was a mere whisper. "I—I appreciate your quick response."

"Eloise?" He swallowed. *Little El Bell?* He hadn't thought about her in years... That was after the years it had taken to get over the hurt she'd caused. Now, here she was. And he was reeling.

"Yes... Hi..." She ran a hand over her thick, brown hair. "As you can see, this was all a misunderstanding."

Right. Business. What had *almost* happened here tonight. He cleared his throat and said, "I'm glad it played out the way it did." The kids were fine, that was what mattered most.

Eloise's kids. He was still trying to wrap his mind around the fact that this was Eloise. The last time he'd seen her, there'd been tears and heartbreak and now...she was here. And he didn't know how to feel about it. He shouldn't *feel* anything—period.

Her gaze, a mossy green he remembered so well, swept over his face. "I do know that this is my fault. And, clearly, you feel the same way. I can see it." She pointed at his face, her posture stiffening. "Thank you for not denying it."

She was calling him out? And he was speechless. But, if memory served, she'd always been on the sassy side. In fact, that's what Quincy had called her back then. *Sassy.*

"You mentioned something about papers?" Eloise asked, brushing past him and heading down the hall to the front door. "I'm sure you have other people to help... And judge." She crossed her arms over her chest and stared up at him, eyes flashing.

It had been years, but hearing her accuse him of being judgy was like the pot calling the kettle black. All he could do was stare back at her.

"Mikey." Quincy came down the hall. "Hold up." He held out his hand. "Thanks for helping out."

"No problem." He shook the older man's hand. "How's Dandelion?" His gaze darted back to Eloise, who was looking everywhere but him.

"Vet said to keep an eye on her. If she gets groggy, to call again." He shook his head. "She's clean—the kids are drying her off. They feel pretty bad. But I know they meant well." He cleared his throat then. "I feel terrible, El. I thought I'd locked that bottle up. I told you I would and I forgot."

"Grandpa." Eloise placed a hand on his arm. "It's all okay."

"No, now, it's not." Quincy took an unsteady breath. "It's not. You put in all those locks and hooks and such to keep them safe and I… Well, I need to be more careful with the kids around."

"It's okay, Grandpa. Having us underfoot is a big adjustment." Eloise hugged him. "Tonight was tough for all of us."

And just like that, Mike felt lower than dirt. Quincy's words offered a very different viewpoint on the evening's events. Eloise *had* done her due diligence as a parent *and* she was giving her grandfather grace and forgiveness for what could have been a potentially tragic evening.

He'd been quick to pin it all on Eloise, and it left a bad taste in his mouth and a knot in his gut. Immediately blaming her had nothing to do with what happened here tonight and everything to do with his own childhood. Assuming anyone—even Eloise—was like his mother was just plain wrong.

Quincy squeezed her shoulder as he let her go, glancing between Mike and his granddaughter. "I'm guessing you two remember each other?"

Eloise didn't look his way. "Vaguely."

Vaguely? If the edge to her voice hadn't rubbed him the wrong way, he'd have laughed.

Quincy chuckled. "It has been a while. I'd say

ten or more years? A lot has happened between then and now."

It was closer to fifteen years, but he only said, "Isn't that the truth."

"Eloise and her kids—my great-grandkids—Kirby and Archie are living with me now." Quincy beamed as he said this, draping an arm around Eloise's shoulders. "I've got a full house again."

Mike had heard something about Quincy taking in his grandkids. People in a small town liked to talk—especially about new arrivals. It hadn't occurred to him that it was Eloise and her kids. He couldn't help but notice Quincy hadn't mentioned anything about the kids' father. Not that it mattered one way or the other. "Welcome *back* to Garrison."

She seemed to ignore his greeting. "I'm sure you're regretting the invitation, Grandpa."

Quincy chuckled. "Oh now, El. You wouldn't believe the chaos your mother and uncles got into growing up. Let me tell you, this is nothing."

"Here." Terri arrived, a clipboard in hand. "We just need a few signatures." She handed the clipboard to Eloise, flipping the page for more signatures. "And here." She flipped to another page. "We're out of poison control pamphlets, Mike—I looked." She took the clipboard Eloise offered. With a nod, she headed back to the ambulance.

He didn't miss the narrow-eyed glare Eloise sent his way.

Quincy scratched his chin. "How about you bring your pamphlets by tomorrow afternoon? Sit on the porch, have some tea, and talk a spell? El, here, makes perfect iced tea."

Mike heard the slight hiss of Eloise's indrawn breath. If there'd been any doubt of the woman's displeasure at her grandfather's suggestion, one look at her pinched face cleared that right up. But once Quincy Green looked her way, she was all smiles. And what a smile.

Eloise Green had been a pretty girl and now she was a fine-looking woman. "Tomorrow?" Mike found himself nodding. Why was he saying yes? She didn't want him here. He didn't want to be here, either. "I should have time to drop them by."

"Good." Quincy clapped him on the shoulder. "Maybe you'll have time for tea, too."

There was no denying the flash in Eloise's eyes. "Can't wait."

He'd been a jerk tonight, that was true, but any apology stuck in his throat. "I'll see you then." Mike gave her a tight smile and headed back to the ambulance. Tomorrow, he'd force himself to apologize and leave well enough alone. Now that he knew Eloise Green was back in Garrison, he could do his best to make sure their paths wouldn't cross. He was already bracing himself for tomorrow's visit.

CHAPTER TWO

ELOISE KEPT UP her rapid pace as she rounded the corner and headed back up Main Street. The sun was just up, the birds were singing, and cars were beginning to park in front of the Buttermilk Pie Café for breakfast. She scanned the shop windows, reading about sales and upcoming events until one flyer caught her eye.

Hill Country Dance Studio was advertising a Ladies Only Stretch and Yoga class. It sounded like the perfect stress reliever. And, maybe, a way to make friends. She loved her kids and her grandfather, but she was lonely. Not that she had the time—or money to pay for it.

Since her ex-husband, Ted, had been incarcerated, Eloise had lost all of her friends. Not that she could blame them. Ted had managed to get most of their friends and family to invest in his *business*. When the Texas Criminal Investigations Division got involved and Ted's not-so-legit company led to fraud and embezzlement charges, those friends and family lost thousands of dollars, retirement capital, summer homes, and kids' college education funds.

While Eloise had been oblivious to Ted's dealings, not everyone believed that. How could they? She and Ted had seemed so devoted—so in sync with each other. Eloise had thought so, too, until she learned he had a mistress. That was why she'd divorced him. And that was months before everything else came out and he was arrested.

What a joke.

When it came to deceit, Ted's mistress had only been the tip of the iceberg.

No matter what anyone else said, the only thing she was truly guilty of was believing her husband.

No, that's not entirely true. She'd known better but she'd still given Ted her trust. She'd wanted to believe he loved her. That he'd be there for her and support her, no matter what. But wanting something didn't make it real. That's how she'd ended up here—with no one to blame except herself.

Then last night happened… What could have happened turned her blood cold.

She *was* guilty. It was her fault. Thanks to Mike and his big blue I'm-judging-you eyes, it was indelibly etched on her brain. She'd messed up and there was no forgiving herself. If her father and Ted had taught her anything, it was not to trust anyone—Grandpa Quincy included.

Mike Woodard. It was hard to reconcile the sharp-eyed giant of a man with the big-hearted, fun-loving little Mikey she'd believed him to be. There was a time she'd thought he was special. She was wrong, of course. And that wake-up call had pulverized her heart.

It had been an insult to injury that he'd been the one to come in to save the day—and he was bringing her pamphlets to hold her accountable. As if her guilt wasn't real and heavy enough.

"Good morning." A woman stood at the door of the dance studio, keys jangling in her hand. With her long blond hair and sunny smile, she was one of those women who was effortlessly beautiful.

"Morning." Eloise was very aware of her too-big shirt, sloppy bun, and the twenty pounds she'd put on over the last six months. She'd never been eye-catching. Average was more like it and she was okay with that. No, it took effort for Eloise to feel attractive—effort she hadn't put in to go on her morning walk.

"I'm Gretta Williams." The woman introduced herself.

"Nice to meet you. I'm Eloise Green." She ran a hand over her off-center bun.

"I couldn't help but notice—are you interested in the new class?" Gretta shifted the strap of her canvas tote and slid the key in the lock.

"I am." But Eloise wasn't going to get her hopes up. "It's just… I have kids."

"I get it." Gretta laughed. "I have one and he's more than enough. Between running this place and keeping up with him, it's hard to practice self-care."

Eloise smiled. *Self-care? What's that?*

"I'm trying to figure out some sort of a day-care option. I mean, I figure moms would benefit the most." Gretta pulled the door open. "Want to come in? I can make some coffee?"

As much as she wanted to, one look at her watch told her she was running out of time. "I wish but the kids will be up soon. They're a lot for my grandpa to handle on his own."

"Gotcha." Gretta paused. "Single mom, too? It's hard. My dad tries to help but... Well, it's hard."

Too? Meaning this gorgeous woman was a single mom? Eloise probably shouldn't be so excited by this information, but she was. "Yes. It is. Yes."

"Well, now, I really have to figure out a baby-sitter option and let you know."

She laughed.

"How can I reach you?" Gretta smiled.

"Garrison Gardens. That's my grandpa's flower shop. And me, now." She shrugged.

"That's right around the corner. That's great. I'll definitely let you know." She waved. "Have a great day, Eloise."

"You, too. It was really nice to meet you, Gretta." Eloise waved and headed toward home, an extra spring in her step. She and the kids had been here for almost two months now and this was her first interaction with an adult that hadn't centered around a flower order, the kids, or making sure the cashier applied all the coupons the kids and Grandpa Quincy cut out of every Sunday morning newspaper.

She'd almost reached the corner when she spied Mike Woodard. He came out of the Old Towne Books and Coffee shop with a pastry box in one hand. After a full body stretch and yawn, he adjusted his straw cowboy hat on his head. He looked every inch the cowboy. A giant bear of a cowboy, maybe. His black T-shirt clung just enough to emphasize his broad shoulders.

Not that I care about his shoulders.

She didn't. And she didn't want him to see her there—not caring—so she realized she'd better get a move on—

But he turned and saw her.

Why am I frozen? Even from here, she saw him hesitate. Then he… What? He smiled? And it was infuriating. He might not know it but he'd poked at her biggest insecurity: that she was a bad mom.

He lifted a hand in acknowledgment and took a step in her direction.

No. No way. Her morning had gone from sunny and hopeful to irritated and tense, and it was all thanks to him. She spun on her heel and headed, double-time, around the corner and as far away from Mike Woodard as possible. Her near-jog pace had her home in record time—and gasping for breath.

"Momma?" Kirby called out, running down the hall to greet her at the front door. "You're all red."

"I'm fine," she said, panting.

Kirby took her hand. "You're hot and sweaty, too."

"Sorry." It was possible she'd overreacted. And was out of shape.

"It's okay. Come on." Kirby tugged her down the hall to the kitchen. "Look."

There, on the round kitchen table, was one of her mother's china platters covered in a pile of waffles. There was a bowl of fresh fruit, four cups of orange juice, and a steaming mug of coffee by her usual chair.

"What's all this?" she asked, still breathing hard.

"Land sakes, El, you're as red as a beet." Grandpa Quincy looked alarmed. "Take a seat, won't you?"

"I told her." Kirby nodded. "She's so, *so* red."

Archie came over to assess her. "Wow, Momma. Are you sick?"

"No." She took a deep breath, willing her breathing into a pseudo-normal pattern. "But I need to exercise more."

There was a knock on the front door and Eloise froze.

He would not *have followed her. Surely not.*

There was another knock followed by the telltale squeak of the front door's hinges. "Quincy?

It's Mike." His voice rang down the hall. A strong, slightly amused voice.

"Come on in," her grandpa called out.

He would and he had.

"Morning, Mikey." Grandpa Quincy headed to the door. "Come on down. El here might need your medical attention."

She was mortified. "Grandpa." Here she was, a red-faced, heaving, sweaty mess, about to face the man she'd literally panicked over and run away from.

"Is that so?" His voice was closer, the sound of his boots on the wooden floor louder and louder. Until he was standing in the kitchen door—a large red dog at his side. "Good morning. I'm happy to be of service."

Good was not how she'd describe her current state of mind. She stared at the toes of her neon green walking shoes.

"Dad heard about what happened and wanted me to bring over some pastries." There was something warm about Mike's voice.

"Well, that was mighty neighborly," Grandpa Quincy said. "Why not have a seat and have some breakfast?"

"We made Momma an 'I'm sorry' breakfast." Kirby studied Mike for a minute before asking, "Are you a cowboy and a doctor man?"

"I guess I am." Mike was smiling, she could hear it in his voice.

"Is your name Mr. Mike or Mr. Mikey?" Kirby asked.

"Mr. Mike. Only old folk like me and his daddy still call him Mikey." Quincy chuckled.

"And my brother." Mike shook his head. "He gets a real kick out of it."

"Is that your dog?" Archie loved dogs. "Can I pet him? What's his name? What kind of dog is he?" He took a deep breath. "Is it a boy or a girl? Does he like waffles 'cuz we have lots of waffles."

"Archie." She reached out and took her son's hand. "One thing at a time."

Archie shoved his glasses up on his nose. "Sorry, Mr. Mike, sir. I like dogs."

"No apologies necessary. I like dogs, too." Mike chuckled. "His name is Clifford—"

"Like the big red dog?" Kirby was ecstatic. She loved the *Clifford the Big Red Dog* books.

Eloise made the mistake of glancing Mike's way.

"Yup." He patted the dog on the head, his handsome face was animated as he spoke. "He's a big red dog so I figured it fit. He's a golden retriever and, as far as I know, Clifford would enjoy a waffle. Did I answer them all?"

Archie was too entranced by the dog to care.

"You did." Kirby nodded. "Wow. 'Cuz that was a lot."

Mike chuckled again.

Eloise tore her gaze away. It was hard to

be mad at someone who was being nice to her kids. She ran a hand over her hair—her sweat-dampened hair—and pulled the "Books are better than people" shirt away from where it was clinging to her chest.

Grandpa Quincy put a glass of water on the table and pushed it toward her.

"Thank you," she whispered, taking a long drink.

"Can we pet him, Momma? Can we?" Archie was practically shaking with excitement.

"You'll have to ask Mr. Woodard, Archie." She squeezed his hand. "Be gentle. And extra patient." Archie struggled with patience.

Archie nodded. "Yes, ma'am."

"Clifford." Mike squatted and scratched the big dog behind the ear. "You get to make some new friends. This is Kirby and Archie."

Clifford's great plume of a tail swayed rapidly.

"Hi, Clifford." Kirby waved at the dog, then hugged herself. "He's so pretty." This was whispered. "He'd look even prettier with some bows in his fur."

"He doesn't want bows." Archie held his hand out for Clifford's inspection.

Clifford's enthusiastic tail-wagging led to a big, wet doggie kiss on Archie's hand.

Archie giggled, which made Clifford wiggle and move closer to her son.

"I don't know about bows, Kirby." Mike watched

the kids with his dog, a crooked grin on his handsome face. "Clifford has a lot of energy, and he'll play fetch for hours. I'm afraid he might lose any you'd give to him."

Before Eloise knew it, the kids were sitting on the kitchen floor giving Clifford a tummy rub. She wasn't sure who was happier, her kids or Clifford. There was no way she could resist their gleeful smiles and free laughter. She didn't want to. Nothing was better than seeing the two of them this way.

Mike shook his head at the contented groan Clifford made, his eyes bouncing her way. His smile tight as he said, "All I wanted to do was leave those." His gaze held hers but he nodded at the box Grandpa Quincy had put on the kitchen counter. "I didn't mean to intrude."

He was not *serious.* She stared at him, incredulous. There was no way he could have misinterpreted her mad dash to get away from him. And yet, here he was. Very much intruding. He knew it—and he was smiling about it.

"Dad's idea but, I guess, they're also a peace offering of sorts."

Eloise sat back in her chair, curious.

"Peace?" Grandpa Quincy's brow furrowed.

"I might owe El an apology."

For last night. Not for the devastation he'd caused her all those years ago—not for doing the one thing he knew she couldn't accept or forgive.

Where did that come from? Why was she thinking about something that doesn't matter? Why was he still smiling at her? And why had he called her El? El was reserved for her family. Her closest friends. Not…him. He needed to stop smiling, stop looking so…like he did. She needed a shower. But mostly, she needed him to leave so she could get on with her day. A day that, with any luck, wouldn't include any more time with Mike Woodard, his smile, tight black shirt, big blue non-judgy eyes, or the pain-filled and anger-laden memories his appearance had stirred up.

IF HIS DAD hadn't threatened to do this pastry delivery himself, Mike wouldn't be here. His dad didn't care about his doctor's orders to rest—or that he wasn't supposed to be driving. That's how Mike ended up here, on the receiving end of El's frigid glare, wishing he was just about anyplace else.

He'd been headed to the Greens' place to appease his father when he'd spied her on the street. When she hadn't waved back, he'd headed over to get it over with, give her the pastries and get on with his day. By the time he'd crossed the street, she was a speck in the distance.

Eloise was fast. Like fast, fast.

He didn't know if her red cheeks were from her sprint home or if she was just that mad he was here. It's not like he was thrilled about it, either.

"Is that so? An apology?" Grandpa Quincy asked. "Did I miss something? It wouldn't have been the first time."

"You were doing your job." Eloise was avoiding eye contact—and she wasn't exactly being subtle about it. "We need to eat and get ready for school, kids."

He got the hint. He was all too happy to hit the road.

"But, Momma…" Archie's disappointment was almost comical. "Clifford is here."

"And he's so, so soft," Kirby added, continuing to rub Clifford's stomach.

"I'm sure Clifford will understand." Eloise's mom voice was impressive.

With sighs and groans, the kids returned to their seats at the table.

"I'll get another plate." Quincy pulled a plate from the cabinet.

"I appreciate the offer, sir, but I've got to open up the hardware shop this morning. As Dad says, Old Towne Hardware and Appliances won't operate itself." He stifled a yawn. "Until Doc Johnston gives him the *all clear*, my brother and I are running the place." Between his EMT shifts, working with the high school rodeo team, and helping out at the shop while his dad recuperates, he was plumb tuckered out.

"I hope he's listening to doctor's orders."

Quincy's brow creased with concern. "You tell him poker night wasn't the same without him."

"I'll tell him. You know how he is, Quincy. But Rusty and I are keeping a close eye on him." He chuckled. He and his brother had their work cut out for them. "We keep reminding him he was just released from the hospital a week ago."

Two weeks ago, life had been very different. He'd been in final job negotiations with the National Rodeo League. In the industry, Mike was well-respected, well-liked and both an experienced pick-up rider and an EMT. He was beyond flattered that they'd come to him. And the offer had been too good to refuse. He'd always wanted to see more of the country so, with his father's and brother's full support, he'd accepted. Sure, it'd keep him on the road for more than half the year, but he'd make sure to spend as much time back home as he could.

Then his dad had a stroke, the world had tipped, and his plans had come to a hard stop. He'd fully expected the NRL to withdraw the job offer when he explained his situation and that he couldn't consider leaving for at least a month. Instead, they'd given him their total understanding. They'd told him to take the month, more if he needed it. As grateful as he was for their flexibility, he was no longer sure about taking the job. His father, his family, came first.

"May I ask what happened to your father?" Eloise's question interrupted his mental musings.

"He had a stroke a couple of weeks ago. A small one." Thankfully, his father hadn't been left with any lingering maladies or side effects. "Good thing he's strong and stubborn—both attributes will work in his favor."

"I'm glad to hear he's recovering." For the first time, Eloise's expression softened.

"Thank you. Me, too." Seeing his father in a hospital bed had hit him hard. The man was his rock.

"He's determined to be back in fighting shape for Founder's Day. You know how involved he gets with the festivals. But that's his favorite. He loves dressing up and being one of the Founding Fathers." He broke off, chuckling. "Rusty and I are hoping the doc gives him the okay or we're going to be fighting Dad *and* Miss Martha."

"I don't envy you that. Just because she can push around the members of the Ladies Guild, she thinks she can go ordering everyone else around. Not me. I see her coming, I'll duck and cover." Quincy opened the pastry box. "My goodness, muffins and donuts and more. Looks like you cleared out the place."

"I didn't know what the kids would like." Mike watched as Archie stealthily slipped Clifford a bite of waffle.

Clifford gobbled up the waffle and sat, ears perked, all alert, hoping for more.

"I like donuts." Kirby frowned at her plate. "I like donuts more than waffles."

"Kirby is a picky eater." Archie pushed up his glasses. "*Very* picky."

"She likes sugar," Eloise murmured. "Eat up your waffle and fruit and I'll save you a donut for an after-school snack."

Kirby's sigh was pitiful. "'Kay, Momma." She speared a strawberry, put it in her mouth, and chewed slowly. "Will Clifford be here after school?"

"No, sweetie. I'm sure Clifford and Mr. Wood-ard have lots to do today—just like you and Archie." Eloise blew a strand of hair from her forehead.

She'd always had thick chestnut hair. Soft, too. Mike frowned.

"Oh." Kirby looked and sounded heartbroken.

"Don't fret, Freckles." Quincy placed a hand on the little girl's shoulder. "I bet we can stop by and visit Clifford sometime." He paused, sitting back in his chair. "Maybe, if you think it wouldn't be too much for him, we could stop by and visit your pa tonight, Mikey? I'll get him a new cross-word book."

"I'd be obliged." His father would enjoy seeing his buddy—and the kids, too. Of course, having the kids in the mix might backfire. His dad was already on him and Rusty about needing to get married and have kids. He said it was high time for him to have grandkids to spoil. *Like it was easy to find someone you could trust for a lifetime.* "And Clifford would, too."

"I can take him for a walk. Or a run. I can run real fast." Archie sat up on his knees. "Or we can play fetch. Dad says I can throw the ball really far. My dad's always right. He says I should play softball. Right, Momma?"

Eloise's smile was forced. "We'll make sure to get you signed up for softball this year."

"Dad will come see me play." Archie was all smiles. "I bet he will."

"We'll see," Eloise murmured.

Eloise's response struck Mike as unusual. Why wouldn't the boy's father come watch his son play? If he had a son, he'd be at every game— cheering him on and likely embarrassing his boy to the high heavens.

"Okay." Archie dropped another piece of waffle on the floor. "Can I play with Clifford later?"

"I'd be mighty grateful, Archie. Clifford here is still a puppy. Sometimes I tire out before he does." Quincy was always welcome at his place and the kids were pretty darn cute, so, for his dad's sake, he'd make peace with her tagging along. "Only when your momma says it's convenient, of course." He glanced at Eloise.

Eloise propped her elbow on the table and

rested her chin, her eyes meeting his. "We'll be there. Something tells me they'll both get their chores and homework done tonight without arguing."

He couldn't tell if he'd gotten her feathers ruffled again or not.

"No arguing." Kirby pretended to lock her lips. "Tell her, Archie," she whispered.

"Nope. Not from me." Archie adjusted his glasses. "I never argue."

"Glad to hear it." Mike saw Quincy roll his eyes—followed by Eloise—and grinned.

"Dad says respect…" Archie paused, thinking. "Respect makes a man." Archie fed Clifford another piece of waffle. "I don't know what respect is, but it's important."

Mike didn't miss the way Eloise's lips thinned. So, things between Eloise and the kids' father weren't…great. For one thing, Eloise and the kids were living here without the man. Then there was the other thing. A quick look at her hand showed she wasn't wearing a wedding ring.

She caught the look. Her hands slipped off the table and into her lap. "Finish up. We've got…" She glanced at the big sunshine-shaped clock on the wall. "Ten minutes until we need to head to school." With that, she stood, glanced around the table, then hesitated.

"I've got this." Quincy sat between the kids and sipped his coffee. "You go and take a shower."

"You're still all sweaty, Momma," Kirby pointed out. "Ew."

Eloise's cheeks, which had almost returned to a normal hue, flared red again. And yet, she lingered.

"You know, I've got a few minutes before I need to get to the shop. If that offer of a cup of coffee's still good, I'd be mighty appreciative, Quincy. I've got a long day ahead of me." He wasn't offering to help Eloise, he was helping *Quincy*. Kirby and Archie were a hoot. Plus, Clifford was all too content eating waffles and being spoiled.

"Make yourself at home and help yourself, Mikey. And get yourself something to eat, too. You brought enough to feed an army." Quincy waved him to the cabinet. "See now, El, you go on. Clifford, Mikey, and I are on the job."

With a sigh, Eloise held up her hands. "Okay. I'll be quick." Not that she looked happy about it. With that, she headed out of the kitchen and down the hall.

"Poor Momma." Kirby shook her head, working her way through her waffle. "She's so, so, *so* tired."

"Yeah." Archie served himself another waffle, cut it into bites, and fed a piece to Clifford. "Dad says we have to go easy on her—since he can't be here."

Mike returned to the table with a blueberry

muffin and a full mug of coffee. He didn't ask any of the questions he had, but he'd be lying if he said he wasn't curious about the man that *can't* be here for his kids.

Quincy took another sip of his coffee. "Little things like not talking in class—" Quincy glanced at Archie "—and eating up the food on your plate—" he looked at Kirby now "—go a long way for your sweet momma."

Mike took a sip of coffee to hide his grin. It was easy to imagine Archie talking in class. He was precocious and, he suspected, full of energy. Growing up, Mike had been a lot like the boy.

"Dad also said we'll be going on a vacation soon. The mountains or the beach with a big water slide and swimming with the dolphins." Archie said this to Kirby, then took another bite. "And he said Momma can go to a spa for ladies."

"He said that, did he?" Quincy's expression was further affirmation that things weren't right with the kids' father. Instead of wearing a big, excited smile, the older man looked concerned—maybe even upset.

"Something like that." Archie shrugged. "Maybe. Sort of."

"Hmm." Quincy sighed. "It's likely to be a while. You know that, Archie. Don't you?"

Archie sighed heavily, then nodded.

Mike wasn't sure what to make of it.

"What's a spa?" Kirby asked around her mouthful of waffle. "Can Momma go spa-ing here?" Kirby glanced at him, dropped a big piece of waffle on the floor, then giggled as Clifford gobbled it up.

"Hmm." Mike scratched the back of his head. "Not that I know of. I'll ask around, see if there's one hereabouts?"

Kirby nodded. "Yes, please."

"Will do." He took a bite of muffin—which elicited a mumbled groan from Clifford. "No, sir. I know better. You're not starving. I'm pretty sure Archie's fed you a whole waffle—and then some. Don't go giving me those sad eyes." He reached over and gave the dog a pat. "You lay down and rest a while."

Clifford yawned, stretched, then flopped on the tile floor.

"Good boy," Kirby said. "Good, good boy."

"Dogs can understand a hundred words." Archie pushed his glasses up on his nose. "I bet Clifford can understand a hundred and one."

"A hundred?" Mike glanced down at his snoozing dog. "I didn't know that."

"Archie knows lots and lots." Kirby ate the last strawberry from her plate, put her fork down, and held her hands up. "Done. I'll go get dressed, Grandpa."

"You do that, sweetheart." Quincy smiled. "Make sure to wash your face—"

"And brush my teeth." Kirby gave him a thumbs-up and slid from her chair. "Be right back, Clifford." And she ran from the room.

"I'm done, too." Archie took a last bite—a bite so big it should have been two or three bites.

Mike watched, stunned at the amount of food the boy managed to fit into his mouth.

"Chew, son. Slow down. It's not a race." Quincy shook his head. "I guess it's a good thing Mikey is here. He can give you the Heimlich if you choke."

The older man was joking but Mike found himself holding his breath.

"Okay." Archie chewed and chewed—then swallowed. "Done."

Crisis averted. Mike went back to eating his muffin.

"All right." Quincy chuckled. "You go on and get yourself ready."

"Yessir." Archie paused by Clifford. "I'll be back, too. I bet you understand that, don't you?"

Clifford wagged his tail.

"See." Archie was grinning from ear to ear. "He does." Then he ran from the room, yelling, "Don't squeeze out all the toothpaste, Kirby."

"There's been some big changes since I last visited you." Mike held out his mug when Quincy carried the coffeepot to the table and offered him a refill.

"You could say that again." Quincy filled his cup, put the coffeepot back, and returned to his seat. "Having El and the kids here has been a jolt to the system. A good kind. I like seeing them every day. I like feeling useful and helping out." He smiled. "They're full of spirit, those kids. After the mess they've been through, I'm glad that hasn't changed. I only wish I could say the same about El. She's not my Sassy anymore. Some spark is…missing." His smile faded and he shook his head. "I can't blame her, though. That big heart of hers has taken a beating—makes sense she's got her guard up." He shrugged and took a sip of coffee. "I guess you're chomping at the bit to get started on your new job?"

But Mike was still mulling over Quincy's words. It was on the tip of his tongue to ask what sort of mess Quincy was alluding to when Kirby reappeared. Her brown plaid dress was inside out and her shoes didn't match, but she flopped down next to Clifford without a care in the world.

"Wanna read, Clifford?" She pulled a book from her backpack and opened it. "This book is about Harvey." She pointed at a picture. "He's a squirrel."

Clifford was on his feet then. His ears perked up and his tail wagged at frenzied speed as he barked and spun in a circle.

Kirby watched, then glanced at Mike. "What's he doing?"

"You said the magic word." Mike patted the dog on the back. "You can't say the 's' word or Clifford wants to chase it."

"The 's' word?" Kirby cocked her head to one side. "What's the 's' word?" she whispered.

Mike pointed at her book. "What kind of animal is Harvey?"

"A squir—" Kirby broke off the second she understood what he was saying. *"Ooh."* She nodded. "Oops."

"Are we ready?" Eloise appeared in the kitchen door. "Kirby, sweetie." She sighed. "Come on, let's fix your dress." She held her hand out. "And shoes. And your hair."

Kirby's long-suffering sigh implied she wasn't thrilled with this announcement. "Okay, Momma."

Archie appeared, immediately at Clifford's side. "Your dress is wrong-side out, Kirby." He pointed at his sister. "And your shoes don't match. But I'm ready."

Kirby shrugged. "Clifford doesn't care. Me neither." She took Eloise's hand and followed her mother from the room.

Quincy's house phone started ringing. Like the Woodard home, there was still a landline in the Green house. Mike believed it was a generational thing—as most of his father's friends had the same.

"I bet that's Dad." Archie ran to the phone.

Quincy headed for the phone. "He normally calls on weekends, Arch."

"Yeah, but it might be him." He waited, smiling, as Quincy answered.

"Quincy Green here." He glanced at Archie and shook his head. "Morning, morning. I heard about the meeting. I'll be there."

If the boy was upset, Clifford's presence seemed to buoy Archie's mood. "Dad's real important," he explained to the dog. "He's real busy. All the time. He travels for work." The boy looked at Mike then. "But he calls lots. He likes to hear about our day and school and stuff."

"My dad likes hearing that stuff, too—from me and my brother." No matter what the circumstances were, it was obvious the boy adored his father.

"Now we're ready." Eloise re-entered the kitchen with properly dressed and matching Kirby. "Ready, Archie?"

Archie pointed at the phone. "It's not Dad."

For a split second, Eloise's brow creased and her jaw flexed tight. "No, probably not today, sweetie." Her gaze bounced from Archie to Kirby to Clifford. "Now, give Grandpa a hug and I'll get you two to school."

"Yes, ma'am." They spoke in unison.

He watched as the kids hugged their grandpa, hugged Clifford, then hugged him, too. "That's a surprise." He patted Kirby's back.

"Momma says sharing kindness and hugs will make the world a better place." Kirby beamed up at him.

"Except strangers. We don't talk to strangers. Or

hug them." Archie pushed his glasses up. "But we can talk to and hug people we know. Or Momma knows. Or Grandpa knows."

"That's a good rule." Mike saw the way Eloise smiled at her kids—there was so much love and pride on her face his heart ached. His father had always loved them unconditionally and, for the most part, that was enough. But there was a piece of him that had yet to heal over his mother's abandonment. Most of the time, he accepted her leaving was the best thing for him, Rusty, and their father. Most of the time, the hurt didn't gnaw at his insides and make him ponder "what-ifs." This wasn't one of those times.

He'd heard what had been said this morning. As much as he wanted to keep his distance, he was sorry to hear she'd been through tough times and it had taken a toll on her. Life wasn't always fair. He knew that firsthand. But the support of family, friends, and time to heal could make a world of difference. That being said, they weren't family, he no longer considered her a friend, and his time here was limited. All he could do was wish her well and hope that Garrison gave her the fresh start she and her kids needed.

CHAPTER THREE

"FOUNDER'S DAY?" Eloise asked, snipping the ends off the stems of six perfect pink roses. "It's a big deal?"

"Any festival in Garrison is a big deal, El." Her grandfather chuckled. "Small towns rely on those sorts of things to keep the community strong and bring in some tourism dollars. This year is extra special. Not only has it been one hundred and seventy-five years since Garrison was founded, it's also been a year since the whole county rallied to save erste Baum." He glanced over the rim of his reading glasses. "Some smooth talker came into town trying to buy up erste Baum Park and build one of those big-box store chains. You can imagine how that went over. It was a big to-do, El. The whole town was in an uproar. Newspapers and reporters from all over showed up. Big news—for these parts, anyways. You and the kids missed it by a couple of months."

Thank goodness. Eloise had had enough of newspapers and reporters to last a lifetime.

While Garrison was rallying to save their beloved tree, her world had been completely falling apart. She'd been making ends meet, barely. Her credit card debt had skyrocketed but, after selling her little flower and tea shop, she'd been managing to make payments and keep food in the house.

Things would have been okay if their house had sold. But the five-thousand-square-foot monstrosity, with fifteen-foot ceilings that cost a small fortune to heat and cool, had been on the market for almost six months and there hadn't been a single offer.

She'd thought waking up to find her minivan had been repossessed in the middle of the night was bad. But bringing the kids home after school to find the locks changed on the house—while their neighbors watched from their front yards and windows—had subjected her to abject humiliation. She'd had no idea they were months behind on the mortgage. Thanks to Ted. It was only when the bank foreclosed on the house that she learned he'd managed to sweet-talk their banker, a friend and investor in Ted's scam, into giving them extension after extension.

"That's why Miss Martha Bossy-pants Zeigler has declared this Founder's Day Festival will be the biggest one yet." Grandpa Quincy seemed blissfully unaware that her thoughts had drifted— for which she was thankful. "I don't know what sort of changes she's thinking, but it's a little too late to overhaul the whole dang thing. And, if she's got all sorts of harebrained ideas, I've a mind to tell her just that."

"That sounds exciting." She tried to imagine her sweet grandfather taking on the town's battle-ax but couldn't do it. "Any idea what she's thinking?" She tucked one rose into the green glass vase, adding a sprig of white-tufted baby's breath, then another rose.

"We'll find out at tomorrow night's planning meeting." He paused, glancing her way. "It'll give you a chance to get to know some of our Main Street neighbors."

She met his gaze. He meant well, he did, but she was still processing the shame of…everything. Meeting new people was nerve-racking.

"I know things have been real tough, El, but no one knows about Ted's…shenanigans in these parts. You don't have to worry about that." He shook his head. "And, even if they did, why would anyone hold it against you?"

They might not hold it against her but they'd *know*, and knowing meant long, curious looks, whispers, and, eventually, an interrogation. Once her dirty laundry was aired, she was forever linked to the pain and embarrassment she'd like to leave in the past.

"You're too young to wall yourself up with just me and the kids. Besides, those young 'uns need to meet folk and make friends, too." He cleared his throat. "Hattie's in charge of the Junior Rangers—I think I've mentioned them a time or two? Anyhow, Kirby and Archie would probably enjoy it. Being outdoors, learning stuff, doing projects, and spending time with other kids."

She wanted them to have friends—for Garrison to feel like home. "I'm not against it, Grandpa. I'd need to know the details—"

"I was getting to that. It just so happens there's a Junior Ranger meeting the same time Martha Zeigler's set for the festival planning meeting. Archie and Kirby can have fun and you'll have a whole hour to yourself." He chuckled.

Junior Rangers was a good idea; it was this planning meeting she wasn't so sure about. But her grandfather asked so little of her, there was no way she could refuse. With a sigh, she tucked the last rose in, stepped back to see her handiwork, then added another sprig of baby's breath.

"More like an hour with me and all the Main Street business owners, that is. And since you are part-owner of the shop now, you should be there." He pushed through the swinging doors that separated the workroom from the shop front.

Working at Garrison Gardens was a comfort. She and her grandfather both shared a deep love of all things green and flowering, but she sensed he was tired. That was why she took the phone orders and put together the bouquets and arrangements in the workroom and Grandpa Quincy manned the front. Besides creating two birthday flower arrangements she'd have to deliver later that afternoon, it was a slow morning. That was the way of things in Garrison—slow and steady. After the nonstop stress of the last eight months, it was a relief.

About noon, she heard the doorbell chime.

"Morning, Mr. Green."

"Morning, Miss Gretta," her grandfather answered. "What can we do for you today?"

"Actually, I thought I'd stop by with lunch. For you, me, and Eloise."

Eloise wiped her hands on the green apron she wore and pushed through the swinging doors. "Hey, Gretta."

"Hi." Gretta held two brown paper bags. "I come bearing food. From the Buttermilk Pie Café fall menu. Apple and pecan salad, chicken and dumplings, and yummy yeast rolls."

"That sounds like a feast." Her grandfather patted his stomach. "That's mighty kind of you, Gretta." He flipped the sign on the door from Open to Closed. "I've learned never to say no to a meal—especially when it comes with good company."

"There's plenty of room in the back." Eloise waved them both through the swinging doors. "Let me clean off one of the tables." She moved the ribbons, wires, and bud vases aside, then wiped down the metal surface with a disinfecting wipe.

"I've never been back here before." Gretta set the bags on the table, staring around the room.

"El's done a lot of work since arriving." Her grandfather sat in one of the chairs. "I didn't have these, what do you call them? Vision boards? Those and scraps and clippings and stuff all over."

"They're for inspiration, Grandpa." She winked at her grandfather. "And it was a little dark and dreary." She helped Gretta unpack the bags.

"Without windows, you have to do something to brighten the place up." Gretta passed out the individual packets of plastic utensils. "I like the vision boards." She scanned El's handiwork. "They're gorgeous. I love that one." She pointed at one with a variety of blues and bits of lace. "If I do ever get married again, I'll let you do the decorations. Not that it's likely to happen any-time soon—I haven't been on a date in a couple of years." She shuddered. "Dating. Ugh."

Eloise laughed. "My thoughts exactly." The very idea of dating turned her stomach.

"I don't know what's wrong with men these days." Her grandfather shook his head, dismayed. "There should be a line of fine suitors wrapped around the block for the both of you."

"Can I be honest with you, Mr. Green?" Gretta sat, opening her salad.

"Please do." He waited.

"I don't want a line of suitors. I'd be happy with

one. One good man with infinite patience and a great sense of humor." Gretta's sigh was wistful.

Grandpa Quincy was frowning. "I can come up with a half-dozen men that fit that description."

"What about you, Eloise?" Gretta poured salad dressing on her salad. "What's on your wish list?"

Eloise took a bite of salad, pondering the question as she chewed, then swallowed. "I don't have a list but honesty is a must—like my number one." She shrugged. "That's all I've got, for now. But I think I'm going to steal yours, Gretta. A sense of humor and patience are both necessary qualities."

Gretta tucked a long strand of blond hair behind her ear. "I think so."

Grandpa Quincy wiped his mouth with his napkin. "Well, I've got a few names for both of you—"

"Since we are being honest—" she gave her grandfather a long look "—I'm not interested in dating. Not a bit. Zero."

Her grandfather's sigh was all disappointment, making Eloise and Gretta laugh.

"I'm a strong, independent woman, Grandpa." She was a long way from independent but she was trying. "I don't need a man. Well, other than you." She reached over and patted his hand. "I don't know what we'd have done—would do—without you. You're the only knight in shining armor me and the kids need."

"Knight in shining armor, huh? I like that." He

speared some lettuce with his fork before asking, "Gretta, your boy is a Junior Ranger, isn't he?"

"He is. And Hattie Carmichael is a saint, that's all I can say." Gretta took a sip of her tea. "I love my son, dearly, but he's…a lot."

"Oh, I get it. How old is he?" Eloise took a bite of the yeast roll and regretted it. Carbs were her weakness. Bread, pasta, cakes, cookies… The pastry box Mike had delivered was pure temptation. If she didn't get rid of it, she'd likely eat them all and add to the extra pounds that now resided on her not-so-toned thighs and tummy.

"Levi likes to say he's almost seven. But he's six. First grade." Gretta finished off her salad. "I regularly send thank-you notes to his teacher. And cookies or candy or gift cards or whatever I think might help. He tends to get into mischief." She held her hand up. "His teacher says he has an abundance of curiosity."

Grandpa Quincy chuckled. "Sounds like he and Archie would get on just fine."

"Oh?" Gretta perked up. "Really?"

"Archie is in second grade." Eloise smiled. "He's seven and a talker. He likes to tell stories—and embellish them. I had to explain to his teacher that Archie's father was not starting a polar bear farm in Antarctica. Only that his father had seen a polar bear when he was on a cruise in the arctic—Alaska, specifically." A trend seemed to be developing as most of her son's embellishments revolved around his father.

"Aw, now. There's no harm meant. He's good at story-telling." Grandpa Quincy set aside his salad container and reached for his soup. "Maybe, one day, he'll grow up and be a writer."

"Maybe. But, for now, there's a fine line between storytelling and lying, Grandpa. It's important he knows the difference." It wasn't Archie's fault. Ted had been the same—he loved adding dramatic flair to his stories for the kids. In the end, Eloise wasn't sure there was a hint of truth to anything Ted had said. "You're the one who taught me a man's only as good as his word."

"But he's just a boy, El." Her grandfather was loyal to her kids—to a fault. "I've been tellin' El that Archie and Kirby might make some new friends at Junior Rangers." He blew on his soup. "And, with the Founder's Day meeting coming up, I figured it was as good a time as any for them to give it a try."

"Oh, yes. The Founder's Day Festival." Gretta shook her head. "So far, we're doing a clogging extravaganza and a line dance, too."

"So far?"

"Miss Martha hasn't weighed in yet. In case no one's told you, she's sort of the boss of…everything. Somehow." Gretta chuckled. "She always has something more in mind."

"I'm getting that. She sounds…interesting."

Eloise reached for her soup bowl. "Clogging and line dancing sound fun. My daughter, Kirby, was in dance back... Well, Kirby used to be in dance." Eloise opened her soup container and stirred the creamy contents. She had fond memories of her little girl in glittery tutus, spinning on the stage and smiling with pride.

"There'd be room for her if she wants to join one of my classes."

"That's sweet of you." Too bad Eloise was trying to keep a tight rein on their spending.

Grandpa Quincy wasn't asking for rent or help with any of the bills. Instead, he'd insisted on making her co-owner of the shop and paying her for her work there. He said he was getting forgetful and tired so having her and the kids was a help to him, but she knew better. Yes, his memory wasn't what it used to be, but he was still more than capable of living on his own.

Since they'd invaded his home, his life had been turned upside down. Her kids were constant noise and chaos, including that scary visit from the local EMTs. He said they gave him a renewed sense of purpose but what else could he say? He knew she had no place else to go. It was painful but true.

After Ted, she hadn't wanted to be reliant on anyone ever again... Now she was entirely reliant on her grandfather's kindness and generosity. In time, she hoped, somehow, in some way, she could repay him for all he'd done for them.

"I haven't eaten so well in a long time." Grandpa Quincy sat back with a sigh. "First Mikey's delivery and now this." He patted his stomach. "At this rate, I could play Santa come Christmastime."

And there he was. Mike Woodard popping up, again. This morning had been a catastrophe. Seeing him, running from him, and him following her? How had he not gotten the hint? She hadn't wanted to see him or talk to him. She certainly hadn't wanted him in the kitchen while she was red-faced and dripping sweat. Then he'd had to go and be handsome and charming and handsome. She frowned. He wasn't that handsome.

He had been awfully sweet to Archie and Kirby, enchanting them with his dog and the promise of more Clifford playtime. *Why had I agreed to that?*

"Santa? We have to get past the Founder's Day Festival before I can start thinking about Christmas, Mr. Green." Gretta wiped her hands on her napkin. "Believe me, I start rehearsing for our Christmas Jamboree the day after we wrap up the Founder's Day show." She started collecting her trash. "And, Eloise, not that you asked me, but you should let the kids go to Junior Rangers this week. The high school football team will be there to help them make paper chain streamers to decorate erste Baum for the festival. There will be lots of helping hands and less for you to worry about."

Gretta was easy to talk to. The two of them

were chatting and laughing the entire time they cleaned up.

"Thanks for the lunch. It was fun." Eloise walked Gretta to the front door.

"Kirby is welcome to come visit the studio— no obligation," Gretta said on her way out of the shop.

After Eloise turned the Closed sign back to Open, she was feeling the tiniest bit hopeful. Sure, the day wasn't over and there was still a chance she'd get a call about Archie from the school— and she'd have to deal with Mike this evening... But she'd had an entire conversation without Ted or the path of ruin he'd left in his wake coming up. And it felt good.

"Is your daddy getting better, Mr. Mike? I miss him. He's funny." Little Samantha Crawley was one of his father's favorite clients at their family's hardware and appliance shop. Well, her father, Jensen Crawley, was the client. But Samantha went everywhere he did so the little girl was a frequent visitor. His father said she was a ray of sunshine that always made his day bright. "He told me about his pet dragon, Bongo."

"He did?" Mike typed in the price on the tools on the register. "You know, my dad told me a little something about you." He reached under the counter for the glass jar his father kept full of lollipops. "He said you liked lollipops. Red ones." He pulled one out and offered it to the little girl.

"He 'membered." Samantha's smile was oh-so-sweet as she took the lollipop. "Thank you, Mr. Mike. And thank Mr. Nolan, too."

"You're welcome. And I'll tell my dad, too."

"'Kay." Samantha pulled off the wrapper and put the lollipop in her mouth.

"Anything else?" he asked Jensen. "What's all this for?"

"Microwave." Jensen sighed. "I'm going to try to fix it this time." He ran a hand along the back of his neck. "But chances are I'll be in here next week ordering a new one."

Samantha took the lollipop out of her mouth. "Another new one. Aunt Twyla always breaks them."

"Is that so?" Mike chuckled. "Well, that happens, I hear."

Jensen slid his credit card across the counter. "Four microwaves in less than two years?"

Samantha tugged on her dad's sleeve. "But this one didn't explode, Daddy."

"That's something, I guess." Mike was laughing as he bagged up Jensen's purchases and handed over his credit card and the brown paper bag of supplies. "Good luck."

"Thank you." Jensen took the bag. "Give your father our best, please."

"Will do. Y'all have a good night." Mike followed them to the front door, all too happy to turn off the illuminated Open sign and lock the front door.

He was tired. "And it's only Monday." Then again, it had been a long Monday. He made his way to the back of the store, flipping off lights as he went. After locking up Old Towne Hardware and Appliances, he climbed into his truck and headed to his dad's little place a couple of blocks off Main Street. He had an old farmhouse with some acreage he'd been fixing up, but since his father's stroke, he'd been spending most of his nights on his father's couch.

As soon as he parked, he heard Clifford's bark hello and smiled. The dog had been intended to be their father's companion. Instead, the dog stuck to him like glue, and Mike was pretty attached to the dog. Thankfully, his father was content with his bearded dragon, Bongo, and his aquarium full of fish.

He was halfway up the path when he heard voices—kid voices. Archie and Kirby? Already? Meaning, Eloise was likely here, too.

Eloise. He paused, running a hand along the back of his neck. His father's hardware shop always had steady customers but, during downtime, his conversation with Quincy and the odd exchanges about the kids' father tugged at his brain. He didn't like it but Eloise had been weighing on his mind. And now... He'd had no right to look her up online but that's exactly what he'd done. After a few minutes, he'd learned more than he wanted. He'd closed down the browser and walked away from the computer.

Eloise had been married to Ted Barnes. The man came from old Highland Park money and had more connections than most politicians. Apparently, he was good-looking and smooth-talking enough to get a whole lot of people to hand over a whole lot of their money and "invest." But not long after he and Eloise divorced, the man was arrested for his not-so-legit investments. Mike didn't linger over the headlines of Ted's trial and conviction or the stricken images of Eloise; they had made his stomach churn.

The truth was the man was serving time for first-degree felony fraud and embezzlement charges. But since Archie and Kirby thought their father was traveling for work, they must not know.

Then again, how would you go about explaining all that to your kids?

Still, Ted Barnes wasn't a complete fool. There's no way the man could have gotten away with his scheme for so long if he'd been dim-witted. And he'd had the good sense to marry Eloise.

Mike scrubbed a hand over his face but he couldn't scrub the images or the knowledge from his brain. It ate at him.

The last few times she'd visited, she'd told him how tough things had become with her father. His drinking and his unpredictable moods—and his temper... It was her father's addiction that had driven them, forcefully, apart.

Then she marries some charming, sweet-talking yahoo who'd rather con people than do an honest day's work.

She had every reason to be standoffish and prickly. Yes, he'd gotten her back up that first night but her hostility toward him for doing his job and assessing the situation had seemed...extreme. Could her attitude be colored by the big blow-up that ended their relationship? For the most part, he'd moved on. But if he thought about the things they'd said to each other, it still stung something fierce.

He was reading too much into it. Eloise had more things to worry about than dwelling on long-ago hateful words and teen heartbreak—his internet search results had said as much.

The thing is, his search hadn't been out of idle curiosity. This wasn't some stranger—this was Eloise. Before that awful fight, she'd been...well, she'd been everything. He'd lain awake for most of last night, sifting through memories he'd locked up years ago.

Clifford's mumbled groan was audible through the door. When he pulled it open, Archie, Kirby, and Clifford all poured out onto the front porch.

"Good evening." He smiled down at them.

"Evening." Kirby hopped up and down. "We're here to see Clifford."

"So, I see." He tipped his cowboy hat back on his head. "You three having fun?"

Archie stood, pushing his glasses up on his nose. "Yep. But Momma said I can't take him for a walk."

"'Cuz he got in trouble for talking." Kirby crossed her arms over her chest and gave her brother a disapproving face. She looked a whole lot like her momma when she did that. "Momma said we should be happy we got to visit Clifford at all."

"I know." Archie sighed. "I can't help it." He shrugged. "I...talk."

Mike did his best not to smile or chuckle at that.

"You're letting all the bought air out." His father sat in his leather recliner. "Come on in and tell me about your day."

"He means, tell him what happened at the store." Rusty sat on the couch beside Quincy Green but there was no sign of Eloise.

Mike pulled the front door closed, stepped over the kids and dog, and headed into the front parlor. "Not much to tell. The place is still standing, if that's what you're worried about." He winked at his father.

"I didn't think I had to worry about that." His father wasn't amused.

"You don't." He gave his father's shoulder a squeeze. "How're you feeling?"

"Fed up and tired over people asking me how I'm feeling." His father sighed. "Other than that, I can't complain. I've got Quincy here filling me in on what I'm missing and these kids here to put a smile on my face."

Mike glanced back to see Clifford, on his back, with Archie and Kirby smoothing his fur and giving him a belly rub. "I don't think a dog could get much happier."

"Ain't that the truth?" Quincy chuckled.

"Did you see the flowers they brought?" His father pointed at the buffet table against the wall. "Sunflowers. And those pretty blue flowers there. What are those?"

"Delphinium. They're one of my favorite flowers." Eloise carried a refreshment tray into the parlor. "A snack and some tea." She set the tray on the coffee table, smiling.

Mike found himself lingering over how her green shirt made her eyes seem even bigger— greener. He tore his gaze from her and stared at the tray she'd brought in. He was pretty sure the contents of this morning's pastry box had been artfully arranged on one of his mother's serving platters, but he didn't say as much.

"It looks like we're one glass short." She headed into the kitchen before he could argue.

He wasn't sure what he was doing or why he

was doing it but he followed her. "I appreciate that but you don't have to wait on me, Eloise."

She opened the refrigerator and pulled out his mother's glass tea pitcher. "I appreciate you letting the kids smother your poor dog with affection." Her gaze bounced from his to the tea.

"Clifford's happy as a clam." He nodded his thanks as she filled up a glass for him.

"Well, we won't stay too much longer. The kids have school tomorrow and I like to keep them on a routine." She put the tea back in the refrigerator and closed the door.

"I get that." Mike sipped his tea and tried not to study the woman before him.

Did she really only have *vague* memories of him? It was a hard pill to swallow. Once upon a time, Eloise had a hold of his heart. Each one of her visits to Garrison had only deepened his affection for her. So much so that he'd married her beneath the sprawling branches of erste Baum. He might have been fourteen but, at the time, he'd been certain it would last forever. Instead, it was the last time he saw her—before their fight.

He realized he was staring and, for a second, she stared right back. "You…you and your grandfather going to the meeting tomorrow night?"

"It would appear so. Grandpa keeps telling me it's a big deal." She crossed her arms over her chest.

Mike grinned. "Garrison's a small town that

values its traditions. Do you remember the egg hunts at Easter? The caroling along Main Street at Christmas. Or watching the fireworks in the summertime?" Holding hands during a hayride? Sharing a kiss under erste Baum?

"Vaguely." There was a ghost of a smile on her face.

That word again. "That's what makes this place special. It's about the memories you make and the community you forge. I'm sure it's a mite different than Highland Park, but it's a good place to raise a family."

Her eyes locked with his, searching. "That's why I'm here. For the kids."

"For Quincy, too, I'm thinking." He leaned against the kitchen counter. "He's perked up since you got here."

She rubbed her upper arms. "I don't know about that."

"I do." He sipped his tea. "It's good you're here, El-Eloise." The nickname almost slipped out.

For a split second, he thought she was going to say something. Then her lips pressed tight and she focused on the window over the kitchen sink.

"Momma, Momma." Kirby came running into the kitchen, with Archie on her heels. "Clifford shook. He did. He shook my hand."

Eloise squatted beside her daughter, all smiles. "He did?"

"He has a big paw." Kirby held up her hands

for scale. "Mr. Nolan said it's 'cuz he's going to get bigger and bigger."

"He didn't shake with me." From the looks of it, Archie was pretty devastated.

Something about the boy reminded him of Rusty when he was young: a little high-strung and sensitive. He didn't like seeing his little brother upset then—he didn't like seeing Archie upset now. "He didn't, huh?" He scrambled to come up with a reason. When it came to tricks, Clifford was pretty treat-driven. "Remember what I said about Clifford being a puppy?"

Archie nodded, his frown too much for Mike.

"He's still learning things—like shake." He put his glass on the counter. "I bet I can get him to shake with you, too." He headed out of the kitchen, waving Archie after him.

Archie followed, dragging his feet and sighing heavily.

Clifford was sound asleep on the floor.

"I don't want to wake him up." Archie rubbed his nose with the back of his arm. "Momma says sleep is important."

"Amen to that," Mike's father sounded off. "But I'm pretty sure he'd rather play with you two while you're here."

"Are you sure?" The boy looked to be on the verge of tears.

"Yup." Mike opened the closet and, before he could pull the treats out, Clifford was wide awake.

"All he has to do is hear that door open and he knows it means food."

"He's just like you, Archie." Eloise laughed. "Once you're awake, you're awake and wanting breakfast."

Mike handed Archie a treat. "Now, don't give him that until he shakes. Okay?"

"Okay." Archie stood in front of Clifford, uncertain. "Hi, Clifford. Shake?"

Clifford's tail was wagging but he didn't lift a paw.

Mike squatted behind the boy. "Almost. Use a strong, firm voice and I bet he'll do it."

"Okay." Archie cleared his throat. "Clifford. Shake."

Clifford lifted his paw.

Archie shook the dog's paw. "Good boy." He fed the dog his treat. "He's not like me, Momma. He's like Kirby. She'll do almost anything for a cupcake." He paused. "Except eat salad or peas or green things."

Mike was laughing then. And so was everyone else. His father's big booming laugh had been so absent, it was a joy to hear. From the looks of it, Rusty felt the same.

Then another laugh grabbed his attention. A high, free breeze of a laugh he recognized in an instant. There she was. El-Bell. She was sitting on the floor, with her kids in her lap, hugging them close while they giggled—carefree and happy and beautiful. Entirely present in the moment. After everything he'd learned, he agreed wholeheartedly with what Quincy had said this morning. She deserved better. She deserved this.

Mike drew in a slow breath, pushing against the sudden pressure in his chest. He wasn't some naïve sixteen-year-old anymore, but he was having a sudden rush of his sixteen-year-old self's feelings. He didn't know what to do with that but he'd get over it. Like Eloise, he had too much going on in his life to add further complications. Something told him El-Bell and her sweet kids would be one big complication.

CHAPTER FOUR

"You're sure?" Eloise stood outside a jam-packed classroom of the Garrison Community Center. It wasn't the noise or crowd that got to her, it was the realization that this was the first time she'd leave her kids since they'd moved to Garrison. Other than school, of course. She couldn't help it, she worried—all the time. *A little too much, maybe?*

"I'm sure." Archie's enthusiasm was obvious.

"Look, Momma, there's Samantha. She's in my class." Kirby was almost jumping up and down with excitement as she pointed out a little girl with curly hair. "She's nice and she never gets in trouble."

"Hi, there. I don't suppose you're Eloise Green?" A woman wearing a khaki Game Warden uniform and baseball cap approached her.

"Yes, that's me." Eloise nodded, reading the woman's name badge. Carmichael.

"I'm Hattie Carmichael. Gretta mentioned you might be stopping by." She shook her hand. "I think we've spoken on the phone a time or two about the big to-do this weekend."

"Of course." Hattie Carmichael was the one getting married this weekend. It was nice to put a face with a voice. "It's so nice to meet you. Are you getting excited?"

"Not really—but don't tell anyone." Hattie had an infectious laugh. Even more so when a snort slipped out. "Forrest and I would be fine getting hitched down at City Hall." She shrugged. "But our families wanted to be involved so we sort of let them take the lead. That's how we ended up with a guest list that included all of Garrison and having our ceremony and reception under erste Baum."

There was something instantly likable about the woman.

Hattie tipped her cap back and put her hands on her hips. "I'm guessing these two fine young people belong to you?"

"Yes. Archie and Kirby. Say hello to… Warden Carmichael." She smiled at Kirby's wide eyes and slightly starstruck reaction to the woman.

"Are you a police person?" Kirby asked.

"What's a warden?" Archie pushed his glasses up, inspecting Hattie's uniform with interest.

Hattie nodded. "Well, Archie. I'm a Game Warden for the state of Texas. My main job is to make sure the animals and land in these parts are respected and looked after. But I'm also a licensed police officer, so I can arrest someone if the need arises."

"Wow." Kirby was impressed. "You're like a superhero."

"She doesn't have a cape." Archie pointed.

"Capes are dangerous, Archie." Kirby shook her head. "'Member in the movie? It showed that capes could get all tangled up and so it was better for superheroes not to have them?"

"Right." Archie nodded. "Are game wardens superheroes?"

About that time, a very tall, very handsome cowboy joined them. "I'd say so. I've seen Hattie here rescue baby deer, turtles, even an alligator once."

"An alligator?" Even Archie was impressed now.

"This is Forrest Briscoe." Hattie smiled up at the man. "He might be a little biased."

Eloise smiled. "I should hope so, you are getting married on Saturday. I'm Eloise, I have the great privilege of putting together your wedding flowers." She held her hand out. "It's nice to meet you, Mr. Briscoe."

"Forrest, please. It's a pleasure." He shook her hand. "Looks like we've got two new recruits?"

"Can we, Momma?" Archie asked. "Warden Carmichael is here and she'll make sure nothing bad happens. And if I act up, she can arrest me."

Hattie laughed at that. Forrest, however, looked slightly concerned.

"He talks a lot. His teacher sends notes to

Momma all the time," Kirby explained. "Can he get arrested for that?"

Forrest relaxed now, grinning. "As long as he doesn't talk when Warden Carmichael does, we should be okay."

"Can you do that, Archie?" Eloise crossed her arms over her chest. "Because if you can't, you can just come along with me to the meeting—"

"I can. I can." Archie nodded, then pretended to lock his mouth shut.

"All righty, then let's find you a partner." Forrest ushered the kids into the room.

Eloise lingered, watching as Kirby took a seat by Samantha. Samantha squealed with glee, they hugged, and the two of them started chatting. Archie sat where Forrest indicated, beside a boy who appeared close in age. They looked at each other, nodded, then started talking.

"There you have it." Hattie smiled. "If only it was that easy for adults."

"Isn't that the truth." Eloise shook her head. "I appreciate this. I'm right down the hall if there's a problem."

Hattie glanced at Kirby, then Archie. "There won't be. You go on to your meeting and take notes so you can fill me in on what's happening." She grinned. "I'm sure there will be something to tell, there always is."

Eloise left the classroom, headed down the hall and turned left, into the main hall of the Community Center. It, like the classroom, was packed but with adults instead of children. She couldn't help the unease that settled over her. For almost a year, social outings included pushy photographers or tabloid journalists shouting questions about every detail of her old life. But that was over now and she was here. Besides, Ted's antics were old news for the rest of the world. He'd been incarcerated for over a year now.

"You look so pretty, Eloise. I mean, you look like a deer in headlights—but a pretty deer." Gretta placed a hand on her arm. "I felt exactly the same when I attended my first planning meeting."

"I wasn't expecting so many people. I thought this meeting was for the Main Street Association?" Surely, all of Garrison was here. She let Gretta steer her into the room.

"Technically." Gretta gave her a reassuring smile. "But Miss Martha made some calls. I guess it makes sense for everyone involved in the Founder's Day Festival to be here—it cuts down on the number of meetings, anyway. Now, let me introduce you to some folk."

She could do this. This was her home now, she couldn't keep hiding in her grandfather's house. She had to engage and network and, hopefully, have a life again. She'd dressed up, put on a light dusting of makeup, and done her hair—wanting to make an overall good impression. Grandpa

Quincy had said she shined up prettier than a new copper penny. Kirby said she looked pretty. Archie, on the other hand, had no comment on her appearance.

But despite her best efforts, she still felt off-balance. All she could do was dig deep and paste on her hostess smile. It was one of the things she'd perfected when she'd been unknowingly helping Ted schmooze and swindle potential investors. She knew how to be just the right amount of gracious and engaging—things that had also helped her little flower and tea shop be successful.

"This is my father, Buck Williams." Gretta introduced a dashingly handsome older man. "Daddy, this is Eloise Green."

"I've been hearing quite a bit about you." Buck had a mischievous sparkle to his eye that reminded her a bit of Archie. "All good things, of course."

"Oh." Quite a bit? About what? From who? "That's nice to know."

"Making the rounds, Daddy." Gretta steered her on before anything else could be said.

"Eloise Green, this is Brooke Briscoe, Mabel Briscoe, and Kitty and Twyla Crawley."

"Brooke?" Eloise smiled. Brooke Young, now Briscoe, hadn't changed much. Except for the very round, very pregnant stomach, that is.

"Eloise? Oh, my goodness." Brooke hugged her. "It's been forever since I saw you last."

Gretta and Brooke introduced Eloise to a group of women close to her age. It was exciting and terrifying at the same time.

"Don't worry, the only one who bites here is my sister, Twyla, and she's on her best behavior." Kitty Crawley smiled at her.

Twyla shot her sister a narrow-eyed look. "I haven't bitten anyone since first grade. And RJ Malloy deserved it." She turned a guarded smile toward Eloise. "As long as you don't go putting gum in my hair, we will get along just fine."

"I promise," Eloise assured the woman.

"I can't believe you're here. It's been years." Brooke squeezed her hand. "Christmas, I think?"

Brooke had been a part of a lot of Eloise's adventures in Garrison. Not as much as Mike, but almost. "That was a long time ago."

"Time flies. Now I own the town beauty shop, Young's Beauty Salon. Kitty and Twyla own the Calico Pig boutique." She pointed at Mabel. "Mabel doesn't have a Main Street storefront."

"I'm here for moral support." Mabel had a warm, curious gaze. "And because I figure I have to represent the Briscoe family. Not to imply you're not a Briscoe, Brooke." She glanced down at Brooke's belly. "You are one. And you're carrying one, too."

"Congratulations." Eloise had loved being pregnant. She'd been lucky to breeze through both of her pregnancies. "Your first?"

"We have a daughter through adoption but, yes, first pregnancy. Though, Audy is already talking about the next four." Brooke shook her head. "He said something about having our own basketball team."

"He doesn't even like basketball." Mabel looked confused.

"I might be married to him but that doesn't mean I understand the way he thinks." Brooke arched back and placed a hand in the middle of her back.

"You should sit." That was one thing Eloise did remember, backaches.

"I won't argue." Brooke rolled her shoulders.

"Watch out, move aside." Twyla had no problem making space. "Lady with a baby."

Not only did people make room for them, several folk offered up chairs and refreshment to Brooke.

"That's why Garrison is special," Gretta said for her ears alone. "When my father is getting on my last nerve and I'm dying to go watch a professional ballet in a real performance hall with a live orchestra, I have to remind myself that this sweet little town would rally around me, my son, or my father in a heartbeat. It makes the two-hour-plus drive into any place with a decent ballet company worth it."

Once they'd all found seats at one of the large

round tables, Eloise found herself searching the room for her grandfather.

"They're over there." Mabel looked toward the far wall. "My uncle Felix calls it the Old Cowboys club. Where there's one, the rest are soon to gather."

Sure enough, her grandfather was wedged in among a group of white- and silver-haired men seated along the edge of the room.

"Now that handsome fella there is my uncle." Mabel pointed. "You met Gretta's father, Buck?"

Eloise nodded.

"Then you've got Nolan Woodard—it's so good to see him out and about—and Doc Johnson. He's been practicing medicine since I was little." She went on. "Dickie Schneider is one of the young ones, but they tolerate him. He and his wife own the grocery store. That one is Earl Ellis. He owns the feedstore in town. And there's Bart Carmichael. He's Hattie's daddy and a real sweetheart." Mabel listed off a few more, offering up a tidbit of information about each one.

Eloise listened but there was no way she was going to keep everyone straight. She'd reached her limit and the meeting had yet to start. People were still milling around the refreshments table, clustered together and talking, with no hint of urgency. She glanced at her watch. Junior Rangers only lasted an hour.

It was only when a gray-haired woman came

through the doors that the commotion died down a little. A distinguished older man trailed behind her, using a wooden cane for balance.

"Daddy came," Kitty whispered to Twyla. "I can't believe it."

But Twyla was smiling. "Good for Miss Martha."

"Miss Martha Zeigler and Dwight Crawley are quite the pair," Gretta whispered. "No one could have imagined it but…love finds a way."

As nice as that sounded, Eloise wasn't the romantic she once was.

"I think it's sweet." Mabel's smile indicated she *was* a romantic. "It's never too late to find the right person."

That part might be true. She liked the idea of finding the right person eventually. Way, way down the road. Now? No. She wasn't ready to open herself up for more disillusionment and pain.

From the corner of her eye, she saw Grandpa Quincy wave.

She turned and waved back.

But, between where she was and where Grandpa Quincy was sitting, stood a group she hadn't noticed before. A group Mike Woodard happened to be a part of. Fine. She could be neighborly. That's what being in a small town was all about. She'd set aside the hostility and whatever else his blue eyes might stir up and focused on the meeting.

"Oh, Eloise, how's that been going? Seeing Mike?" Brooke leaned forward to rest her elbows on the table. "Tough? That was a long time ago."

It had been years ago. Her father had her sent to Garrison under the guise of giving her a normal Christmas but that wasn't true. Her mother had been recovering from her first heart attack and her father was drinking more than ever to cope. If it wasn't for the alcohol, her father never would have hit her. But he had—and it forever changed their relationship. He'd had a hard time looking at her and she'd been wary of him. That was why her father had sent her to Garrison.

As soon as she'd arrived, she'd gone looking for Mike. She needed him, needed his gentle words and strong embrace. When she'd found Mike drunk with his friends, the betrayal was more than she could bear. He'd *known* how her father's alcoholism made her feel and how anti-drinking she was. The unexpected death of Gene Briscoe, the oldest Briscoe boy, had rocked the small town. Grieving was to be expected but drinking? Getting drunk? That's what her father had done. And, if her father could hit her, there was no guarantee Mike wouldn't do the same. It scared her. That had been *the* fight—the one that got heated and mean and ended it all.

When her mother had suffered a second heart attack and died a few days later, she'd been called back home. Her whole world had collapsed—taking all sense of security in the process.

She and her father never talked about what happened, how to grieve her mother, or how to heal. In fact, they never talked about much of anything. Instead, her father married Eloise's first stepmother and moved them halfway across the country from her home, friends, and family. After two more moves and two more stepmothers, she'd become pretty good at bottling things up.

"All of that is ancient history." And Eloise wanted to leave it that way.

"Mike Woodard is such a sweetheart." Mabel's gaze bounced between Eloise and Mike. "I can't believe he's single. He's quite a catch."

"That wasn't subtle. At all." Kitty Crawley patted Mabel's hand.

"That was painful." Twyla sighed, shaking her head.

Eloise would have agreed but she found herself laughing instead. Laughter was good. She needed more of it. So, she was going to enjoy herself, listen to what the formidable Martha Zeigler had to say and what was decided about Founder's Day, and ignore the odd looks Mike Woodard seemed to be sending her way.

"You know, growing up, Dad said it was rude to stare." Rusty nudged his elbow.

The nudge almost had Mike dropping his cup.

Instead, he splashed a good portion of his tea on his long-sleeve button-up.

"See." Rusty shook his head. "If you'd been paying less attention to her and more attention to what you're doing, you wouldn't have tea staining the shirt you spent thirty minutes ironing."

Mike shot his brother a look.

Rusty smiled back. "What?"

"Sometimes I wonder what it'd be like to be an only child." He used napkins to blot his shirt.

"Lonely." Rusty was unfazed. "Sad." He shrugged. "You couldn't make it without me."

Mike sighed. "Probably not."

"What's going on over there?" Tyson Ellis joined them, his gaze trained on the table where Eloise sat—the table Mike had been staring at. "You seem awfully concerned about whatever's happening over there, Mike."

"Told ya," Rusty murmured. "People are gonna notice."

"Wait." Tyson moved to Mike's other side. "Oh. I get it."

Don't ask. Don't say a word.

"Get what?" Rusty was grinning.

Tyson leveled a long, assessing look Mike's way. "That's Mike's El-Bell, isn't it? That's answer enough."

El-Bell was his nickname for Eloise. His and only his. Everyone who'd known them back then knew that and how devoted he'd been to her. Especially Rusty and Tyson.

Growing up, the three of them had always been getting into trouble and covering for each other. The point both Rusty and Tyson were trying, miserably, to make was his present behavior was going to lead to a whole lot of embarrassment and poking and prodding at old wounds.

"I don't know what you're talking about." Mike turned his back on Eloise. "What are you doing here, Tyson? How'd Martha Zeigler drag you into this?"

Tyson tipped his hat back on his head. "Something about a Founder's Day rodeo."

"A rodeo?" Mike knew the woman was ambitious but to organize a rodeo in two weeks' time was impossible. "She's serious?"

"It would seem so." Tyson took a cookie from the expansive refreshments table. "I'll hear her out but I'm not promising a thing."

"I'd say it can't happen but Miss Zeigler does have a way of making the impossible, possible." Rusty reached for a cookie, too.

"I think that's the nicest compliment I've ever received, Rusty Woodard." Martha Zeigler stood behind them, a white baker's box in her hands. "I came to add my contribution."

Out of habit, all three of them froze. Over the years, Martha Zeigler had doled out many a deserved punishment for their youthful shenanigans. Whether it was riding their bikes through her flower beds, setting off firecrackers under her porch, or crashing the golf cart Tyson had borrowed, without his father's permission, into her white picket fence, she'd made them work hard to repair the damage and teach them respect. At the time, Mike hadn't appreciated the way she'd handled it. Now, he did.

"Allow me." Mike took the box.

"I appreciate that, Mr. Woodard." The woman glanced between the three of them. "I declare, you three are acting mighty guilty."

"Guilty?" Tyson's chuckle was forced. "No, ma'am."

"We're just talking, is all." Rusty's cheeks were red.

"Uh-huh." She gave them each a long, assessing look. "I'm keeping my eyes on you all so you'd best behave."

Mike had always admired her ability to put someone in their place with a look. She didn't have to raise her voice or carry on. Nope, one look, and that was the end of it.

"I see your sweet father is here." Her tone softened. "I'm glad he's on the mend." She pointed at the box. "You add those to that tray and don't eat them all yourself." And with that, she headed for the podium at the front of the room.

"Every time." Rusty shook his head. "Every

time I see her, I feel like I've been caught with my hand in the cookie jar."

Tyson chuckled. "Don't I know it."

Mike chuckled as he put the box on the table, using the serving tongs to move the cookies from the box to the serving tray. He'd just finished when the crackling static of the microphone brought the room to absolute silence.

"Good evening, everyone." Martha Zeigler took a moment to look over the room.

Mike could almost imagine her taking note of those who hadn't attended.

"We have a lot to discuss and not a lot of time to do it, so let's begin." She lifted a yellow-paged legal tablet from the podium and turned the top page.

Mike was impressed with the woman's efficiency. The celebrations started with dawn's chuck-wagon breakfast and ended with fireworks at the fairgrounds. Somehow, she managed to convince all the Main Street shop owners to wear frontier attire, arrange for a farmer's market on the courthouse lawn, and have interactive historical booths and activities for children in the park around erste Baum. There would be hayrides from the main square to erste Baum and back, and a cattle drive down Main Street to the fairgrounds, and more.

By the time the meeting was all over, he had his phone out and was making notes.

"At least you don't have to put together a rodeo." Rusty sat back in his chair.

Tyson's brows rose. "Nope, just make sure there's no fire concerns and that the cattle are out of there before the fireworks start." He ran a hand over his face. "That's all."

"I'll help." Rusty slapped Tyson on the arm. "I'm sure the Briscoes will help out, too. And Jensen."

As much as Mike would have liked to lend a hand, he knew that he'd have to work. Big crowds meant a high risk for injury and a high need for EMT services. In all of Colton County, there were only four ambulances, a half-dozen certified paramedics, and a handful more of volunteer firefighters and medical professionals that could help out in an emergency. A festival wouldn't classify as an emergency, so he and Terri would be on duty.

All this was assuming he'd still be here. And that was up to his father. Until his father was hale and hearty, Mike wasn't going anywhere. He scanned the room and saw his father making his way toward them. And, from the looks of it, he was tuckered out. Quincy was walking along with him but if Dad went down, Quincy would probably go down, too. He headed that way but Eloise beat him.

"Is that the way these planning meetings always go?" Eloise asked. "I'm not sure I managed to process everything Miss Zeigler said."

A smile creased his father's face when Eloise hooked her arm through his. "That's understandable. It's taken me years to figure out how to sift through everything and find that piece of her grand design that's my responsibility."

When Eloise smiled up at his father, Mike's throat went dry. She was beautiful. Her hair was free, a glossy chestnut wave that rested on her shoulders. Her lips were a bold red—the same as her dress. A wide leather belt encircled her waist, showing off curves that had him tongue-tied and admiring.

"Ahem." Rusty nudged him in the side. He coughed, cleared his throat, and nudged him again.

"Yeah, yeah. I get it." Mike tore his gaze from Eloise.

Rusty and Tyson were laughing so hard, there was no way his father, Eloise, and Quincy could miss it.

"What's so funny?" Quincy Green was already smiling.

"Mike," Tyson managed, then started laughing again.

"What about him?" His father shot Mike a curious look.

"Nothing. You know how these two get." Mike sighed, hoping that would be the end of it.

"Eloise, you remember Tyson Ellis? He was always running around with the Woodard boys when you'd come to visit. And, for the most part, he's still running around with them." Quincy patted Tyson on the shoulder.

"Nice to see you, Tyson. I admit, after that—" Eloise pointed at the podium "—my brain's short-circuiting."

"Understandable." Tyson touched the brim of his hat. "I remember you. You still scared of spiders?"

Eloise blinked, her mouth opening, then closing. All of a sudden, her gaze shifted and locked with Mike's. Was she thinking about that time a huge tarantula went crawling into their path and she'd climbed up onto his back—making Tyson and Rusty laugh so hard they had tears running down their cheeks? He sure was.

"You have a seat, Nolan." Quincy pulled out a chair as he spoke. "No need taxing yourself while the young folk converse a spell."

When his old man didn't argue and sat, Mike knew it was time to head home. He poured a glass of tea, grabbed a napkin, and took two ginger-snap cookies off the tray. "Have a little snack. Keep your blood sugar up." He set the cookies on the napkin before his father and handed over the drink.

"I'm fine." But his father took a long sip of tea and nibbled on the cookie.

"I'll bring the truck around." Mike waited for Rusty's nod. "It was nice seeing you all." He tipped his hat at Eloise and forced himself across the room and down the hall to the front door.

He'd almost reached it when he saw Brooke leaning against a column and fanning herself. He paused. "You okay?"

"I'm great. I'd be better if everyone stopped looking at me like a ticking time bomb. I know I'm huge but I still have another six weeks." She patted his arm, then folded her hands across her pregnant belly. "Leaving?"

"I think Dad's done in for the night." He paused, giving her a nod.

She glanced around, then stepped closer. "You doing okay?"

"Good. With Dad on the mend, I've got no complaints."

"I'm glad he's getting better—we all are." There was a pause. "You know I'm not a fan of gossiping, Mike, but Eloise's grandpa's been worrying out loud." She was whispering now. "All about how hard she is on herself, how closed off she is around folk, and not reaching out to old friends." She hesitated, then added, "I figure that stings a little, all things considered."

It did, but he wasn't going to say as much. "Considering how things were left, it's no surprise."

"Mr. Mike, Mr. Mike. I'm a Junior Ranger." Kirby came running toward him. "We made all sorts of stuff for the Founding Day festival. And

I got to sit with Samantha. She likes horses and princesses. I like horses and princesses, too."

"Sounds like you had quite an evening, Kirby." He smiled down at the little girl. "Did you have fun?"

"Yes. It was the bestest time." She looked as delighted as she sounded. "Was your meeting fun?"

Mike chuckled. "It was…something. We didn't make anything but there were snacks."

"Any cupcakes?" Kirby asked.

"Mr. Mike." Archie arrived, turning this way and that as if he were searching for something, with Hattie Carmichael trailing behind him. "Is Clifford here? Can I say hi?"

"Clifford's still tuckered out from your visit last night." Mike winked at the boy. "But I'll be sure to give him an extra treat from you."

"Okay." Archie's disappointment was obvious. "I hope he won't forget us. I hope Momma lets us visit again."

"Let's go find your momma and find out." Hattie waved as she led the kids down the hall. "Night, y'all."

"Cute kids. Who do they belong to?" Brooke asked, watching them go.

"Eloise."

Brooke arched her back. "They sure seem to like you."

"They like my dog." He laughed. "If you'll excuse me, I'm going to bring the truck up for Dad.

You put your feet up and take it easy—let that husband of yours wait on you."

"Oh, he does." She pointed. "See."

Audy had pulled his truck right up to the front door of the Community Center. He was grinning from ear to ear when he reached Brooke's side. "There's my wife."

"I'm so big, it's impossible to miss me." But Brooke melted into his embrace.

"You're not big, you're perfect. My boy needs room to grow." Audy kissed her nose.

"Your boy? What if it turns out to be your girl?" Brooke asked.

"She needs room to grow, too." Audy turned. "Mike, didn't see you there. Too blinded by my wife's beauty."

Mike was still laughing when he reached his truck. It was a wonder the way things worked out sometimes. Not all that long ago, Brooke and Audy couldn't stand each other. Now, they seemed about as well suited as a couple could be. And he was happy for them.

He pulled up and parked in the spot Audy had vacated. When his father and Rusty didn't come right out, he went in to find his dad sitting in the same chair. He was smiling at something Archie was saying, but there was a definite droop to his shoulders. Tonight had been too much, too soon.

He didn't realize Eloise had come to stand by

him until she spoke. "I think he'll need a hand getting to the truck."

Mike nodded.

"Is there anything I can do?" The concern on her face touched him.

"I appreciate that, El." He shook his head, then paused. "Your visit last night sure lifted his spirits. If you have the time, you and the kids are welcome."

She glanced his way. "I'm sure Grandpa would be happy to bring them."

His eyes met hers. "I'm pretty sure he enjoyed your company, too."

"*He* did?" She'd turned to face him.

Okay, if they were being honest—he hadn't exactly hated her being there. But he didn't say as much.

"It's best if they come with my grandfather." She took a deep breath. "I don't want people talking about me. Or me and you. With our history, I don't want people thinking we're pursuing..." She faltered.

Pursuing what? What was she getting at? "Friendship?" He frowned.

"I don't see how that's possible." Her full lips pressed tight.

"Maybe not." He cleared his throat. "But we were pretty good friends, once."

Her gaze was hard and her tone was brittle as

she said, "Friends don't treat each other the way we did."

"We were both hurting. Both young." When he looked back on their fight, he felt as wounded and betrayed as he had the day it happened. They'd both been grieving and raw—too caught up in their own suffering to see how much they needed each other. And that grief broke them. He cleared his throat again, eager to leave. "I'd best get my father home to rest. I'm sure I'll see you around, El-Bell. You take care of yourself." He touched the brim of his hat only to find her staring up at him.

But she didn't say anything. Just stared at him with those big, wary eyes.

Even after he'd gotten his father home and into bed, he couldn't help thinking about that look. Had he done something? Said something? Did it even matter? She'd made it plain she had no interest in having anything to do with him. It was probably for the best. He'd follow her lead, leave the past in the past, and leave well enough alone.

CHAPTER FIVE

ELOISE BACKED IN the front door, a full grocery bag in each hand. "I'm back," she called out, only to find her grandfather and both kids sitting on the couch. "What are you three up to?" She pushed the door shut behind her.

"I'm showing them a little about Garrison and a little bit about you when you'd come visit." He smiled up at her.

"Grandpa says you're about my age in this picture." Kirby pointed at one of the pictures.

"How about I get some help putting everything away and then I'll come look at the pictures with you?"

"Now that's a plan." Her grandfather stood, took a bag, and headed for the kitchen.

Archie did the same, while Kirby skipped along beside her down the hall.

"The pictures Grandpa was showing us were real old." Archie started unpacking the bag onto the counter.

Eloise had to laugh at Archie's announcement.

"I thought you were looking at pictures of me when I was young?"

"Yep." Archie pushed his glasses up on his nose. "Grandpa said you took your first hayride at the Founder's Day Festival. Me and Kirby will, too."

"That's true." She put the milk and orange juice in the refrigerator.

"Is it scary?" Kirby asked, taking the eggs from Grandpa Quincy and carrying them, with extreme care, to Eloise. "Archie says the wagon is pulled by horses and sometimes, horses can take off running for no reason. They can buck and bite and be wild."

Eloise paused, glancing at her son. "Where did you hear that?"

"Levi told me." Archie shrugged. "He's a real cowboy and he lives on a real ranch so he knows about horses and cows—cattle—and stuff."

"Who is Levi?" When had Archie been talking to a cowboy?

"He's so cool. He was at Junior Rangers. He knew all sorts of stuff."

"He was a helper?" Eloise had a hard time imagining Hattie being okay with one of the helpers telling the kids something like that.

"No, he's a Junior Ranger." Archie folded up the shopping bag.

"Levi Williams." Grandpa Quincy nodded. "Gretta's boy."

"Oh." Eloise put the yogurt in the refrigerator

and closed the door. "I don't live on a real ranch *but* I know the horses pulling the wagon for the hayride will be gentle and won't take off running, Kirby."

"You promise?" Kirby didn't look convinced.

"I do." Eloise smiled. "I learned how important Founder's Day is at that meeting Grandpa and I went to. They wouldn't want anyone to get hurt. They will only pick the most gentle and best wagon-pulling horses around."

"Okay." Kirby relaxed. "Then can we go on the hayride?"

She nodded.

"Yay!" Kirby clapped and jumped up and down. "Samantha is going on the hayride, too."

"She keeps talking about Samantha." Archie rolled his eyes.

"She's nice. Levi's not." Kirby crossed her arms over her chest. "He said girls are stinky."

"I told him you didn't stink." Archie sighed.

"I think we're all done in here." Grandpa Quincy took the recyclable shopping bag from Archie and stored it away. "How about we go look at more pictures?" He waved the kids down the hall and smiled at her. "That Levi is a handful. From what Doc was saying, that boy tells tall tales that might just rival our Archie."

"Great." Just what Archie needed—a co-conspirator. She flipped off the kitchen light and followed her grandfather back down the hall to the living room.

Once they were all comfortable, Grandpa Quincy lifted the oversized album off the top of the stack. "Your great-grandmother used to get so much joy putting these things together." He ran his hand over the fabric cover. "She had some sort of subscription that sent her stickers and fancy scissors and stencils and such. I can't tell you how many stories we shared while she was making these books."

Eloise draped an arm along the back of the sofa so she could give her grandfather's shoulder a squeeze.

"She'd be tickled pink to know her great-grandchildren were looking at them." He chuckled. "Now, let's see." He flipped a few pages. "Here we go." He tapped one photo. "That's your momma. She was about six here. It was Founder's Day."

Eloise studied the picture. Another lifetime. A happy one—before her mother died.

Her memories of Garrison were warm and real and comforting. That's why she'd brought the kids here. She wanted them to grow up feeling connected and seen. And, maybe, she wanted that for herself, too.

"And that's your great-grandmother," her grandpa was saying. "There's always something fun happening. You'll see. Your momma always had a real good time when she visited."

"Did you, Momma?" Kirby stared up at her, waiting for her answer.

"I did, Freckles."

"What about Dad? Did Dad ever come here?" Archie went from concerned to panicked. "Wait, will Dad know how to find us?"

"He has the address. I know, when he's able, he'll come see you both." She gave him a reassuring smile. Her sweet boy had always been anxious. The divorce didn't help. Ted "traveling" didn't help. But Archie's counselor thought that explanation would cause Archie less stress and anxiety than knowing his father was in prison. Prison was a scary and dangerous place—and, for the time being, too much for Archie's fragile psyche. Ted had, of course, been on board with this recommendation.

"Do you think he will move here, too?" Archie flipped the page. "He should."

"I don't know, sweetie. That will be his decision." Eloise couldn't imagine her ex settling here. "I know he'll do his best to be close to you and see you whenever he can." She hoped that would be the end of it.

"What's that?" Kirby was all too happy to get back to the pictures.

"That was a World Hat Day party." Grandpa Quincy shook his head. "Something the Garrison Ladies Guild put together one year."

Eloise smiled over the pictures of her grandparents. "Gramma Beryl looks so glamorous."

"She always was a looker." He smiled at the picture. "But your momma wasn't here for that so…" He flipped a few pages. "Here we go. Christmas."

The picture was like stepping back in time. "We were caroling." She ran a finger along the edge of the photo. "I was trying to sing. But I'd been practicing so much that my voice was almost gone." Caroling was one of her favorite parts of Christmas and she'd been so sad.

"You sounded like a rooster trying to crow." Her grandfather chuckled. "If I recall correctly, the other kids sang off-key and real loud to make you feel better."

He was right, they had—at Mike's suggestion.

"Who's that?" Archie leaned forward to frown at the picture.

"That's Mike Woodard and your momma." Grandpa Quincy shook his head. "I'd say that boy's done some growing."

"*That's* Mr. Mike?" Kirby giggled. "He's little. Was he your friend, Momma?"

"Why does he have his arm around you?" Archie wasn't happy.

"He and your momma were sweethearts." Grandpa Quincy chuckled.

Archie crossed his arms over his chest, displeasure lining his face.

"I was cold." She hurried to explain, surprised

by Archie's reaction. "He let me wear his coat but my teeth were chattering."

"That's a good friend." Kirby patted the picture. "I like Mr. Mike. And Clifford."

We were friends once.

Yes, they were. There were plenty of pictures of them together to prove that. Page after page of the holidays and festivals she'd spent here. Whether it'd been a Fourth of July picnic, hunting for Easter eggs, or caroling along Main Street, Mike always found her and—just like that—things were more fun. He'd included her in the shenanigans he and his brother got into and she'd loved laughing at all of his bad jokes and silly faces. He'd been sweet and funny and the person she'd looked forward to seeing most when she visited her grandparents.

Later, he'd been so much more than her friend. She'd loved him—really loved him. She'd loved the way her hand fit in his. She'd loved the way his arms had felt around her and how breathless she'd get from his kisses. He'd loved her, too. At least, she thought he had. She'd honestly thought he'd always be there for her. That he understood and respected her.

I was so naïve. He'd hurt her. A lot.

Grandpa Quincy was her mother's father. When her mother died, her father couldn't bear to have contact with anyone associated with her. Which meant Eloise lost contact, too. In a way it had been good—she hadn't known how she'd face Mike after what happened.

"I'm hungry." Archie was still frowning at the picture. "What's for dinner?"

"Chicken Alfredo." Eloise pushed off the couch. "Which I should start cooking."

"Do you need any help?" Archie stood, too. "I'm done looking at pictures."

"I'm not." Kirby leaned against Grandpa Quincy's side. "Show me more, Grandpa."

"You bet, Freckles."

Eloise waited until they reached the kitchen to ask, "Is everything okay? You seem kind of glum."

"Fine." He sat at the kitchen table, draped his arms across the surface, and rested his chin on the tabletop. Clearly, he wasn't fine.

"Bad day at school?" She filled the large stainless steel pot with water and put it on the stove burner. "Or something else?" With a turn of the knob, the blue fire of the gas range started. "Talking will help." She wanted to make sure her kids felt safe enough to talk and share their emotions—even when it was hard.

"I got another note," he mumbled.

She didn't want to be upset but she was tired of having the same conversation with her son. "What happened?"

"Some kid said we were poor and that's why we're living with Grandpa Quincy. I told him to shut up." He pushed his glasses up, then looked at her. "Are we poor? Is that why we live with Grandpa Quincy? But we can't be poor since Dad's always working so much."

Oh boy. Eloise walked over and knelt beside him. "We live with Grandpa Quincy because we're helping each other out. I help him at the shop and he helps us by letting us live here. It's what family does, you know? Look out for one another."

"Then why is Dad gone all the time? He should be looking out for me and Kirby."

She rested her hand on his back. "Your father loves you and your sister more than anything in the whole world. Don't you ever forget that." That was the one thing she never doubted about Ted: his love for his children. "Sometimes, being a grown-up is hard."

"Some dads have jobs that let them stay home. Why can't he have one of those jobs? Why, Momma?" He sniffed, rubbing his nose with the back of his arm. "I miss him."

"I know you do, sweetie." She leaned forward and drew him into a big, long hug. Archie wrapped his arms around her neck and held on tight. Her heart ached for him. As a mother, she wanted to take away her son's hurt. But this was one of those times where that was impossible. "I'm sorry about what happened in class today." She held him away from her and tried to smile.

The tip of his nose was red and there were tears on his cheeks. "What can I do to cheer you up?" She wiped away the tears.

He was quiet for a while. "Can we have pizza for dinner?"

She was pretty sure there wasn't a pizza delivery place in Garrison. "Let's go ask Grandpa Quincy if there's someplace to get pizza."

"Okay. I'll go ask." Archie perked up a little. "Kirby likes pizza." He hopped down from the chair and ran down the hall into the family room.

"She does." Eloise turned off the burner. Surely there was someplace with pizza in Garrison. It would be nice to have a night out and not have to clean up the kitchen. And she could make chicken Alfredo tomorrow.

"Yay!" Archie's excited voice carried down the hallway.

She grabbed her purse and headed down the hall. "Are we going to get pizza?"

It took a good five minutes to find Kirby's shoes, but then they were on the sidewalk making the short walk to Main Street.

"I like walking, Momma." Kirby held her hand, skipping at her side. "My teacher Miss Rowe says that's one of the things she likes best about living here."

"I agree. I love that we don't have to drive everywhere." Garrison was such a pretty little town. Her grandfather's neighborhood was neat as a pin.

It didn't matter if it was the grandest house on the block or one an eighth that size, people took pride in their homes. Yards were neatly mowed, sidewalks swept clean—there was even the occasional white picket fence. "And I love the trees." The town was full of tall oak trees that provided shade even on the hottest days.

"Erste Baum is even bigger. Miss Rowe says it's the biggest tree ever." Kirby kept on skipping. "In Garrison."

"It is." Grandpa Quincy was walking with Archie right behind them. "You'll get to see just how big it is this weekend at the wedding. And I bet you'll get to see some of your school friends, too. From the sounds of it, the whole town will be there."

"Do you think Mr. Mike will bring Clifford?" For the first time since earlier, Archie sounded happy.

"Well, now, I don't know about that. But I was thinking of stopping in on Nolan tomorrow, anyway. Seeing how he's feeling." Grandpa Quincy was close to Nolan Woodard. "I'm sure he'd be happy to see you all. I'll tell you a secret."

"What, Grandpa?" Kirby stopped and turned to face them. "I'm a good secret keeper."

"Me, too." Archie stared up at his grandfather, waiting.

"Well, maybe it's not a secret. More like life advice." He chuckled. "When you get as old as

I am, you learn how important the little things are. Like making time for your friends and family. Nothing, I mean nothing, says you care or lifts a person's spirits as much as spending time with them."

It sounded so simple. Most of the people she'd loved hadn't wanted her time or her company, they'd wanted something from her or her compliance. It wasn't about *her*. But that was a different time and place. If she was truly going to make Garrison her home, she couldn't be so jaded. She had to give this place and these people a chance. She'd even try, for the kids and her grandfather, to get along with Mike Woodard. She'd try. But there was no guarantee.

Mike's horse, Chuck, snorted and pawed at the dirt of the arena. "Yeah, I'm ready to go home, too." He patted the horse on the shoulder. "Not too much longer." He tipped his hat forward to shield the setting sun from his eyes.

From the stands, Tyson waved.

He nodded back, stifling a yawn.

He wasn't worrying over his father tonight—thanks to the Garrison Ladies Guild. Patsy Monahan had called the shop to tell Rusty the whole guild was coming to his father's place to lend a hand. According to Rusty, they were going to cook and clean and who knows what else. Unfortunately, Mike's plan to head home and turn in early had been foiled when Audy Briscoe had texted him a reminder about the high school rodeo teams' practice. Being an EMT and a pick-up rider, the team relied on him to keep everyone safe. Most of the time he enjoyed it. There was nothing like seeing a kid have a good ride or set a new personal best record and get a confidence boost. But he was dragging and it was only Wednesday.

"Good." Audy Briscoe called out to the teen on horseback. "Keep a hold of that rein, Hans." He rode closer to Martha Zeigler's grandson and adjusted the boy's grip on the thick braided material of the reins. "Believe me, you'll need to keep a hold. It might be eight seconds, but it'll feel a whole lot longer."

"Yes, sir." The boy nodded, listening as Audy gave him some more pointers.

With a light squeeze, Mike steered Chuck to the pipe fence that surrounded the entire arena.

Tyson walked down the bleacher stairs, a clipboard hanging from one hand. "How'd you get wrangled into this? Don't you have enough going on?"

He chuckled. "I gave my word I'd be at all the practices."

"I'm sure Audy and the kids appreciate it. Looks like the Zeigler boy has some talent." He nodded at the boy working with Audy.

"Yep. And Audy's a good coach." He yawned again. "What are you working on?"

"Making a list of repairs. That row needs replacing." Tyson lifted the top page. "The whole place could use an overhaul but we don't have the budget."

"Put Miss Martha on it. She'll put together some fundraiser and you'll have all the money you need—and then some." Mike was only partly kidding.

Audy whistled, catching Mike's attention, and signaled they were wrapping things up.

"You eaten yet? I'm hungry." Tyson glanced at his watch. "You can turn Chuck loose in one of the corrals and come back and get him after we eat."

Mike rested his hands on the pommel of the saddle and looked at his friend. "You buying?"

Tyson laughed. "I didn't say that."

Twenty minutes later, he and Tyson were walking into the Buttermilk Pie Café.

"Evenings, boys." Miss Lucille waved from behind the counter. "You go on and find yourself a table and we'll get you taken care of."

"I'm gonna go wash up." Mike headed for the bathroom. He needed to splash some cold water on his face or he'd fall asleep at the table. On the way out of the restroom, he heard an excited squeal.

"Mr. Mike, Mr. Mike." Kirby came running

and hugged him around the knees. "Are you here to have pizza, too?"

"Oh. Kirby, honey." Eloise reached for her daughter's hand. "I'm sorry," she said to him.

He wasn't. Kirby's cheery disposition perked him right up. "It's not very often I get such an enthusiastic greeting." He grinned down at Kirby. "Pizza, huh?"

"Uh-huh. I like pizza."

"It might be waiting for us at the table." Eloise wiggled her daughter's arm. "We should go wash our hands."

"Okay. You have to wash your hands to stay healthy." Kirby pulled against her mother. "Oh, and it's important to eat breakfast, lunch, and dinner. Miss Rowe says it's how you keep your brain and body healthy and strong." The little girl paused. "Miss Rowe is my teacher."

"Sounds like she's pretty smart." Mike got tired just thinking about corralling a classroom full of bouncy, curious five-year-olds.

"She's a teacher. Teachers are smart." The little girl nodded.

"Come on, Kirby. I'm sure Mr. Mike is as eager for his dinner as you are for yours." Eloise steered her daughter to the ladies' restroom.

Before the door closed, Kirby waved at him.

He was still smiling when he joined Tyson at their booth.

"What's that about?" Tyson glanced up from his menu. "That smile?"

"Can't a man smile?" Mike set his menu aside. He was so hungry, he knew exactly what he wanted.

"Hey, hey now. Someone's sounding hangry." Tyson cocked an eyebrow.

"Hangry, huh? I think you've been hanging around with the rodeo club kids too much." He hung his hat on the hook Lucille had added to the outside of each booth. She knew her clientele well.

"It means angry and hungry."

"I know what it means." Mike shook his head, chuckling. "I just never thought I'd hear you say it."

"What can I get you two?" Myrna Ingells stood at the end of their booth, a pad in hand.

"Hey, Myrna. When did you start working here?" Tyson set his menu down. "Things slowing down at the salon?"

Myrna was one of the beauticians that rented booth space in Brooke's salon. She'd been there as long as Mike could remember, long before the place was Brooke's—so seeing her waitressing was a first.

"Slowing down?" Myrna's snort was dismissive. "No, sir. I'm picking up some shifts. Trying to help my little sister finish college."

"That's mighty nice of you." Mike meant it. "What's she studying again?"

"She's going to be a nurse practitioner, whatever that means exactly." Myrna shrugged. "All I know is she's helping sick people get better and I'm proud to help her do that. So, you two know what you'd like?"

"Hamburger special. And a chocolate shake. And tea." Tyson handed over his menu.

"I think I'm hungry enough to go for it." Mike handed her the menu. "I'll take the Texas-sized chicken fried steak dinner. And a tea."

Myrna blinked. "You sure about that?"

"I'm sure." He smiled.

"Okay. It's your heartburn." Myrna took the menus and walked to the counter to put in their orders.

"Think your dad's surviving with the ladies?" Tyson asked, his gaze wandering around the restaurant.

"Oh, he's probably enjoying having a houseful of women taking care of him." He paused, thinking. "But he'll be just as happy when they go home."

"Uh-huh." Tyson's attention returned to him. "I see why you were smiling."

"Can we talk about anything else?" Mike heard Kirby's infectious laugh from somewhere behind him but didn't turn around. He did, however, smile.

"You wanna tell me why we're not talking about…that." Tyson pointed at his face.

"There's nothing to tell." Mike wasn't smiling now. "Whatever happened was fifteen years ago—it doesn't mean a thing now."

Tyson's eyes narrowed and his mouth tightened, like he was holding something back.

"Go on and say it." He propped himself up on one elbow. "You're going to anyway."

"For something that doesn't mean a thing, you're awful riled up about it." Tyson smiled his thanks as Myrna put their drinks on the table.

"Riled up about what?" Myrna asked.

Mike glared at Tyson. If the man opened his mouth, he'd kick him in the shin—but good.

"Oh, you know how it is. Your friends start getting married and people start asking you when you're going to get married, that sort of thing." Tyson grinned up at Myrna.

"Wait a few years and people will stop asking." Myrna tucked her pencil behind her ear. "You reach a certain age and you're past your prime. Believe me, I know. And, boy howdy, am I grateful." She laughed. "There's nothing wrong with being your own person."

"That's what I was telling Mike. He shouldn't cave to any pressure." Tyson's smile meant trouble. "You see, he's always been a ladies' man. A heartbreaker. Not the marrying type." Tyson was having way too much fun. Mike was no ladies' man and they both knew it. Tyson liked to give him grief for being too nice—saying that's why Mike always ended up stuck in the friend zone. "A no-count love-'em-and-leave-'em sort of man, that's him. Starting back, oh, in high school, I'd say."

"Well, Mike Woodard, I'm surprised." Myrna's brows rose high.

Mike opened his mouth to contradict Tyson's load of horse pucky but his friend cut him off.

"Oh, he is. Believe me." Tyson was near laughing now. "Not me, though. People say I'm too nice for my own good. I didn't think a person could be too nice."

Which is what Mike would say to him when Tyson would throw the whole "too nice" thing in his face.

"You can't be too nice." Eloise's brittle voice came out of nowhere.

And, just like that, things were no longer funny.

He leaned forward to see Eloise and her kids standing around the side of the booth.

"What's a ladies' man?" Kirby asked. "Or a heartbreaker? Doesn't sound very nice."

"I'm going to go check on your food." Myrna made a beeline for the kitchen.

Tyson was no help; he'd gone as still as a statue. *Now's a fine time to stop talking.* Mike took a deep breath. "Tyson was teasing—even though it's not funny."

"Why is he teasing?" Kirby looked confused. For that matter, so did Eloise. Archie, on the other hand, looked upset.

"Well." He swallowed. "Sometimes friends do that." Which sounded pretty pathetic.

"That's not nice." The little girl shook her head. "Or friendly."

Mike turned to Tyson, silently pleading for help.

"You're right," Tyson managed, pulling at the neck of his shirt. "I'm sorry, Mike. I shouldn't have said that... Sorry." He took a sip of tea.

"Archie had something he wanted to tell you." Eloise nodded at her son, barely glancing Mike's way as she said, "Hurry up, before our pizza comes."

But Archie didn't say a word. Mike had never been on the receiving end of such anger. But it was rolling off the boy—at him.

"Go on, Archie." Kirby patted her brother. "Don't be mad."

"Why do you love 'em and leave 'em?" Archie crossed his arms over his chest. "If you love someone, you shouldn't leave." Then the boy burst into angry tears. "You should stay. You should take care of them. That's what love means."

It didn't matter that every person in the restaurant heard the boy's outburst, Mike *felt* it. Every one of the boy's words was a cut to his heart. He knew that kind of anger. He knew that kind of hurt. It'd taken years to grow and heal before he could let it go. "You're right, Archie. I'm sorry. I'm so sorry." He didn't know what to do or say, but he had to do something.

Before he could move, Eloise had dropped to her knees beside her son and pulled him into her arms. "It's okay, sweetie." She ran a hand over his hair. "It's okay."

"I wanna go home, Momma." Archie's words were muffled against her shoulder. "I want to go *now*."

"Okay." Her arms stayed tight around the boy. "Kirby, please go tell Grandpa we want to take our pizza home, okay, sweetie?"

"Is Archie going to be okay, Momma?" Kirby was on the verge of tears now.

"He will be just fine." She managed a reassuring smile. "Don't you worry."

"'Kay. I'll go tell Grandpa." Kirby ran across the restaurant, too upset to keep her voice down. "Grandpa, we need to take the pizza home in a pizza box because Archie's crying."

"I don't want to go back to Grandpa's." Archie pulled back enough to see his mother. "I want to go to our real home. I want my old friends. I—I want Daddy."

Eloise blinked rapidly, the muscle in her jaw tight. "I know, Archie. I know you do. Change is hard." She smoothed the hair from his forehead. "It's okay to be upset. I'm so proud of you for telling me what you're feeling. If there was a way I could give you everything you want, I would. But, I promise you, we'll figure this out together.

Me and you and Kirby. And Grandpa Quincy, too. Okay?"

Mike was in awe of the woman. She didn't hush her son or get embarrassed over his outburst or care about the stares and whispers of the restaurant patrons. Her son hurt and that was all that mattered to her.

And Mike felt lower than dirt that he'd been the one to trigger such pain.

"Okay." Archie sniffed and wiped his nose.

"Okay." She smiled, squeezing his shoulders.

"I wanted to tell you that we walked here and I saw your brother walking Clifford so we said hi." Archie barely looked at him. "That's all."

Eloise stood and said, "You two have a nice evening." She kept her eyes on her son as they walked away.

He sat, trying to figure out what to do now. What to say. He couldn't just leave things this way. That boy… He swallowed hard against the jagged lump in his throat.

"Well, I hope you're hungry." Myrna slid his platter-sized plate in front of him. "You know the deal. If you eat it all, it's free." She eyed the plate and shook her head. "And your burger special." She glanced over her shoulder. "Oh, they're leaving." She sighed. "That poor boy. And his sweet momma. I don't know much about that family but something tells me they've been through a world of hurt." She patted the end of the table. "Let me know if y'all need anything."

Mike stared down at the mountain of food he'd been starving for not ten minutes ago. His appetite was long gone.

"I am sorry, man." Tyson groaned. "I didn't think... How was I to know... I'm sorry."

Mike nodded. It had been an accident. There was no way to know Archie had heard them, let alone how he'd react. But it didn't matter. The boy had heard. And his reaction would haunt Mike for the rest of his days. He couldn't let the boy think the worst of him. He had to fix it.

CHAPTER SIX

SATURDAY WAS A perfect outdoor wedding day. The sun was out, the clouds were fluffy and white, and there was enough chill in the air to keep things comfortable. Eloise hoped this was a good indicator for the day ahead of them.

"Where do these go?" Grandpa Quincy held a large white wicker basket overflowing with dahlias, hydrangea, lily of the valley, and white roses.

"I'll weave them into the arch." She pointed at the large wooden arch wrapped in green and brown vines. "But I can get it, Grandpa." As much as he refused to admit it, she knew lifting and carrying things was a struggle for him.

"Of course you can," he grumbled. "But so can I. That's what my cart is for." He set the basket in his collapsible red wagon. "There's no shame in making life a little easier."

"No, sir, there is not." She smiled. "Archie, would you and Kirby pick up all the flowers that fell inside the van and put them in Grandpa's wagon? Then you can blow bubbles all you want."

She stood back to assess her work so far. Each of the white folding chairs had a swath of tulle across the back. The end of each row had a distressed metal milk churn ready and waiting for the arrangements Eloise had waiting in the truck—along with the dozen flower balls to hang from the canopy-like branches of erste Baum.

She stared up at the tree overhead, marveling at its size. She'd never seen a tree this big before. It had seemed huge when she was little but children often see things as bigger than they are. Erste Baum was the exception to this. It really was huge. Kirby said it was big enough for a whole village of elves to live in. Eloise agreed.

"Ready for the ladder?" Her grandfather headed back to the van.

"Sure." While she climbed up to tie each of the flower balls to a branch, Grandpa Quincy held the ladder steady. "How does it look?" she asked, staying on the ladder in case she needed to adjust the twine length.

"I'd say it's just about perfect." Grandpa Quincy shook his head. "You're a creative one, Eloise Green."

She climbed down the ladder and smiled at him. "I'd say we're a pretty good team."

"Isn't that the truth?" He chuckled. "What else?"

She put Grandpa Quincy in charge of placing the aisle arrangements, made sure the kids were okay, then started on the arch. It was a painstaking process. Making sure each flower was visible while ensuring the cascade pattern hung in just the right way.

She was halfway through when she heard voices.

"Holy cow. This...this is incredible." Hattie Carmichael stood at the end of what would be the aisle with Mabel, Brooke, and Gretta.

"Oh, Eloise." Mabel placed a hand over her heart. "It's beautiful. It's like the flowers just sort of bloomed here—like they belong."

It always thrilled her to hear her work praised. "I was told to make it glamorous rustic." Which was a term she'd never heard before. "I hope this works."

"I don't know what you'd call it, but it's beautiful." Brooke was taking everything in, turning slowly.

"It's settled, if I ever do get married again, you're doing my flowers." Gretta stared up at the hanging flower balls. "*Just* like this."

"Can we help?" Hattie asked.

"Um..." Eloise wasn't sure she was serious. "You're the bride."

"Don't I know it." Hattie shrugged. "I can't see Forrest. I don't want to get into that dress until I have to. My parents keep giving me these teary-eyed looks... Something you should know about me, I like to do things. I'm a doer. I can't just sit and wait or watch others do."

There was no way Eloise was going to let them help with the arch—she had a very particular layout. But her grandpa did seem to be slowing down. "If you're sure?" She waited for Hattie to nod. "Grandpa, you can go play with the kids, if you want?"

"I don't mind if I do." He grinned. "I'll leave you ladies to it."

It was only when the four women started helping that Eloise realized how quiet things had been. Now, the chatter and laughter made the work feel less like work and more like fun. She stayed busy, kneeling and crouching and bending to get the flowers onto the arch just right, while listening in on the conversation.

"I can't believe you're not nervous, Hattie," Gretta said.

"I didn't say that." Hattie's sigh was long and drawn out. "I'm nervous. I could trip in that big ol' poofy dress."

Eloise smiled, tucking a white rose and a cluster of baby's breath into the vines of the arch.

"That's not what I meant." But Gretta was laughing.

"I wasn't nervous when I married Audy." Brooke was sitting in a chair close to Eloise, her hands resting on her stomach. "I was…happy."

"And as long as I make it down the aisle without tripping, I'll be happy, too." Clearly, Hattie was worried about her wedding dress.

"You won't trip." Brooke laughed. "Go slow. One step at a time."

Archie came running up. "Momma, we're out of bubble juice."

"Already?" Eloise stopped working and sat back on her heels. "There's a big jug in the van. But let Grandpa pour it, okay? If you get some on your hands and wipe your eyes, it'll make your eyes burn."

"Yes, ma'am." He ran over and climbed into the van. "Hey, Warden Carmichael."

"Hey, Archie. You looking for this?" She handed over the jug.

"Thank you." He held the bottle close. "Are you getting married in that?"

Hattie looked down at her jeans and too big T-shirt. "I wish."

"It's all right by me." Archie shrugged, jumped out of the van, and ran back into the field where Kirby and Grandpa Quincy were waiting.

"Maybe I will get married in this." Hattie slid from the van, holding the last of the vases. "Then I wouldn't worry about tripping."

"You know Forrest won't care." Mabel came over to Eloise's side and sat on the grass next to where she was working. "My brother still gets tongue-tied whenever you wear a dress. He'll probably pass out when he sees you in your wedding dress."

Hattie dropped down in the grass beside Mabel,

then lay flat. "I do kind of want to see his face when he sees me."

"That's the look." Brooke nodded. "That look that tells you he loves you more than anything and he's proud that you're his."

"Audy's always looking at you like that." Hattie groaned. "And Jensen's all googly-eyed as soon as he sees you, Mabel." She looked at Eloise. "I think we owe it to Eloise and Gretta to find them men who'll look at them like that."

"Oh, let's." Mabel perked up a little too much for Eloise's liking.

"You two sound like a younger version of the Garrison Ladies Guild." At least Brooke didn't sound excited. "Of course, if *we* don't find them their perfect men, then the Garrison Ladies Guild will hound them until they're satisfied."

Eloise paused, a lily in her hands. "That sounds ominous."

"Have you met them?" Mabel wrinkled up her nose.

"Grandpa Quincy told me to stay out of their way. He said they loved to stir up gossip and spread it all over everyone." Eloise glanced into the field where the kids were chasing bubbles.

"Your grandpa is a smart man." Hattie rolled onto her side. "I'm sure he'd agree with what Mabel and I are proposing."

"Oh, I'm sure he would, too." Eloise went back to work. "But I've made it clear that I'm not interested in dating—or finding the perfect man. Even if he does give me the look."

"Same." Gretta held up her hand. "No, thank you. I've got my hands full with Levi and the studio. I'm supposed to add dating?"

The rumble of a truck engine drew all eyes.

"It's not Forrest, is it?" Hattie hid behind Mabel. "He can't see me."

"It's not," Mabel assured her. "It's Audy and the Woodard brothers."

The Woodard brothers. And she'd been having such a nice morning. When she was being rational, she knew that the conversation hadn't been meant for her children's ears. But the overprotective, irrational part of her didn't care. She also didn't care if Mike was or was not some cowboy Casanova. What she did care about was her kids and how upset Archie had been.

"What are you all doing here?" Brooke tried to stand.

"Checking on you. You stay just like that, Brooke Briscoe." Audy hopped over one of the chairs to get to her. "How's my gorgeous wife?" He kissed her forehead.

"Pregnant." She sighed. "Very pregnant."

"What?" Audy jumped back. "When did this happen?"

They all laughed then. Audy Briscoe was a character. His open adoration for Brooke suggested things like love and commitment might still mean something.

"We were on the way out to the ranch and wanted to see if you needed help with anything." Rusty Woodard paused. "Did you do all this, Eloise?"

"I had some help." Eloise tucked the last bud into the arch and stood, dusting off her green overalls. "Let's see how it turned out."

She walked down the aisle, stopped at the end, and turned to take it all in.

Everyone but Brooke and Audy followed suit, standing alongside her.

Rusty gave a long, slow whistle. "It looks *good*."

"It looks beautiful." Mabel grabbed Eloise's arm. "I don't think erste Baum has ever looked so grand."

This was punctuated by a bark.

"Sounds like Clifford agrees." Mike scratched the dog behind the ear. "This is…something." He turned in a slow circle, then shook his head. "You've done it now."

"Done what?" She tucked a strand of hair behind her ear but refused to make eye contact. He had nice eyes—warm and likable—and she really didn't want to like him at the moment.

"When Miss Martha gets a load of this, you're going to get put on every decorating committee for every festival for the rest of your life." Mike scratched his jaw.

"That's not at all dramatic." Eloise laughed, then realized no one else was laughing.

"Oh, Eloise." Mabel frowned. "He's right. It's too good."

"I'm so sorry." Hattie ran a hand over her curly hair. "Forrest and I should have eloped—that's what we wanted to do anyway."

"Hattie Carmichael." Eloise put a hand on Hattie's shoulder. "I forbid you to be anything but happy today. I did this for you and Forrest and your families and no one else. If you're happy, that's all that matters." She paused. "I can handle Miss Martha so don't you worry about that."

"Oh, I'm happy. I didn't know it could be this perfect." She smiled. "Now I definitely can't trip on my dress."

Clifford barked again, whimpering at the sight of the kids.

"Is it okay if he says hello?" Mike asked.

She nodded, but continued not to make eye contact.

"Let's go." Mike released Clifford from his leash and the dog ran toward the kids. "I think he's excited."

She watched, smiling as Archie and Kirby saw the dog and cried out, "Clifford!" in unison. If only they didn't love the dog. She sighed, her gaze accidentally tangling up on Mike's. If only he wasn't such a handsome…ladies' man? Heartbreaker? It was possible. After fifteen years, she couldn't claim to know Mike Woodard. Not that she cared, she didn't. She paid an inordinate amount of attention to an imaginary speck of dust on the front of her overalls. "I guess we're all done here."

"I can't thank you enough, Eloise." Hattie hugged her. "You should know, I don't hug people."

"I'm glad you think this is hug worthy." Eloise laughed and hugged her back. "I should get the kids so we can clean up."

"I'll walk with you." Mike waited. "I was hoping to talk to Archie."

She didn't slow for him but he matched her stride soon enough. If he thought her pace was brisk, he didn't comment. When she glanced his way, his waiting smile was a little too warm and a little too genuine to be a love-'em-and-leave-'em type.

Come on, Eloise. Just because she wanted everything she'd heard to be a joke didn't make it so. Wait. No. When it came to Mike Woodard, she didn't want anything. Well, that wasn't entirely true. "It's no secret Archie was upset the other night."

"I understand what he's feeling." He ran a hand along the back of his neck. "I was sixteen when my mom left us—I knew she was gone and not coming back. I was angry from the time I woke up until the time I went to bed." His gaze wandered to where the kids and Clifford were playing. "My dad tried but he never said anything like what you said to Archie. You keep talking to him like that, letting him get his feelings out, letting him be angry and sitting with him through it, and he'll be okay." He paused, then added, "It's good he knows you're on his side. Always. Even if it's hard, even though he's young, it matters now—and it will years from now."

And before Eloise could think of a single thing to say, Mike left her standing in the middle of the field and headed for her kids.

Mike's mom had left him? She'd lost her mother but her mother hadn't chosen to go. Mike's mom had. That was a pain she couldn't wrap her head around. And yet, it was his reality. It also offered up some explanation as to why Mike would be a player—assuming Tyson hadn't been teasing. And even though it was none of her business and she didn't care, she hoped Tyson had been teasing.

"MR. MIKE." Kirby greeted Mike with her usual exuberance, giving him an around-the-knee hug and a big grin. "You're here. And you brought Clifford."

"I knew he'd want to see you." He nodded at the dog, running around them in a circle. "He's so excited, he can't sit still."

"He's silly." Kirby giggled and ran after the dog.

"Quincy." Mike nodded in his direction.

"It'll be interesting to see who wears who out." The older man stood with his hand on his hips, watching Kirby and Clifford running.

But Mike was on a mission. "Hey, Archie." He cleared his throat. "I was hoping I could talk to you for a second? Man to man?"

Archie pushed his glasses up on his nose and nodded. "Okay."

He tipped his cowboy hat back on his head. "What you heard Tyson say about me sounded bad. Horrible, even."

Archie nodded.

"And I got to thinking, if I were in your shoes, I'd have been upset, too." He shook his head. "Tyson was teasing me—making up stuff to make me sound…"

"Like a jerk?" Archie shoved his hands into his pockets.

"Yep." Mike smiled. "He thought it was funny because everything he said was the opposite of who I am."

Archie's brow creased and he cocked his head to one side, like he was thinking.

"Kinda like if you or your grandpa said Kirby doesn't like donuts or cupcakes." He was pretty sure he was going about this all wrong. "It'd be funny to you because you know it's not true."

"She loves donuts and cupcakes." Archie nodded slowly.

"Exactly." He took a deep breath. "I wanted to

set the record straight. None of that stuff was true. I'd never leave someone I love—not if I could help it. Not ever." He couldn't help the gruffness of his tone.

"Grandpa said you and Momma were sweethearts in high school. Did you break her heart?" He crossed his arms over his chest.

Mike swallowed. "I don't think so." If anything, she'd broken his.

Archie was silent for a long time. "Mr. Mike, if someone does leave, does that mean they don't love you anymore?"

There it was, Archie's fear laid bare. And it was a knife to the heart.

Mike squatted by the boy and looked him in the eyes. "No, sir. Not at all. My daddy loved us but he had to leave when he was a soldier. He went off to do his duty to the Army but he still loved us and he came back just as soon as he could."

Archie thought about this for a moment, then nodded. "Okay." And he took off after Kirby and Clifford.

"I guess that's that." Mike chuckled and stood up—to find he had an audience. Quincy, Eloise, and Rusty stood, each of them wearing a very different expression. He took off his hat and ran his fingers through his hair. Had he messed up? Again?

Quincy came forward and clapped him on the

shoulder. "You took a load off that boy's shoulders. And I thank you for that."

"That was some heavy stuff." Rusty ran a hand along the back of his neck. "I get the feeling I missed something."

"Tyson…being Tyson." Mike broke off, his gaze shifting to Eloise.

There was a smile on her face as she watched her kids running and playing and laughing with Clifford. When she smiled, it was easy to remember the girl he'd once adored. Time had passed, but she hadn't changed much. With her hair up in a ponytail and her green overalls, she didn't look old enough to be a mother. But the love she had for Kirby and Archie was all over her face.

"Anyway, we should be heading out. Gotta get back to the groom and all." Rusty shook his head. "I still can't believe Forrest's getting hitched." Forrest and Rusty had been team roping together since high school. While Forrest was pleased as punch to be marrying Hattie, Rusty was having a surprisingly hard time with it.

"It happens." Mike chuckled. "It's not like the world's coming to an end, Rusty. I hear some people even like being married."

Rusty's snort was answer enough.

Surprisingly, Eloise laughed. "I'm with Rusty on this one. Marriage isn't for everyone."

"Now, Eloise." Quincy shook his head. "You

can't let one bad apple ruin the whole bunch. No man, or woman, is meant to be alone."

"Oh, really? What about you, Grandpa Quincy?" Eloise hooked her arm though his. "You've been single for a long time now."

"That's different. What me and your grandmother had gave me enough love and happiness to last the rest of my life." He patted her hand.

Eloise rested her head on his shoulder. "That's the sweetest thing I've ever heard." There was just a hint of wistfulness in her voice. "Well, I've got Archie and Kirby. And you. So I'm not alone. What else could I need or want?" She smiled up at him.

"A man." Her grandfather answered so quickly, they all laughed. "A good man. One who'll treat you right and love those kids and—"

"That was a rhetorical question." She hugged his arm.

Quincy sighed as he let her go. "I'll tell you one thing, Eloise Lynn Green. You're as stubborn as your grandmother."

"Considering how much you adored her, I'll take that as a compliment." She released him and headed across the field. "I'll get the kids. If you're really set on coming to the wedding, I'm going to need time to get them ready—then myself."

"I want to show off my great-grandchildren and my talented granddaughter. Of course we're coming." He was frowning, his hands on his hips as he turned around.

"Whatever I did, I'm sorry." Rusty held up his hands.

"I'm not mad at you, boy. You didn't do a thing," Quincy muttered, his voice low and gruff. "You didn't have to. It started with her selfish father dragging her all over and taking her away from family. And that no good, lying, cheating, waste of a space she was married to made good and sure she'd never trust again. That's why she won't find the right fella. And it chaps my hide something fierce."

Mike and Rusty exchanged a look. Their whole life, Quincy Green had always been a generous and even-tempered man. It was a bit of a shock to hear him insult someone with such vigor— even if it sounded like the insults were deserved.

This new bit of information sparked Mike's temper.

Bad things had happened to the carefree, fun-loving El-Bell he'd pledged his heart to under erste Baum so many years ago. She'd had her heart stomped on over and over. Her father. Ted. *And me*.

He glanced across the field to where El was. She was talking to the kids, pointing at something in the sky, her ponytail blowing in the morning breeze. She was more than just a strong, beautiful woman. She was a loving mother and granddaughter and an accomplished businesswoman. If she was happy, that was all that mattered.

"I shouldn't have run my mouth." Quincy's agitation was obvious. "Do me a favor and forget I said all that, will ya? I'd no right. El would never forgive me for airing her dirty laundry that way. It was wrong. I just… I—"

"We won't say a thing, Quincy." Mike rested a hand on the older man's shoulder. "I imagine I'd have a few choice words to say myself, if I were in your shoes."

"What my brother said, Quincy." Rusty nodded, his expression grave. "She's lucky to have you in her corner."

"I'm the only one." Quincy shook his head.

"She's in Garrison now, Quincy. It won't be too long before she has the whole town watching her back." Mike hurried to offer Quincy reassurance. After his father's stroke, he was all too aware of what stress could do to a person.

"I know you're leaving soon, Mike, but…" Quincy gave each of them a long, hard look. "I'd be mighty grateful to you both if you'd help with that. I know she's prickly and stubborn and likely won't take too kindly to—"

"I will." Mike answered before he'd thought about what he was saying. Quincy was asking him to do the very thing Eloise had asked him not to do.

Quincy's posture relaxed and he took a deep

breath. "Good. Good. I knew I could count on you, Mike."

"I'm not the only one." That last comment seemed a little too pointed. "Seems like she's made friends with Gretta. Hattie and Brooke, too." He ignored the way his brother was looking at him but suspected he'd get an earful later.

Clifford was panting when he reached them, turning every so often to make sure Eloise and the kids were still following.

"You keeping an eye on them?" Mike asked, giving the dog a scratch behind the ear.

Clifford's tail wagged.

"We have to get ready to go to the wedding," Kirby announced. "Momma says we have to use our manners."

"You always do, Freckles." Quincy chuckled.

"I've never been to a wedding before." Kirby shrugged. "I hope there's dancing. I like to dance."

"There is." Rusty nodded, smiling at the little girl.

"You know what else there is?" Mike crouched. "It's something I think you'll really like."

"What is it?" Kirby waited, her hands clasped in front of her as she leaned forward to hear him.

"There will be cake. A gigantic one, too." Mike held his hands apart.

"That big?" Kirby was impressed.

"What's that big?" Archie asked, only now reaching them.

"The cake." Kirby jumped up and down. "There's gonna be cake, Momma. And lots of it." She grabbed Eloise's hand and tugged. "Come on, Momma, we need to get ready."

"I'm coming." Eloise laughed and tucked a strand of hair behind her ear. "Say your good-byes and thank Mr. Mike for letting you play with Clifford."

"Thank you, Mr. Mike." Kirby gave him a big hug.

He was getting awfully fond of the little girl's hugs.

"All right, let's go. I guess we'll see you later." Eloise's gaze wasn't frigid—it was warm and clear when she glanced his way.

He nodded, touching the brim of his hat. "Yes, ma'am."

She smiled at that, then steered the kids—with Quincy bringing up the rear—back across the field to where the van was parked. Clifford ran after them, accepting more hugs and pats before they climbed into the van, then ran to Audy.

"You done staring?" Rusty adjusted his hat. "Or should I give you a minute?"

He glared at his brother and started walking. "Let's go."

The Garrison Gardens van pulled away and Clifford trotted back to them, staying by his side. "Get all that running out." He smiled down at his dog. "You get tired enough, maybe you won't chew up

any more of the couch while I'm at the wedding."
Not that Mike was overly upset about the couch—
it was years past needing to be replaced.

"What was that?" Rusty fell in step beside him.
"With the kid?"

"I know he's a kid and it might not make much
sense to you." He glanced at his brother. "Didn't
want him thinking ill of me, is all."

"Okay." Rusty looked like he was holding back
a smile, but he let it be.

They made their way back to Audy without
another word being said.

"I have to go." Gretta held up her phone. "Dad
texted. Levi's asking if he can help cook and Dad
said yes. I hope the fire extinguisher works." She
all but ran down the path to her car.

"Mike." Hattie's tone suggested something was
awry. And Mabel and Hattie were both wearing
the oddest expression.

He stopped. "Something tells me I'm not going
to want to hear what you two have to say."

"Oh, trust me, it's good." Audy chuckled.

"Behave." Brooke shook her head and said,
"This is all Hattie and Mabel. Just so you know."

Rusty tipped his hat back, smiling. "This *will*
be good."

"You know how the Garrison Ladies Guild is
always tending to other peoples' business? Well,
we were thinking, this time, it might be better

if we interceded." Mabel glanced at Hattie, who nodded.

"That'd be kind of you." Mike knew Eloise would appreciate it, too.

"It's just you know they'll hound Eloise until they've got her paired up and married." Hattie put her hands on her hips. "Like they're trying to do with Gretta."

"With Gretta? Who are they pairing her up with?" Rusty's brows rose. "I haven't heard anything."

"Then you're not listening." Hattie rolled her eyes. "They're convinced she and Fritz Koch were a match made in heaven. He's got little Abigail. She's got Levi."

"Fritz? The high school teacher? Isn't he a little old for her?" Rusty scratched his stubbled jaw.

"Not really. And he's a nice man. But poor Abigail cries all the time." Mabel shook her head. "And Levi loves to make her cry. That alone is reason enough for them to find someone else for her."

"What does this have to do with me?" Mike had a sinking suspicion.

"You and Eloise." Hattie, being Hattie, cut to the chase.

"No." He crossed his arms over his chest.

"But it's you." Mabel acted like this explained everything. "I mean, Brooke and Audy filled me in—"

"Then you should know why it's impossible."

Mike leveled a hard look at Audy. He couldn't bring himself to do the same to Brooke. "Besides, as soon as my dad is back on his feet, I'm leaving."

"You're really going to take that job?" Hattie was stunned.

"It's a good job." Rusty jumped to his defense. "He'll get to see more of the country, do what he loves, and get really paid for it. Why wouldn't he take the job?"

"Because we're all here." Hattie shook her head.

Mike saw the way they were watching him then. Except Rusty. Rusty was staring at his boots, his jaw clenched tight. When he'd told them about the job offer, they'd all been excited for him. He took a deep breath. "Back to Eloise." He adjusted his hat, antsy. "I think it's best if we respect what she wants. Friends. Not dating. That sort of thing." He didn't pause too long before he said, "We need to go. Forrest is waiting and, if I recall correctly, there's a wedding in less than three hours." With that, he headed to Audy's truck feeling uneasy. Today wasn't the day to second-guess his career choices or worry about Hattie and Mabel pairing Eloise up with someone else in town. Today, two of his best friends were getting married and he wanted to celebrate that.

CHAPTER SEVEN

"Did you wear a big white dress when you and Daddy got married, Momma?" Kirby sat on the stool in front of the antique vanity in Eloise's room. She was swinging her legs, chattering away, while Eloise braided her hair.

"I did." Her wedding had been quite a production. Big and over-the-top in every way. She didn't want to think about how much money it'd cost—or where the money had come from. Thinking back, she had so many questions about her life with Ted. But she was pretty sure she wouldn't like any of the answers.

"Was the dress poofy like a cloud?" Kirby picked up one of Eloise's makeup brushes.

"It was. It was so big it was hard to dance at the reception."

That made Kirby smile. "What's a reception?"

"The party after the wedding." She used a hair tie to secure the braid that hung halfway down her daughter's back. "All done."

Kirby looked in the mirror. "I like it. Thank

you, Momma." She turned on her stool. "Mr. Mike said there will be dancing. I want to dance."

"We will." Eloise started pulling the hot rollers from her hair and frowned. Her hair was hopeless. It was mousy brown, too thick, and had no natural curl. It went frizzy when it rained or was too humid. No matter what she tried to do with it, it didn't work—like now. The few curls that had set were too tight. Out of habit, she pulled some bobby pins from the jar on the vanity and picked up her brush. She'd worn her hair up every day in Highland Park, but now she paused.

She put the bobby pins away and ran a brush through it, pondering options. The headband she'd bought for Kirby, which her daughter refused to wear, hung on the necklace stand on the vanity top. She reached for it and slid it into her hair and sat back. Was she too old for headbands?

"You look pretty, Momma." Kirby smiled up at her. "You do."

"Thank you, sweetie." Kirby approved and that was enough. "I think we're ready."

"Yay. Time for cake and dancing. And cake." Kirby clapped her hands and ran from Eloise's bedroom.

Her grandfather and Archie were in the family room. Eloise had picked up a puzzle the last time she was at the store and it had been a hit for the whole family. The coffee table was now the puzzle table. Archie sat on the floor with a puzzle piece in his hand. Grandpa Quincy perched on the edge of the sofa, sorting through a pile of pieces. They were both too focused to notice their arrival.

"No fair." Kirby ran to the coffee table. "We're supposed to work on it together."

"I was only sorting through the piles here, Freckles." Her grandfather stood. "My, my, aren't I the luckiest man in town? I get to escort the two loveliest women in all of Garrison."

Eloise rolled her eyes but Kirby was all smiles as she spun in her pink dress with tiny blue flowers.

"You do look nice." Archie stood, shoving his hands into his pockets. "Momma, do I have to dance? Levi said you get cooties from dancing with girls."

Eloise managed not to smile. "Cooties?" The fear of cooties had been around since she was a kid.

"Levi said it'll make you sick. Your hands turn green and you throw up and your eyes bulge out." And Archie believed every word of it. "He said he wouldn't dance with anyone. Not even his mom."

Poor Gretta.

"Didn't you get the kids their cootie vaccine when they had their last doctor visit, Eloise?" Grandpa Quincy asked, his expression grave. "You got some shots, didn't you?"

She was impressed that her grandfather managed to keep a straight face.

Archie thought for a minute. "Yes."

"And they hurt." Kirby rubbed her upper arm like she was still sore.

"Well, there you go." Grandpa Quincy nodded. "You don't need to worry about cooties. You can dance all you want."

Archie relaxed. "Okay, then. You should tell Levi's mom so he can get one, too."

"We need to scoot or we'll be late." Grandpa Quincy led them to the front door, giving her a wink.

Sometimes her grandfather was almost as mischievous as her kids. Maybe Archie didn't get all of his storytelling abilities from his father after all.

The kids chattered about weddings the whole way to erste Baum Park. Archie was set on having his wedding in outer space. He wanted aliens to shoot firework laser guns and his guests would all bring bubbles. Kirby said she wanted to get married underwater with mermaids and sea turtles. Then she would ride off on a pink dolphin. They were still talking about it when they parked in the nearly full parking lot.

"But I want bubbles, too," Kirby said, waiting for her mother to unbuckle her from her booster seat.

"Copycat." Archie jumped out of the back seat of Grandpa Quincy's car.

"Archie." Eloise used her mom voice. "Remember what I said about today?"

"I need to be on my best behavior." Archie nodded. "Sorry, Kirby."

"It's okay. I was copycatting. I like bubbles, like you." Kirby grinned at her brother.

Archie smiled back.

This was one of those rare moments where Eloise was content.

Grandpa Quincy took Kirby's hand and Eloise held Archie's before the four of them walked the long path from the parking lot to the shade of erste Baum.

"Hattie wasn't kidding." Eloise was stunned at the number of people. "This has to be the whole town."

"Looks like it." Her grandfather nodded. "And all of them are going to be tickled pink by what you did for Hattie and Forrest's wedding."

"*We* did."

Grandpa Quincy snorted. "You came up with the plans, El. I just did what you told me to do."

"I'm sorry. I didn't mean to take over—"

"Hold up, now. I wasn't complaining. Not one bit. I kinda liked it." He patted her shoulder. "I'm not as creative as I once was. You've got more creativity in your little finger than…well, I do." He chuckled.

"You're sure?" The last thing she'd ever want to do is run ramrod over her precious grandfather. "You'd tell me if I stepped on your toes?"

"Why would you step on Grandpa's toes?" Kirby asked.

"That hurts." Archie looked up at her.

"It's an expression." Grandpa Quincy was laughing now. "Your momma would never step on my toes. Your momma wouldn't hurt a fly." He paused. "That's another expression. It means she's nice to everyone."

"Oh." Kirby's expression was pure confusion.

"I see Levi." Archie tugged on her hand. "He's right there."

Eloise glanced in the direction he was pointing. Sure enough, there was Gretta and her father. The little boy in the too-big cowboy hat sitting between them had to be Levi.

"And there's Samantha." Kirby's squeal was pure delight.

Samantha sat at the end of one row, a big bow in her curly hair. She'd seen Kirby and was waving excitedly.

Kirby waved back.

"Let's go find us some seats before there aren't any." Grandpa Quincy led them down the rest of the hill to the rows of chairs Eloise had decorated earlier.

"Quincy." The voice was commanding. "I have a bone to pick with you."

Eloise recognized Martha Zeigler but not the handful of women following in her wake. Was this the dreaded Garrison Ladies Guild?

"And a good afternoon to you, Martha." Her grandfather smiled at the woman.

"Why didn't you tell me what your granddaughter was capable of?" The woman turned and gave Eloise a head-to-toe inspection. Her gaze was shrewd, assessing. "This is…well, this is… I mean to say… This is a wonder."

"Thank you?" Eloise glanced at her grandfather for translation.

"No, no, thank you." Martha Zeigler was openly studying her. "I'm so glad you've moved to Garrison."

The way she said it made Eloise nervous. "Thank you." She swallowed.

A woman with fire-engine-red hair joined them. "Brooke was telling me all about you." She rested a hand against her bountiful chest. "We're the Garrison Ladies Guild. I'm sure your grandpa has told you all about us?"

If they only knew what her grandpa had said about them. Eloise only smiled and nodded.

"Well, I'm Miss Patsy. That's Dorris Kaye—watch out, she's a bit of a gossip." She pointed at the woman wearing a bold flower-print dress. "That tall string bean over there is Pearl Johnston. Don't let that face fool you, she's got a wicked sense of humor. And somewhere around here is Barbara Eldridge."

"The service is about to start, but I'll find you

during the reception." Miss Martha continued to study her. "I have a proposition for you."

And just like that, the ladies left.

"There they go, waddling off all proud-like," her grandpa whispered.

"They're not that bad." She glanced his way, saw the look on his face, and asked, "Are they?"

He shrugged. "Let's find our seats."

It took time and a little maneuvering to get four chairs together but, finally, they were seated. Not ten seconds later, the groom and his groomsmen took their place on the right side of the arch.

Forrest Briscoe stood proud and tall, his eyes fixed on the path of rose petals serving as the aisle. His groomsmen, Audy and Rusty, were at his side. Of all of them, Rusty seemed nervous—shifting from foot to foot while his gaze never stopped moving.

"That's Mr. Forrest," Kirby whispered loudly. "He was at Junior Rangers."

Eloise nodded and patted her daughter's leg.

The strum of a guitar echoed from the back and Eloise turned to see who was playing.

Mike. He sat on a stool, one leg kicked up, playing the strings of his classic acoustic guitar with ease. Like the groomsmen, he wore black jeans, a starched white button down, black boots, and a black felt cowboy hat. Only, on Mike, it was more…he was more… He was the very definition of a handsome, manly man.

Eloise swallowed hard. She'd heard every word he'd said to Archie. While he'd cleared the air with Archie, he'd left her more confounded than ever. Did he believe what he'd said? That he hadn't broken her heart?

Everyone stood, blocking Eloise's view and making her acutely aware of how distracted she'd been by the man.

"I can't see, Momma." Kirby tugged on her arm.

Eloise lifted Kirby onto her hip. "Better?"

Kirby nodded, staring with wide, curious eyes. "She looks so pretty."

But Eloise didn't look at Hattie, not yet. Instead, she waited to see Forrest's reaction. And when he looked up, Eloise felt tears stinging the corners of her eyes. To see such a big, brawny man gasp was powerful. He shook his head, one hand covering his mouth—struggling to control his emotions.

Eloise wasn't a romantic anymore, but this... It was hard not to be when faced with such love.

When she turned her attention to Hattie, her eyes burned all the more. Hattie Carmichael was a beautiful bride. Yes, her dress was big and poofy, but she needn't have worried about tripping. With her father's help, she was gliding down the aisle— solely focused on the man waiting for her.

"Why are you crying, Momma?" Kirby whispered.

"They're happy tears," Eloise whispered back. "I'm so happy for them."

Kirby didn't say a thing, she just hugged her tight and rested her head on Eloise's shoulder.

Eloise pressed a kiss to the top of her daughter's head and, with the rest of the guests, sat when Hattie reached her groom. Kirby crawled back into her seat and sat up on her knees, transfixed.

The service was short and sweet. Hattie and Forrest were oblivious to everyone else. Mabel and Brooke, Hattie's bridesmaids, cried. Audy spent most of the time staring at his wife while Rusty pulled at his collar. When Hattie and Forrest kissed, the crowd erupted and that was that.

"Ew. They kissed." Archie's wrinkled-up nose was all disgust.

"That's how you seal the deal." Grandpa Quincy chuckled. "One day, you won't mind kissing so much."

Archie stuck his tongue out. "No way, Grandpa. Now what?"

"Now, we move the chairs to those tables over there and we get the dance floor set up." He paused, smiling. "Nolan made it."

"You can go keep him company, Grandpa. I'm sure Rusty and Mike would appreciate someone keeping an eye on him—so he doesn't get over-tired." It wouldn't hurt for her grandfather to sit a while, either.

"If you're sure?" He waited for her nod, then

patted her on the cheek and headed toward his friend.

"Are we supposed to help?" Kirby was already trying to pick up her chair.

"I can do it." Archie lifted his. "See?"

"And you're doing a good job, too." Eloise's words trailed off as Mike approached. Why was he heading their way? And why did he have to smile that way?

"Need a hand?" He reached for Kirby's chair.

"I can do it." Kirby's arms shook beneath the weight of the chair.

"I believe it." He crouched. "But I'm a gentleman, Kirby. That means I like to do chivalrous things. Like opening doors for ladies. Or carrying their chairs for them."

"Oh." Kirby seemed to think about this for a second, then offered him the chair. "Thank you, Mr. Mike."

He smiled and stood, those warm eyes of his locking with hers. "Eloise."

She swallowed, hard. "Mike."

"You're beautiful." He cleared his throat, then said, "You and Kirby both...are. Let's move these chairs, Archie." And with that, he folded and carried four chairs while Archie carried one.

Eloise tried not to notice what a fine figure he made as he walked and talked to her son. She tried not to think about the sweetness of his awkward compliment or what a truly handsome man he was. She tried. But it didn't work.

HE'D MADE A deal with Quincy and he'd honor it. He'd be Eloise's friend. That's all. Friends helped each other out and gave each other compliments. Friends didn't get tongue-tied and doe-eyed over each other. He was pretty sure he'd just done both.

It'd help if she wasn't the prettiest woman here. But she was. Seeing her under erste Baum, with tears in her eyes and a gentle smile on her lips, had dragged him back to the last time he'd seen her here, all those years ago. He'd been so caught off guard, he'd played the wrong notes. No one noticed. At least, he hoped no one had.

He had to stop this. The staring was bad enough. But getting sentimental over things best left in the past was asking for trouble. She was his first love and, for that reason, she'd always be special to him. But no one met their soulmate when they were nine years old. It was ridiculous to even think it.

"Mr. Mike?" Archie was staring at him. "You okay?"

Mike realized he'd been standing next to a table, holding the chairs, and staring off into space. *Not at all conspicuous.* "I am." He started setting up chairs. "How's your day been going, Archie?"

"Okay, I guess." He shrugged. "I'm kinda bored. And my stomach hurts a little."

"You okay?" A quick inspection showed the boy's color was normal, he wasn't sweating, and there was no labored breathing or signs of distress.

"Yeah." He sighed. "Too bad you didn't bring Clifford."

"I didn't want him eating the wedding cake before the bride and groom cut it." Mike set up the last chair. "And, believe me, he would have. He's fast and sneaky. That cake wouldn't have stood a chance."

That had Archie smiling. "You should take him a piece."

"I don't know. He's got enough energy without giving him sugar." He glanced back in the direction they'd come.

Eloise was talking with Mabel while Samantha and Kirby were going row by row, smelling the bouquets at each end.

"Should we get some more chairs?" Archie tugged on his arm, glancing back and forth between Mike and Eloise.

"How about we get your grandpa and my dad to come sit over here first?" He pointed out where the old men sat. "Then maybe get some punch?"

"I like punch." Archie walked with him. "Do you think you'll get married, Mr. Mike?"

"Oh, maybe someday." If his father had it his

way, it would be sooner rather than later. "Why are you asking?"

"Will you kiss her?" Archie's disgusted expression had Mike swallowing down his laughter.

"Well, now…" He paused, nodding slowly. "I guess I will."

"You will?" Archie shuddered. "If I ever get married, I'm not kissing her. No way."

Mike couldn't help but laugh then. He'd have to check in with Archie in another eight or nine years and see how the boy felt then.

Mike stayed busy. Once he got his father and Quincy set up at a table with Archie, he went back to moving chairs. When that was done, he helped set up the dance floor. If there was something that needed doing, he volunteered. But, through it all, he was acutely aware of Eloise. Her voice. Her laugh. The way she'd run her fingers through her hair or tuck a strand behind her ear.

He forced himself to focus on Hattie and Forrest as they cut the wedding cake.

"Be nice." Hattie shot Forrest a warning look as he prepared to feed her a bite of cake.

"I'm always nice." True to his word, Forrest was careful.

Hattie, on the other hand, got great joy out of smearing frosting across Forrest's chin.

"You knew she was going to do that." Tyson gave Mike a firm nudge in the ribs.

"Ow." He rubbed his side. "Forrest doesn't seem to mind."

Forrest had pulled Hattie into his arms and was kissing her, making sure she wasn't frosting-free before it was all over.

"Your brother holding up? He looked like he was going to hyperventilate up there."

"I don't think I realized how much Rusty hates weddings until today." He and his brother had both been affected by their mother's desertion. "Unless something changes, I don't see him walking down an aisle any time soon." Or ever.

"I'm not saying it would have been funny if he'd passed out but… I'd have laughed." Tyson shrugged and headed toward the giant six-layer wedding cake. "I'm getting some cake."

Mike followed. He and his brother tried to limit their heart-to-heart talks, but this might be one of those times. Mike struggled with the wounds his mother had caused, but he was pretty sure it wouldn't interfere with him having a future—a family. With Rusty, he wasn't so sure.

He got enough plates for his father and Quincy and reached the table to find it occupied with all of his father's cronies. "Sorry. I only brought two." He put a plate in front of his father and Quincy.

There was a lot of general grumbling and some heckling, but Mike brushed it off.

"There's a chair over here." Brooke waved him

over. "And I won't be mad at you for not getting me cake."

Mike paused, taking in the other occupants at the table. Mabel. Gretta. And Eloise. "I can get you cake."

"Audy is." She smiled up at him. "But you're a sweetheart for offering."

"Anyone else?" He glanced around the table, hoping one of them would send him on his way.

"Nope." Mabel shook her head.

"Already had some." Gretta smiled. "But it's nice of you to ask."

"No cake for me." Eloise sighed. "Not if I'm ever going to fit into my jeans again."

Mike frowned. Was that some sort of dig at her weight? As far as he was concerned, she was perfect. Any less and she'd be too skinny. But nobody asked him and he was doing his best not to offer up his opinion unsolicited.

"It's bad luck." Gretta turned to Eloise.

"That's birthday cake. Everyone has to have a bite for good luck. Not weddings." Eloise smiled, then paused. "Isn't it?"

"Don't ask me." Brooke shrugged. "Mike?"

"As a general rule, if there's cake, I eat it." He loved to hear Eloise laugh. Too much. "So, no cake?"

"Now I'm worried." Eloise stood. "But I can get it myself, thank you. And I should probably check on Archie."

He hadn't intended to watch her walk away.

"Mike Woodard." Brooke hissed. "Sit down, right now."

He sat.

"You should ask her to dance." Mabel propped her elbow on the table and rested her chin in her hand.

"No, he should not." Brooke sighed. "You should dance with anyone except Eloise."

Mabel huffed. "But Brooke—"

"Mabel, Dorris Kaye already asked if Eloise was the little girl Mike used to follow around like a puppy. And Pearl Johnston said something about first loves lasting forever. Then Nolan said something about her being Mike's first love." Brooke shook her head. "Mike's not interested. He needs to be careful."

Mike seriously regretted sitting down. "Where's Audy?" If Audy were here, this conversation wouldn't be happening.

"He's coming." Brooke's forehead smoothed. "With the biggest piece of cake I've ever seen." But she was smiling.

When Audy sat, Mike sighed in relief.

"These ladies grilling you?" Audy asked. "You were panicking." He scooped up a bite of Brooke's cake with a fork. "Not as bad as Rusty was earlier—but I'm not sure I've ever seen someone that uneasy."

"Poor Rusty." Brooke took a bite of cake. "Oh, this is too good."

Audy nodded. "Where'd he run off to? Rusty, I mean?"

Mike hadn't realized his brother had left. He scanned the crowd, but no Rusty. Now he was concerned. "I'm not sure. But I think I'll go find out." He stood. "If you'll excuse me."

"You want some help?" Gretta's concern was sincere.

"I don't think so." He touched the brim of his hat. "But I'll let you know if that changes." He did his best to be casual about his search, making small talk as he worked through the tables and doing his best to fly under the radar. But he made the mistake of standing too close to a table he should have avoided altogether.

"Mike Woodard." It was Martha Zeigler. "You've been running around like a chicken with its head cut off all afternoon. Come, sit a spell, won't you?"

It was only Martha and Dorris Kaye, but that was enough to make him scramble for an excuse not to sit. Since he couldn't come up with one, he sat.

"A little bird told me you're leaving Garrison." Martha's brows drew close together. "This was news to me."

"I'm not leaving. I'll just be on the road six months out of the year." He shrugged. "Garrison is my home. It always will be."

"What are we going to do without you?" Dorris Kaye was downright indignant. "I don't trust any of the EMTs but you." Unfortunately, Dorris Kaye called 911 enough to know all the EMTs in the county. From bad heartburn to sciatica to hiccups that wouldn't go away, Dorris seemed to prefer having the paramedics come to her versus her going to a doctor. "That Terri is never nice to me—but you are."

"She's a good EMT, Miss Kaye. She's the only partner I'd want with me in an emergency." He couldn't exactly blame Terri for being brusque with the older woman. So far, none of her calls had been real emergencies.

"What about the high school rodeo team?" Martha's tone was sharper now. "My grandson is on that team. I can't, in good conscience, let him participate if his safety is in question."

"My brother Rusty is taking my place." He didn't appreciate her tone, but he did respect her concern. Her grandson was her pride and joy—and the only family she hadn't chased off with her less than cordial ways.

"Rusty?" Martha's brows rose high but she didn't say anything for a long minute. "And your father?"

"I'm not leaving until after the Founder's Day Festival, Miss Martha." He ran a hand along the back of his neck. "By then, Dad will be back to his normal self. He and Rusty both support my decision."

"All any parent wants is for their child to be happy. Even at the cost of their own happiness." Martha patted the edge of the table. "Now, if you'll excuse me. Dwight is here and I have some dancing to do." She stood, staring down at him. "But, Mike Woodard, you listen to me. Garrison needs you. Your daddy and brother need you. I'm not sure what itch you're hoping to scratch with this new job, but you might want to think about that before you go running off."

They left and he sat, alone, at the table. How two women could make a person feel so shell-shocked he didn't know. Somehow, those two women had managed just that.

"Mr. Mike?" Kirby patted him on the arm.

"Hey, Kirby." It was impossible to be angry when this little girl was smiling up at him. "Having fun?"

"I am." She patted her tummy. "I ate cake. And it was yummy."

"It was."

"And I was having fun with Samantha but now she's dancing with her daddy." She pointed at the dance floor. "Archie won't dance with me. Grandpa Quincy's friends are scary so I can't ask him."

"Would you dance with me, Kirby?" He couldn't

think of a better way to shake off his foul mood. And after, he'd go back to looking for Rusty.

"Oh, yes, please." She bounced on her feet. "Thank you."

"My pleasure, Kirby." He stood and took her hand.

On the dance floor, he soon realized he was too tall. He tried to hunch over but it wasn't working.

"You can pick me up. That's what Samantha's daddy did." Kirby held out her arms. "I don't mind."

Mike chuckled and scooped her up. "That's better." He two-stepped along with the music, spinning them once—and making Kirby giggle.

"You're really tall." She stared up at the tree branches overhead. "I'm almost as tall as the tree."

"That tall, huh?" He spun them again and was rewarded with another giggle. Funny how a little girl laughing could ease all his stress and worry. Instead of letting people get in his head until he was doubting himself, he needed to do this. Take it day by day, minute by minute. And enjoy all the giggles he could.

He was smiling when the music came to an end. He was smiling when he walked Kirby off the dance floor to where Eloise was waiting. Eloise. Looking so beautiful it put a knot in his throat.

"Now it's Momma's turn," Kirby said, grabbing her mother's hand and putting it in his. "Go on, Momma. Mr. Mike's a good dancer."

"Shall we?" he asked, his stomach a ball of nerves. All at once, he was aware of every little thing. The feel of her silky-smooth hand against his calloused palms. The way her hair lifted and moved in the fall breeze. The tiny specks of gold in her mossy green eyes. And the way her full lips tilted up in a smile.

"Sure."

One word and he was happy. Mike led her onto the dance floor knowing full well people were watching and not caring one bit. People would talk. Whether they danced together or not wouldn't change that. He'd been wanting to dance with Eloise for the last fifteen years. Now he had the chance and he was going to savor every last second.

CHAPTER EIGHT

WHAT AM I DOING? She tried not to stiffen as Mike's arm slipped around her waist. He didn't pull her against him or hold her too close—but that didn't stop her heart from picking up or her breath from growing uneven.

"You've got one sweet little girl." Mike's voice was deep and low.

She stared at his chest. "She is that. You made her day." Her eyes darted up to his far too handsome face. "Thank you for that." Her words were a whisper.

"Until now, it was the high point of my day." His eyes trailed slowly over her face.

She swallowed hard. "Mike." But that's all she could say. He was so close, smiling a smile that rattled her to the core, and all she could think about was how good it felt to be in his arms.

"It's just a dance, El-Bell." He shook his head. "Nothing more. Neither of us wants more."

He was right. But, instead of being relieved, she was…disappointed. Because she knew, deep down, that there was something between them. There always had been a connection. In every one of their pictures together, she'd been lit up from the inside. And he...well, he was looking at her like he was right now. Why was it so hard to breathe?

"You know, one of the last times I saw you was right here." The muscle in his jaw tightened.

She stared up at him, memories rushing in on her. Good memories. "It was the summer before my mother died," she managed, the words tight. "Before Dad..." *Got lost in drink and depression.* She shook her head, trying to smile. "Well, that was when the world still made sense. It had been a good summer. The best summer."

Because of Mike. All at once, she was wrapped up in images so vivid she could feel them. His sweet smiles. Holding his hand. Sweet, stolen kisses. She'd been in love with Mike Woodard. Real, true love. So much so that she'd "married" him, right here, beneath the very tree they were now dancing under.

"El." The hand holding hers tightened. "The last time I saw you..." He broke off, the muscle in his jaw going tight. "I didn't know about your mom or what was happening until I came looking for you." His voice was gruff as he added, "All I knew was you were gone."

She wasn't sure she was breathing at all now.

"You came looking for me?" After their fight, she'd assumed he'd never want to see her again.

His brow furrowed and his jaw clenched tighter. "Of course I did, El." Mike's hand squeezed hers. "I looked for you for years—hoping I'd get the chance to tell you I was sorry about your mom. And for what I said to you." He cleared his throat. "Telling you your problems were nothing compared to losing Gene was pretty heartless. So was telling you that you needed to learn to pull yourself up by your own bootstraps and stop making everything about you. You were losing your mom and, thanks to drinking, your dad, too. I'm sorry. It might not matter to you anymore, but it does to me." The space between them seemed to spark and compress. "I drank most of a bottle of whiskey before that night was over." The corner of his mouth kicked up. "If it makes you feel any better, I threw up all night and could barely move for two days after."

"Maybe. A little." His words eased some of the hurt she'd been holding on to all these years. "I was so mean to you, Mike. You'd lost a dear friend and I came in there yelling at you because you were drinking." She took a deep breath. "It scared me. You... My dad was my dad but, when he drank, he wasn't. He got mean and aggressive and..."

"And what?" His hand pressed against her back.

"Nothing." She sucked in a deep breath. "Thinking of you that way scared me. But I had no right to call you selfish or heartless. Or a liar."

"That part was true." His eyes held hers. "I'd promised you I wouldn't drink. Then I did."

"Because you were grieving and trying to cope—"

"It was still a lie, El. And I'm sorry for that." He sighed. "We were too young to know what we were doing—or what we were throwing away."

"You did break my heart." She was horrified. That had been the last thing she'd meant to say.

"No, ma'am." His voice was a soft whisper. "You broke mine."

Something inside her seemed to thaw and shift. Something warm and alive, sparking in her stomach and rising up into her chest. "Was Tyson really teasing you?" She hadn't meant to ask him but...

"I'm the one that's *too nice*." He was smiling now.

"You always have been." And it had been one of the things she'd loved about him. Her heart thumped a little harder, a little faster.

"Interesting that's still weighing on you, though." There was a sparkle in his eye.

Interesting? Or concerning? But it had been weighing on her. The longer they danced, the harder it became to deny the growing pull between them. It was familiar. And disconcerting. More so when his thumb ran along the back of her hand. *Enough*. She scrambled to find a safer topic. "Hattie didn't trip on her dress."

He nodded. "She didn't. Forrest was worried he'd cry. He didn't—but it was close."

"How's your brother?" She couldn't have been the only one who noticed Rusty's discomfort during the ceremony.

"To be honest, I'm not sure. He seems to have disappeared." And Mike's tone implied he was worried about him. "Our mother leaving... Well, he has commitment issues. I didn't realize how much until today."

Her heart hurt for the man. "Parenting is a tricky business. Some of them don't realize that what they say and do will forever impact their kids."

"Or they don't care." His words were hard.

"Or that." It was her turn to squeeze his hand.

"You don't have to worry about that, El-Bell. You're a good mother." His thumb stroked along her back and, for a second, his gaze dipped to her mouth.

Thankfully, the music stopped and Mike led her off the dance floor. Any minute now, she'd find her footing and things would go back to normal. Any second.

"Thanks for the dance." He let go of her hand, that muscle in his jaw tightening again.

"I'm glad Kirby forced us." The spot on her

back felt cold now that his hand was gone. She felt colder.

"Forced?" He chuckled. "No, ma'am." He touched the brim of his hat and took one step away—

"Mike." She swallowed. What now?

He waited, watching her intently.

"I… I'm glad we had a chance to talk." Which was a pretty pathetic reason to stop him.

"That it had to happen after so long makes me sad." His gaze fell from hers.

What was she doing? Her heart had no business reacting to this man. But it did and the realization was more than a little shocking.

"I should probably go find my brother. Enjoy yourself." And with that, he walked into the crowd and away from her.

"Momma." Kirby grabbed her hand. "Archie's sick."

"What?" She frowned. "Where is he?" She'd left him with Gretta and Levi to check on Kirby—then ended up dancing with Mike.

"He's over there." She pointed out into the field. "He says his tummy hurts real bad."

"Probably ate too much cake." She took Kirby's hand. "Let's go check on him." Sure enough, Archie was crumpled up on the grass beside Levi Williams. His face was red and his legs were drawn up and into his chest.

"Archie, honey, are you okay?" She knelt in the grass beside him.

"He's not." Levi shook his head. "He's been moaning and groaning. I think he's real sick." The boy pushed his too-big cowboy hat back. "I figured I should stay with him."

"Thank you, Levi." Eloise pressed a hand to Archie's forehead. "You're hot." Not too much cake, then. "I think I need to get you home."

"Momma." His voice was a croak. "It hurts." He pressed his hands against the right side of his stomach.

"Okay, sweetie." She scooped him up in her arms. "We'll get you some medicine and let you rest."

Levi hopped up. "I'll go get my mom." And he ran across the field to the tables before Eloise could stop him.

"Is Archie going to be okay?" Kirby's chin trembled and her eyes welled up with tears.

"He will be." She cradled Archie close as she started for the parking lot. Unlike Kirby, he was heavy.

Archie's moan worried her. He'd never made that sound before.

"Eloise." Gretta waved her down. "What can I do?"

"I think he'll be okay. I just need to get him home." She kept walking. "Can you get my grandfather?"

"Of course." She pressed a hand to Eloise's

arm. "Call me if you need anything. It's no fun when they get sick."

"Thanks, Gretta." Archie wasn't getting any lighter but she couldn't bring herself to put him down.

The path to the parking lot stretched out before her, ten times as long as it had been when they'd arrived. With every step, Archie's noises became more distressing. *Maybe we should go to the hospital.*

Mike. She kept walking but glanced back, searching the sea of people for him. The one time she'd needed him to pop up and he's nowhere to be found.

It seemed like forever until her grandfather reached them. By then, she had sweat running down her back and her arms were shaking. "He's really sick, Grandpa. I think we need to take him to the hospital."

Grandpa Quincy gave Archie a long look, then nodded. "Then let's go."

He buckled Kirby in while Eloise wedged herself beside her daughter's booster seat and let Archie lay across her lap. Every bump and bounce along the road had Archie crying out—and there was nothing she could do. She smoothed his forehead and murmured words of comfort, but he was sobbing by the time they reached the small emergency clinic.

From there, things picked up.

A gurney was wheeled out and, finally, a familiar face.

"Terri." Eloise almost hugged the woman. "He was fine and then he wasn't. It's his stomach."

Terri gave her a reassuring pat. "Don't you fret. Let the doc look him over and we'll see what's ailing him."

Eloise left Kirby with her grandfather, then went into the ER with Archie. She held his hand, hating how helpless she felt. The tears streaming down his cheeks broke her heart. But seeing him ball up in pain was terrifying.

"It'll be okay, sweetie." She ran her hand across his forehead, smoothing the sweat-slicked hair back. "The doctor will find out what's wrong and fix it."

Archie's nod was slight.

She stood, holding his hand, watching the second hand on the clock tick by. It was taking too long. Her son was in pain. He needed help. It's not like there were wall-to-wall patients. As far as she could tell, they were the only ones here.

What if it was something serious? Was the Colton County Emergency Center and Hospital equipped to handle whatever Archie was struggling with? And, if they weren't, what happened then?

Finally, the curtain moved aside and a middle-aged woman came to the side of Archie's bed. "Hi, Archie. Miss Green. I'm Dr. Rowe." She was already zeroed in on Archie. "I hear your stomach is bothering you?" She put on her stethoscope and leaned forward. "I'm going to listen to your stomach, okay? I'll try to be extra careful."

Archie turned his face into the pillow.

"Did he eat anything unusual?" Dr. Rowe lifted Archie's shirt.

"No. Some wedding cake, maybe. But nothing else out of the ordinary." She saw the way Archie flinched away from the stethoscope.

"How long has he been in pain?" Dr. Rowe rested her hand on the right side of his stomach.

"Not long." Eloise racked her brain for any signs of distress earlier in the day. "He never said anything about it—until ten minutes or so ago. He was crumpled up like this." She took a deep breath. "He's in a lot of pain."

Dr. Rowe nodded. "I think we're dealing with appendicitis. But we need to get a CT scan of his stomach to confirm that." The woman met Eloise's gaze. "Once we get that done, we'll know exactly what we're dealing with and how to treat it."

Eloise nodded. "Can he… Will he be able to be treated here?"

"Yes, ma'am. Now, let's get this CT done." She typed something into the computer on the stand next to Archie's bed. "Order's in." She offered Eloise a smile. "I'll be back to check on him soon."

Eloise went with him to get his CT. He was in too much pain to care what was happening. Instead of taking him back to the ER, Dr. Rowe met them in the hall outside the radiology department.

"The CT confirmed it. Archie is going to need his appendix taken out." Dr. Rowe spoke calmly. "It's a quick surgery—an hour or so."

Surgery. She nodded. If Archie heard he was headed for surgery, she couldn't tell. He lay on the gurney, curled on his side, hugging the pillow.

"All right?" Dr. Rowe asked.

She nodded again.

"We are going to go to pre-op and get an IV started and give him some antibiotics." She started walking, but kept talking. "Then our anesthesiologist will come in and sedate him. He'll sleep through the whole thing."

Eloise followed, keeping a hold of Archie's hand as a nurse pushed the gurney. He'd be okay. In an hour, he'd be out of pain and feeling better. Until then, she had to be strong. For Kirby and her grandfather and Archie, too. They were all counting on her and she wouldn't let them down.

For the first time in a long time, she felt completely alone. There was no shoulder for her to cry on and no one to offer her strength or comfort. She'd get through this on her own, but it would be nice if she didn't have to.

JUST ABOUT THE time Mike had given up on finding Rusty, he found him. He'd climbed up one of the large rock outcroppings and sat on the edge, his legs hanging over the side.

"You sure didn't want to be found," Mike called, searching for the best way up.

"Which begs the question, why are you here?" His tone was all irritation.

"I'm your brother. It's my job to irritate you." Mike climbed up the least treacherous side and stood on the relatively flat top. "Not an easy climb in boots."

Other than a sigh, Rusty didn't acknowledge him.

Rusty wasn't happy he was here, he got that. But something was bothering his little brother and Mike couldn't just sit by and do nothing. He'd never given up on his brother, and he wasn't going to start now. He sat beside Rusty, draping his legs over the edge as well.

"Nice view." It was, too. A clear view of the park below, erste Baum, and the wedding festivities still taking place.

Rusty stayed silent.

"You try the cake?" Mike took off his hat and ran a hand through his hair. "I brought you a piece but dropped the plate. I'm sure there's still plenty, though."

Rusty glanced his way.

"Whenever you're ready." Mike shut up then. He wasn't going to badger his brother. If he sat with him long enough, he'd start talking.

For the next fifteen minutes, Mike watched Hattie and Forrest dance and enjoy their special day. He was too far away to make out their features, but the laughter echoed so loud he could hear them up here.

"I don't get any of this," Rusty muttered. "The vows. The whole 'death do us part' thing doesn't mean a thing. They're just words."

Mike held his peace. He wanted Rusty to get it all out in the open so they could face it together.

"Forrest and Hattie are our friends and it's gonna hurt something fierce when it falls apart. You know that." Rusty glanced his way.

"What if they make it work?" Mike kept his tone casual.

"That's a pretty big if. An 'if' that impacts all of us." He ran his hands along the top of his thighs. "Sure, everything's fine now but it won't last."

"It might." He looked at his brother then.

"Mom left after twenty years, Mike." And Rusty was still angry. "She had a life and kids and a good husband and that didn't stop her from going. Why is Hattie any different? Or Audy?"

"Because Hattie is Hattie. And Audy couldn't survive without Brooke." He took a steadying breath. "Mom might have been there physically all that time but she'd tapped out mentally years before she finally left. You know that." How many times had she left them alone when their father had been working? How many times had Mike made peanut butter and jelly sandwiches because the one time he'd tried to use the stove Rusty had burned his little hand? It was his mother's fault for leaving them alone but he was the one that let his brother get hurt and it had gutted him.

"If it's not a lie, if they all stay married and happy, then the only other explanation is us." Rusty gripped the edge of the rock. "We're the reason she left. Not Dad—she could have left before we were born—but you and me. *We* made our mother want to go." He paused to look at Mike. "If that's the truth then why should we think anyone else would stay? If our mother doesn't want us, who else would?" He broke off, staring blindly ahead of him. "Whether it's all a lie or it's just us, we're not getting a happy ending."

Mike shook his head. All this time and she was still hurting them. "This hit you while you were standing up with Forrest?"

Rusty didn't respond.

"That's an awful lot to contemplate while your best friend is getting married." Mike nudged his brother. "You ever stop to think it was her? That something inside of her snapped—"

"Because of us."

"Because of the way she was wired. We've both wasted too many years trying to make sense of what happened. Who knows why she chose to leave when she did, Rusty? We'll never know.

And, to be honest, I don't care." He managed a smile. "Don't let what she did stop you from living a full life. She's got no right to stand in your way—don't you dare let her."

Rusty was quiet for a long time. They both were. Besides the noises from the wedding below and the occasional gust of wind, it was silent.

"I made a fool out of myself down there, didn't I? I'm sure people were laughing." His brother turned to face him.

"No." Mike rested a hand on his brother's shoulder. "You had some people worried after you—because they care. Nobody was laughing."

Rusty nodded. "I guess we should go back?"

"Probably. If for no other reason than to check on Dad." He stood, offered Rusty his hand, and pulled his brother to his feet.

Conversation was easier on the way back. Mike suggested they try to get their dad to go part-time at the shop once Doc Johnston cleared him to go back to work.

"He'll probably argue." Rusty laughed, following the path down to erste Baum. "That shop is his baby."

"I know it. But it's not like you won't take care of it. You know the place like the back of your hand." Mike paused, watching his brother as he asked, "It's still what you want? To take over the shop? You're not just saying that to make me or Dad feel better?"

"It is." Rusty nodded. "Dad said I have a good eye and a good ear. I can normally see problems before they happen or I can figure out what the problem is by the sound it makes." He shrugged. "I guess that's a good thing."

Mike chuckled. "I'd think so."

"You need to do what makes you happy, too." Rusty stopped before they reached the celebration. "This job." He adjusted his hat, his eyes shifting to the ground before meeting his. "I figure you've got some concerns about leaving—with Dad and all. But you staying here won't stop life from happening. Nothing will. If this job is what you want, if it lights a fire in you, then don't let this opportunity slip away." He didn't wait for Mike to answer. "That's all I wanted to say."

"You're the second person today to give me an earful about this job." Though Martha Zeigler had been a little less supportive than his brother.

"Let me guess, Eloise Green?" Rusty grinned, elbowing his brother.

"No." Mike shook his head. "Why would you think… No. Martha Zeigler."

Rusty's eyes widened. "How'd that go?"

"Not so great." Mike sighed. "She meant well. I think."

Conversation stopped when Audy jogged to them. "Mike. Eloise took Archie to the hospital."

"What?" Mike froze. "What happened?"

"Something about his stomach bothering him?

Gretta said he was curled up, moaning. He was hurting something fierce, Mike." Audy was rarely serious—like he was now. "I— We figured you'd want to know."

Every instinct told him to go. It wasn't his place. She'd have Quincy and Kirby and Archie to look after. Who'd be looking after her? Mike glanced at his brother, scanned the field for his father, then turned back to Rusty. "You got Dad?"

"You go." Rusty nodded. "We'll be fine."

Mike nodded, already heading for the parking lot.

"Call if you need anything," Audy called out.

Mike was a careful driver. He'd seen one too many accidents caused by distracted or speeding drivers. It took every ounce of his self-control not to step on the gas and fly to the Colton County Emergency Center and Hospital. He was kicking himself all the way there. Archie had mentioned his stomach was hurting and Mike hadn't thought much of it.

He tried to stay positive and not focus on the worst-case scenarios. Archie was right where he needed to be.

He spotted Quincy and Kirby as soon as he walked into the waiting room.

"Mike." Quincy stood, shaking his hand. "You get called in or something?"

"I heard about Archie." And he'd come running.

"Thank you, son." Quincy's face crumpled. "El's in the back with him."

Mike didn't hesitate to pull the older man in for a hug. "It'll be fine, Quincy. Archie's young and strong. They'll take care of him, you'll see."

"You're right. Of course you are." Quincy sniffed, a tired smile on his face. "She's worrying mightily over her brother."

Kirby's knees were drawn up and her face was buried in the fabric of her dress. If she knew he was there, she didn't acknowledge him.

"Hey, Kirby." He sat in the chair beside her. "You feeling scared?"

She nodded but kept her face covered.

"About Archie?"

Another nod.

"Your momma is with him. So is the doctor. They're taking good care of Archie." He waited, searching for something to make the little girl feel better.

"He's not going to die?" she whispered.

Mike frowned.

"Levi said one of their horses got a bad tummy ache and he died." Kirby's voice was thick and wavering.

That explained why she was so upset. "Oh, Kirby." Mike reached over and put his arm around the little girl.

Kirby turned toward him, wrapped her arms around his neck, and started to sob.

"Hey, hey." He pulled her into his lap. "Your grandpa and I are right here, Kirby." He rocked her, looking to Quincy for guidance.

The old man shrugged, concern and a hint of panic on his well-lined face.

Mike's shirtfront was wet with tears when Eloise pushed through the doors leading to the ER. She was pale but composed. A smile was in place, but he saw how badly her hands were shaking.

"Kirby, Archie's with the doctor getting fixed up right now." She scooped up Kirby and gave her a squeeze. "That's a good hug."

"Hugs help, Momma." Kirby gave her another tight hug.

"That's perfect. Can you give Grandpa Quincy a hug? I think he needs one, too." She offered her daughter a tired smile.

"Do you, Grandpa?" Kirby sniffed.

"I do, Freckles." Quincy sat and gathered the little girl into his lap.

Mike hesitated. He didn't want to overstep but... Since he was here, he was pretty sure it was too late. No going back now. He was at her side before he could change his mind. "El?"

She blinked, staring up at him. "Mike?"

"How's Archie?" He resisted the urge to take her hand or wrap his arms around her.

"You know... That's why you're here?" She swallowed hard, her smile faltering.

He took her hand and gave it a squeeze.

"He… It's his appendix." She took a deep breath. "He's gone back for surgery now."

"That's good, El-Bell. Great news." He sighed. "He's going to be okay."

"He is." But it sounded more like a question than a statement.

He gave her hand another squeeze. "Are you okay?" He kept his voice low and soothing. "What can I do?"

"Stay?" Then she shook her head. "You don't—"

"I'm not going anywhere." No way, no how was he going to leave her side. She was strong, no denying that. But she'd weathered too much on her own. Not this time. This was where he needed to be. And even though she might not know it yet, this was where she might need him to be.

CHAPTER NINE

ELOISE SIPPED THE tea Mike had gotten her and tried not to worry. Mike was confident everything was going to be fine. Since he was an EMT and had medical training, Eloise believed him. She had to. She'd been in shock since she'd found Archie in the field. Seeing her boy that way… Nothing had prepared her for the panic and terror that threatened to pull her under.

But now Archie was in surgery, Mike had Terri keeping tabs on things, and there was nothing to be done except wait.

In the span of thirty minutes, Mabel had arrived with a care package. She'd packed a snack basket with wedding cake, peanut butter crackers, apples, and punch. But the biggest treat was an oversized coloring book and crayons for Kirby. Grandpa Quincy, Kirby, and Samantha were currently sitting around one of the waiting room's tables coloring away.

"I can't thank you enough." Eloise turned the

paper cup in her hands. "As soon as you and Samantha walked in, Kirby's tears stopped."

"Samantha was worried about her friend. And
I was worried about mine." Mabel's smile was
warm. "Samantha might be my future stepdaugh-
ter but I love her as if she were my own. When
she gets sick, it's horrible. I feel so helpless. I'm
sure this is ten times worse."

Eloise nodded.

"Thank goodness he's going to be okay."

"Mike said an appendectomy is a pretty com-
mon childhood surgery." Eloise glanced at the
man sitting on the opposite side of the waiting
room. He was here—nodding at something Jensen
Crawley said—as if he somehow belonged here.

Technically, he did. He worked at the hospital.
But he wasn't working today. He'd come for Archie—and for her.

"He would know." Mabel glanced at the men.
"He took off running before I knew what was
going on. Once Gretta and Samantha filled me
in, we knew we had to do something. Gretta and
Brooke are already planning to bring some meals
over. You shouldn't have to worry about cooking
and all that."

"Oh, Mabel, that's not necessary."

"Necessary or not, it's happening." She patted
Eloise's hand. "I think it makes people feel better to help and do something in times of upheaval
versus sit and do nothing. So let us do, please."

Eloise's phone started ringing. Ted. She stared at the screen. She'd called and updated Ted's prison warden but hadn't expected Ted to call back. He was the last person she wanted to talk to. "If you'll excuse me." She stood, walked down the hall to the cafeteria, and pressed accept on the screen. "Ted?"

"Eloise? What's going on? Is Archie okay? What happened?" He was frantic.

"He's in surgery. His appendix. The doctor says it's a routine procedure and he'll recover in a couple of weeks." Which is what she'd told the warden. She leaned against the wall, staring up at the fluorescent lights overhead.

"Routine? He's in surgery." His muttered curse was pure frustration. "I should be there."

She pressed her other hand to her forehead.

"I know he's in good hands. You'll handle this better than I ever could. And I'm grateful that my boy has you." His voice broke. "Oh, Eloise, I'm so sorry. I left you alone to carry the weight of the world on your shoulders all this time—"

She didn't want more empty apologies. "I have Grandpa Quincy and my friends here, with me." From the corner of her eye, she saw Mike feeding coins into the vending machine. "Good people who care about me and the kids. I'm not alone." She took a deep breath. "I'll tell Archie you called when he gets out of surgery. I know it would mean the world to him if you call him tomorrow."

"I will. Don't you worry about that." His voice wavered again. "I'll make sure he knows I love him—even if I can't be there in person."

"That will make him happy, Ted."

"Benny, the guard, said he'd pass along any messages you leave." He sniffed. "I'd appreciate you keeping me updated. If you can?"

"I will."

"Thank you, Eloise. Thank you for calling me." He sighed. "You're a good woman—a good person. And I'm the fool that let you go."

She shook her head. Every time she talked to him, he'd say something along these lines. She couldn't decide if he wanted her forgiveness or a second chance but now wasn't the time for either conversation. "Ted, I should let you go. Kirby—"

"Is Freckles around? Can I talk to her? For just a minute?"

While she understood he was missing the kids, she had to put their well-being first. Kirby was understandably fragile. Talking to her father and then saying good-bye would upset her all over again. "She cried for over an hour—she's just calmed down. I don't want to upset her all over again. They have a hard enough time saying good-bye after your weekly talk. It would be too much for her."

"Every time I hang up, it's like having my heart cut out all over again. I just want to talk to my little girl, Eloise." There was an edge to his words.

"She *needs* me. You're telling me I can't talk to her? It's not right."

"Ted—"

"I never expected you to be so cruel." He was definitely angry.

"Cruel?" That hurt. "I'm their mother. I have to do what I think is right, even if you don't agree."

"I don't agree. And I'm their father." His voice rose. "But there's nothing I can do, is there? I don't have any say-so in any decisions in here. Or out there. You're making sure of that."

"I'm doing the best I can." She was exhausted. Scared. Frustrated. Hurt and angry. "I'm trying to be a good mother. Sometimes that means telling half-truths to protect my hypersensitive son and daughter, sometimes it means screening who they talk to when they're vulnerable. That's the way it is—whether or not you agree or think it's fair, Ted."

The silence stretched out until she thought they'd been disconnected.

"I'm sorry. I got angry and I shouldn't have snapped at you. I *am* sorry, Eloise." He cleared his voice. "I'll reach out tomorrow and talk to Archie. You have a lot on your plate, I know. But things will be different—better—soon."

She didn't have the energy to argue.

"You'll tell them that I love them? That I'll be there to hug them just as soon as I can?" He said something, muffled, to someone in the room with him. "I've gotta go. Just… I am sorry, Eloise. For everything. I don't know what I'd do without you. I promise, I'm going to make it up to you." And the line went dead.

She tucked her phone into the pocket of her dress and ran a hand over her face.

"Here." Mike handed her an orange soda. "I don't know if it's still your favorite but the sugar will do you some good."

"It is." She took the can.

"You are a good mother, El-Bell." The way he said her name flooded her with warmth. "You love those kids more than anything."

Did he mean that? Or was he trying to make her feel better? Her gaze met his and she knew. He meant it. For a second, she wanted nothing more than to be wrapped in his big, strong arms—for him to hold her until she was calm. "Did you listen to the entire conversation?"

"I figured… Maybe…" He shrugged, his brown eyes searching hers. "Yeah. I wanted to make sure you were okay."

Oh, Mike. He'd always looked out for her. She could always count on him. Something told her she still could.

No. Now she was letting her emotions get the better of her. It had been a long, hard day, that's all. Nothing would make sense or be right until Archie was safe and sound. "We should get back."

He nodded but didn't move. "If you ever need to talk, I'm a good listener."

"I know." But it would be stupid to start relying on him when he was leaving soon. Without another word, she edged around him and headed for the waiting room.

"Momma." Kirby was standing in the middle of the room with tears running down her cheeks. "Where did you go?" she wailed.

"Oh, baby." She scooped up her daughter. "I had a phone call. I was right there, in the hall. Mike got me an orange soda."

"That's your favorite." Kirby sniffed, wiping at her eyes.

"Want a sip?" Eloise offered her the can.

"Really?" Kirby was surprised. "Sodas are for parties."

"Normally, yes." She hugged her daughter close. "Today is an exception." She carried Kirby back to the table where they'd been coloring. "Show me your picture."

Time ticked away at a snail's pace. Grandpa Quincy dozed in one of the waiting room chairs. Mabel, Samantha, and Jensen said they'd come back to visit Archie later. Mike checked in with Terri but there was no update. Gretta called to check up on things and then Rusty and Nolan Woodard walked into the waiting room with balloons, flowers, and a large gift bag.

"How's the patient?" Mr. Woodard gave her a hug. "How's the patient's mother?"

"He's still in surgery." She tried to smile. "I'm coloring and drinking soda and trying to stay positive."

"That sounds like a plan." Mr. Woodard sat beside her grandfather. "We figured we'd keep you company while you wait."

"You don't have to—"

"You won't talk him out of it." Rusty grinned. "Hey, Kirby. Whatcha doin'?"

"Coloring." She pushed the box of crayons toward him. "You can color this zebra unicorn if you want to?"

Rusty nodded and sat. "Are zebra unicorns a specific color?"

"No." Kirby giggled. "Any color you want."

"Whew." Rusty pulled a crayon from the box. "That's a relief."

"Miss Green?" Dr. Rowe pushed through the doors leading back to the emergency room. "We just finished up."

Eloise hurried to the woman. "How did it go?"

"Archie did great. He's in recovery right now. The nurse will come get you and take you to him in a few minutes. I'm sure he'd like you to be there when he wakes up."

"Yes." Eloise felt the tears starting. "Oh, thank you."

A cheer went up in the waiting room and Kirby clapped and jumped up and down.

"You're welcome." Dr. Rowe smiled. "He'll be staying overnight so I'll see you later." And with that, the doctor went back through the swinging doors.

She'd been so scared. More scared than she realized. "He's okay." Even though she was relieved and happy, she was crying.

"El?" Poor Grandpa Quincy was flustered by her tears. "Oh, Sassy, it's all right now."

She nodded, but they wouldn't stop. "I—I know."

"It scared the daylights out of her," Mr. Woodard murmured. "Of course it would."

"Holding it together for everyone else is hard work." Mike stood beside her. "You take all the time you need—"

She wrapped her arms around his waist and buried her face against his chest. Those big, warm arms of his held her tight against him. Later, she might regret this, but now? This was what she needed. A minute where she didn't have to be strong because Mike would be strong for her.

"Hey, now," he murmured against her ear. "It's all right, El-Bell."

She nodded against his chest.

His hands pressed against her back to anchor her in place. She was safe. Protected. Supported. Because Mike was Mike. It was highly improbable that this handsome bear of a man still had the same heart of gold he'd had fifteen years ago. Too much time had passed… And yet, no matter how long it had been between visits, they'd always picked up right where they'd left off. He'd been true blue, always.

He'd given her his Easter candy. He'd comforted her when she'd fallen and skinned her knee. He'd handed over his coat when it was freezing and never once complained. He'd listened to her dreams and told her to go after them. He'd kissed her once and forever ruined any other kisses she'd have in the future. He'd been constant and loyal, kind and loving.

That boy was not this man.

But what if he was? Was it possible the man currently giving her the comfort she so desperately needed was the same Mike she'd known and loved?

It didn't matter, did it? He was leaving. She wasn't stupid enough to open herself up for certain heartache.

Her emotions were all over the place, that's all this was. She was a mess. Period. And she was making a fool of herself. She pushed out of his arms. "I'm so sorry." She wiped at her face. "I don't know where that came from."

"It's okay, Momma. Sometimes a hug can make things better." Kirby took her hand and smiled up at her. "Mr. Mike gives good hugs."

He gave the *best* hugs. It had felt so good. "But

you give the best hugs." She picked up Kirby and hugged her tight. "You and Archie." She glanced toward the emergency room doors, willing the nurse to come and get her. She needed to see Archie with her own two eyes and know he was okay. Once that happened, this day would be over and things could get back to being relatively stable and calm. Her emotions, too.

A RESTLESS NIGHT on his dad's sofa had left him with a crick in his neck, a headache, and a bad attitude. He'd had two cups of coffee, but it hadn't perked him up the way he'd hoped. But he had a shift starting in an hour so he'd drink the whole pot if he had to. Until then, he'd do his best to wear Clifford out before he had to go.

"His battery never runs out." His father sat in his old wicker rocking chair on the front porch.

"No, sir." Mike smiled at Clifford—who was happily chasing a butterfly. "I could use a little of that energy today."

"Couldn't we all?" His father chuckled, rocking away.

Rusty came out the front door, a coffee cup in his hands. "What are you talking about, Dad? You'll be running circles around the two of us again in no time." He sipped his coffee, then set his cup on the railing and joined Mike on the lawn. "It almost feels like fall."

Texas wasn't known for having much in the

way of seasons. It was hot for most of the year. The few months when the sun wasn't making the air ripple were a treat. Especially for Clifford.

"What's on the agenda for today?" Rusty picked up Clifford's ball and tossed it back and forth between his hands.

"I'm in the rig today." And he was grateful. When he was working, he put everything else aside. That's what he needed—to take a break from his own thoughts.

"If you get a chance to check in on Archie this afternoon, will you?" His father kept on rocking. "Yesterday was tough on that whole family. I'm sure they could use a friendly face. Only wait a bit. Quincy sent me a text that the whole Garrison Ladies Guild was in Archie's room."

As if Eloise needed more difficult personalities to deal with. Like her ex-husband.

Yesterday had been a roller-coaster ride for El. Just about the time she'd seemed calm, her ex had called. And that call had upset her something fierce. Not that Mike blamed her. He only heard her side of the conversation, but it'd been enough. Not only did the man have the nerve to pick a fight with El, he'd said something that made her feel the need to defend herself and her mothering style.

Mike hoped he never came face-to-face with Ted what's-his-name. If he did, they were going to have words. For the first time in his life, Mike disliked someone he'd never even met.

"You good?" Rusty asked.

"Fine." He hadn't meant to snap.

"You can go back now, you know?" Rusty threw the ball and Clifford went tearing across the yard after it.

No. He couldn't. "The Garrison Ladies Guild would love that." He took the ball Clifford brought to him. He'd already spent more time at the hospital than anyone that wasn't family. That alone was sure to cause talk.

"Fair point." His brother sighed. "Why am I the one throwing the ball and you're the one he brings it back to?"

"I'm his favorite." Mike crouched and gave Clifford a good back scratch. "Aren't I?"

Clifford flopped and rolled onto his back. The dog had always preferred tummy rubs to back scratches.

"I know." Mike chuckled and rubbed the dog's stomach. "You're not the least bit spoiled. Are you?"

Clifford's tongue lolled out the side of his mouth.

Mike's phone pinged so he pulled it out of his pocket. It was Audy. The high school rodeo team would be practicing twice this week—to help out with the cattle drive for Founder's Day. "You free tonight?"

"No hot date yet." Rusty grinned.

"Good. Audy needs a hand." He held up his phone so Rusty could read the message.

"Can do."

Mike texted, We'll be there, and hit Send. "Dad, you've got your poker game tonight?"

"You bet I do." And he was tickled pink. "I can't wait to take their money and run."

"How about you take their money and *walk* this time?" Mike put his hands on his hips and faced his father. "Please."

"Oh, fine." His father sighed heavily. "You two act like I'm some porcelain doll or something. I'm not. I won't break."

Mike and Rusty exchanged a long look of understanding. The chances of either of them forgetting just how breakable their father had seemed in that hospital bed were slim to none.

"But I'll be good. Besides, Doc Johnston's playing tonight so, technically, I'll be under medical supervision." He chuckled again.

"Is that how it works?" Rusty scratched the back of his head.

After another cup of coffee, Mike got ready for work. He buttoned up his pale blue shirt with Colton County EMT stitched across the back before tugging on his pants and checking the two large multi-compartment pockets.

He paused on the front porch, buttoning the cuffs on his shirt, and asked, "You sure you're up to going to the shop today, Dad?"

"I don't see why you're worried. I'm only staying until noon." He frowned up at Mike.

"I love you, Dad." Mike leaned forward to drop a kiss on his father's head. "I kinda want to keep you around. Okay?"

His father smiled and nodded. "All right, son. You go save people that need saving."

"Yes, sir." He walked down the steps. "You keep an eye on Dad while I'm gone." He scratched Clifford behind the ear. "I'm counting on you. Now, Clifford, shake." He held his hand out and Clifford put his paw in Mike's palm. "Good boy." He fed the dog a treat. "Good boy," he repeated and gave the dog a final pat on the head before leaving.

He walked to his truck, started the ignition, and pulled out onto the road. He glanced up to see Clifford sitting inside the gate, watching him. Once Archie was home, he'd ask Eloise if he could bring Clifford by.

"Or not," he murmured, as he turned onto Main Street and headed out of town.

Before he let himself get any further invested in Eloise's family, he had to stop and think things through. Rusty was right. Instead of charging into things—this job or his feelings for Eloise and her kids—he had to determine what he wanted. And why.

He pulled into the parking lot of the Colton

County Emergency Center and Hospital, parked around back, and entered through the staff door.

"Right on time." Terri stood at the nurses' station inside.

"Always."

Terri's brows rose and she narrowed her eyes as she gave him a once-over. "Need some coffee?" She cocked her head to one side. "I'm thinking someone woke up on the wrong side of the bed."

"Couch." He scrubbed a hand over his face.

"Stay at your dad's place?" She nodded. "He doing all right?"

"Yep. Getting feistier by the day." He signed in on the clipboard. "We got any calls or is it all paperwork?"

Terri exchanged a quick smile with the nurse at the nurses' station. "You don't need to, I don't know, make a stop real quick? Check on a certain patient?"

He almost groaned. "Nope." Why was she surprised?

"All righty, then." She shrugged. "Don't go biting my head off."

After a quick inventory of the rig's interior and restocking as needed, the two of them headed inside to their office. In a small county with limited resources, they didn't drive around all day waiting for a call. They waited here, centrally located, for any emergency that might come in.

He was working. He needed to keep his mind

clear and focused. In his line of work, there was no room for mistakes—even on paperwork. And, boy, was there a lot of paperwork to catch up on. By noon, he'd finished and offered to help inventory the supply closet.

At one, he and Terri ate lunch in the cafeteria. Besides the two of them, there were a few surgical techs and a doctor. Nobody else.

At two, he wandered down the empty hall to get a snack.

At two thirty, he gave up and headed upstairs to check on Archie. His dad had asked him to check in on the boy. Plus, he wanted to make sure the kid was doing better. Eloise, too.

Mike lingered in the doorway to get a read on the room. Archie had two huge balloon bouquets on either side of his bed. He was propped up with several comic books spread out over his lap. From where he stood, the boy's color was good. That was the thing about kids. They bounced back pretty quickly. A fact he was thankful for.

Kirby sat on the foot of the hospital bed listening as Archie read aloud.

Quincy occupied one of the two chairs in the room. The television was on with the sound turned off and the captions on. The old man was all wrapped up in some sort of fishing show.

There was no sign of Eloise.

"Mike?" Patsy Monahan tapped on his shoulder, then edged into Archie's hospital room. "You come to check up on the patient?"

"Yes, ma'am."

"I've heard all about how sweet you've been with those kids in there. Aren't they the cutest?" She didn't wait for him to answer. "Their poor momma was so tired out, Quincy and I sent her home for a quick shower. Seems like the doc is keeping Archie here another night."

Which was unusual. "Oh?"

"Mike." Quincy saw him. "Come in, come in."

Mike stepped inside the room and headed to Archie's bedside. "I was in the neighborhood and figured I'd check in." He smiled at the boy. "How are you feeling?"

"Fine. Until I sneeze or laugh or cough." Archie held up a pillow. "Then I have to hug this 'cuz my stomach hurts bad."

"Worse than yesterday?" Mike didn't like that Archie was being kept a second night.

"No." Archie shook his head. "Better."

"I'm glad to hear it. Looks like you've got something to read." He nodded at the comic books.

"Levi brought them." Archie held one up. "It's about robot aliens."

"They're scary." Kirby wrinkled up her nose. "They suck people's brains out with their straw mouth."

Which didn't exactly sound like kid-friendly reading.

"They're bad robot aliens." Archie said this like it explained everything. "Levi said they all explode and die."

"They die?" Kirby pushed the comic books away. "I don't like this story."

Mike was acutely aware of the way Patsy Monahan was watching the exchange. It made him nervous.

"You don't have to read them, Freckles. How about we find you something to watch. There's that talking dog show? Or the singing, flying ponies you like?"

"Ponies." Kirby turned so she was able to look at the TV. "Samantha likes ponies and I do, too."

"Well, I like robot aliens." Archie went back to reading his comic books.

"Kids." Patsy smiled. "If you come back in a while, Eloise will be back. She'd love to see you."

Would she? They'd had quite a talk on the dance floor—one that left him hoping. But then she'd pushed out of his arms yesterday and he was more confused than ever. Did she still want him to leave her alone? Did she want him with her? And, if so, as a friend? Or more? Now wasn't the time to ply her with questions—not until Archie was better, anyway. With Patsy watching his every expression, he shouldn't even be thinking about such things. He'd do his best to shut down the talk before it got too out of hand. "That's okay. Now that I see Archie's doing so well, I'll get back to work."

"I'll tell Eloise you stopped by. I'm sure she'll call you." Patsy was determined.

"I don't think she has my number." He shook his head.

This wasn't the news Patsy wanted to hear—but the woman rallied. "I can pass it along to her."

"That's kind of you, Miss Patsy, but Quincy knows how to reach me. If something comes up, that is." He had to bite back a smile when Quincy rolled his eyes. Poor Quincy. "You all have a good day."

"Bye, Mr. Mike." Kirby smiled at him. "I can't hug you. The bed's too high."

"That's all right. Next time." He winked at her. "Enjoy those robot aliens, Archie."

"Okay." Archie nodded, his gaze glued to the pages.

With that, Mike left and headed back downstairs. It was good to see Archie was on the mend, but there was a reason Dr. Rowe was keeping him. And, before Mike could get on with his day, he needed to find out what that was.

CHAPTER TEN

"THESE ARE AWFUL." Eloise skimmed one of the comic books, horrified. "Where did you get these?"

"Levi brought them." Archie fanned out the stack of comic books, all smiles. "He and his grandpa came to visit. They brought these and a water gun and a whole bag of bubble gum."

"Was Levi's mom with them?" She had a hard time believing Gretta would be okay picking these comic books out for a seven-year-old.

"No." Archie shook his head.

"She and Mabel are down cleaning up after the wedding." Grandpa Quincy nodded at the comic books. "I don't think she had any idea. Still, I should have checked myself."

She turned the page to find one gruesome scene of death and dismemberment and shut the book. "I'm sorry, hon, but these are too grown up for you."

"But, Momma, they're a gift from Levi." Archie held the comic books close.

"I know they are, sweetie. He's a good friend

to come and see you—but I don't feel comfortable with you reading about this." Giant lizards with laser-beam eyes that melted their opponents, leaving only the bones behind? Absolutely not.

"The robot aliens suck out people's brains, too, Momma." Kirby shook her head. "I did not like that."

"Archie." She held out her hand.

"You can't throw them away, Momma." He handed over the comic books and drooped back against the pillows.

"I'll put them away—for now." Eloise shoved them into her bag. "What else have you been up to?"

"Miss Patsy kept asking Grandpa questions." Kirby shrugged. "And she tried to braid my hair. Oh, and she had candy in her purse."

"But we only had one piece." Archie huffed. "Only one."

"That's probably for the best, Archie. Too much sugar might make you sick to your stomach. We don't want that." She pushed the hair off his forehead and pressed a kiss there.

He sighed. "You're right, Momma." He lifted the extra-firm pillow the nurse had brought him to hug when his stomach hurt. "It hurts to sneeze. I don't wanna throw up."

"Ew." Kirby stuck her tongue out in distaste. "Gross." She patted her brother's foot. "We can watch that wild animal show you like since you can't read your comics."

"Okay. Thanks, Kirby."

Grandpa Quincy changed the TV channel and stood, stretching.

"You should go home, Grandpa. Get some rest." Eloise lowered her voice. "The antibiotics are working so we should be discharged early in the morning."

"I know, I know. But he's my boy, too. I don't like him having an infection." He glanced at Archie. "I can't help but worry. I'd rather worry here, where I can see him, than sit at home alone."

"I can't argue with that." She smiled at him. "Thank you for putting up with us. I know it's been a lot."

"Aw, El, stop worrying about that, will you?" His hands rested on her shoulders. "I'm happy to have you back in my life, Sassy. I'd do just about anything to help you and these kids out."

"You're the best grandpa. Ever." She felt her phone vibrating in her pocket and pulled it out. "It's Ted," she whispered. "For the kids."

Grandpa Quincy sighed. "That's good. It's good he's consistent on that front. A kid needs to be able to rely on their parents."

"I agree." She answered the phone. "Hello?"

"Eloise. How's Archie doing?"

She turned away and whispered, "He has an infection so we're staying another night. Other than that, he's doing well. Feeling more like his old self."

"Is this infection cause for concern?" He sounded worried.

"No. Dr. Rowe said she wanted to watch him overnight and make sure he was responding to the antibiotics before sending him home." She ran a hand over her hair. "I'd rather be cautious, too."

"Of course. Of course. So he'll still be in the hospital tomorrow?"

"Until Dr. Rowe says he's ready to go, yes. That's it." She turned back to the kids. "Guess who's on the phone?" She infused as much enthusiasm into her voice as she could muster.

"Daddy?" Kirby asked, all smiles.

"Is it? Is it Dad?" Archie was reaching for the phone. "Can I talk to him first?"

"You go first. You're sick." Kirby patted his foot.

"That's very sweet of you, Kirby." Eloise handed the phone to Archie.

"Dad?" Archie's excitement was almost too much for Eloise to bear. She loved that her son loved his father. It was the way it should be. But every week, the lie seemed bigger and heavier than the week before. "Good." Archie put one of his pillows across his lap and played with the tag on the edge of the pillow. "I didn't cry." Another pause. "Yep. I'm a big kid now."

Eloise nodded.

"Momma said they didn't keep it." Archie sighed heavily. "I wanted to. In a jar. Kirby said that would be gross."

She hadn't been disappointed when Dr. Rowe said they had disposed of his appendix. As interesting as the idea was, she didn't relish keeping her son's discarded organ in a glass jar for visitors to appreciate. Though, it would have been a conversation starter.

She sat in the chair beside Archie's bed. It was a habit. When the kids talked to Ted on the phone, she listened in. It wasn't meant as eavesdropping—more like staying informed. If something was said that she needed to handle, she'd rather take care of it immediately versus letting them get upset. They were still so young.

"No. Momma and Grandpa Quincy drove me." He paused. "Or I bet Mr. Mike would take me in the ambulance. He's Momma's friend and he drives an ambulance." Another pause. "He was friends with Momma when she was little, too. I like him a lot, too." This pause lasted longer than the others. Archie's gaze shifted to her, widened, then went back to the tag on the pillow. He took a very deep breath and said, "Okay."

Eloise sat forward. Archie sounded…off. "Everything okay?"

Archie nodded but didn't look at her. "She's asking me if everything is okay," he said into the phone.

Eloise frowned.

"Everything is great, Momma." Archie gave her a thumbs-up. "Okay." He smiled. "I love you, too. Okay. Here's Kirby." He handed the phone to his sister.

"Hi, Daddy." Kirby held the phone with both hands. "He's fine. He has a hug pillow in case his tummy hurts." She was nodding. "Yep. He's super brave."

Eloise's eyes shifted to Archie. He was fidgeting with the pillow tag, his whole body tense. "Archie, sweetie. Is everything okay?"

"Uh-huh." Archie shrugged. "We were just talking about stuff." For a kid who loved to tell every detail of every conversation, he was too quiet. Almost like he was hiding something.

"I'm glad. What sort of stuff?" She moved to sit on the side of the bed.

"Daddy said…" Archie finally looked at her. "Dad said he'll see us real soon." He was practically radiating with excitement.

Eloise, on the other hand, was dismayed. Why would he say such a thing? All he was doing was getting the kids' hopes up—only to disappoint them. Soon? Ted had been sentenced to two years—he'd only served, what, a year? Twelve months was an eternity to a seven-year-old. *Not soon.*

"My new friend Samantha likes ponies. And I have a dog friend named Clifford. He's big and red just like Clifford in the books." She stopped talking and took a breath. "He belongs to Mr. Mike. Yes, Momma's friend." Another pause. "Clifford came to Grandpa's house and we went to Clifford's house and he helped set up the wedding, too." She nodded. "Yes, with Mr. Mike. And Mr. Mike stayed with us yesterday but he didn't bring Clifford to the hospital." She shrugged. "He's nice. He gives good hugs, too." Another pause. "Me and Archie and Mommy."

Eloise's patience was running out.

"Okay, Daddy. I love you more." Kirby giggled. "More and more." She giggled again. "Even more. The most." She nodded. "Okay, bye." Kirby handed her the phone.

Eloise went into the hall. "Ted?" The line was dead. She stared at the phone, grappling with her mounting frustration. "What is he thinking? What is he up to?"

"El?" Gretta was walking down the hall. "You okay?" She reached her and frowned. "You're mad at me, aren't you? I'm so sorry about the comic books. I came to replace them. I was hoping Archie hadn't read them yet."

"He did. But—"

"You have every right to be mad. I can't believe Dad thought his old comic books were okay for the boys." She was so upset. "I'm so sorry. Truly."

"I'm not mad at you, Gretta." She gave her a quick hug. "I figured you didn't know about the comic books." The comic books didn't seem like such a big deal now. "It's…"

"What?" Gretta's brow dipped. "What's happened? Archie's okay?"

"Yes. He's fine." Eloise hesitated. As much as she'd like to keep Ted out of Garrison, it couldn't last. The man would always be a part of the kids' lives. And, through them, her life, too. "My ex," she murmured.

"Oh." Gretta sighed. "Exes are the worst. Is yours a champion gaslighter? Mine misses his visitation days and then shows up when he wants, expecting Levi and I to adjust accordingly." She broke off. "Sorry. Too much?" She frowned. "What did yours do?"

Gretta's rant was exactly what Eloise needed to hear. If anyone would understand how she felt, it was Gretta. "He told Archie he'd see him soon. Which isn't possible because he's…in jail. But the kids don't know that because Archie is hypersensitive and his father being in jail would cause him constant stress." She paused. "Too much?"

"Oh." Gretta blinked. "No. Not at all." She frowned. "Why on earth would he say that? Is he normally careless with their feelings?"

"Not really." Eloise didn't like the knot in her stomach. "He is the best version of himself with them. They adore him, especially Archie. I don't want them disappointed, you know?"

"I do." Gretta looked as confused and upset as

Eloise felt. "I'm here for you. I mean it. Being a single mom... You're single *but* your ex is still around for your kid. A kid that you try to shelter from the bad side of their father. But you understand—I mean, you *really* understand."

"Boy, do I." Eloise smiled. "It's exhausting."

Gretta squeezed her arm. "And you've just been through this scare with Archie, too. How are you holding up? Really?" She paused. "I heard Mike's been watching over you. That's nice, isn't it? He's one of the good guys, you know? Taking care of his dad. Working as an EMT and a pick-up rider. He's the protect-and-shelter type." She shrugged. "If he wasn't moving, I'd say Mike Woodard was someone you could consider dating."

"But he *is* moving." It was hard picturing the place without Mike.

Gretta paused. "Last I heard, that was the plan. Some really good job with one of the national rodeo companies, too. Then his dad had a stroke and he delayed his start date to take care of him." Her smile was almost sad. "Like I said, he really is one of the good guys, isn't he?"

"Yes." He was. Her chest seemed to collapse in on itself, compressing her heart to the point of rupture.

But if he left, this intense *thing* between them would go, too. Wouldn't it? He'd go on to bigger and better things and so would she. They'd both be happy.

But…was it impossible for them to be happy together? The truth was he was *still* her Mikey. Knowing that, could they do what they always did? Pick up where they left off. Together.

Stop it. He was leaving. She was staying and she had no right to ask him to give up this opportunity and stay here, too.

This whole time, Gretta had been watching and waiting for her reaction.

Eloise pinned on her hostess smile. "He deserves only good things." That much was true.

MIKE SPLASHED COLD water on his face. Yesterday's paperwork had been mind-numbingly boring. But today had made up for that. He ran a hand along his forehead, the surge of adrenaline that had carried him through the afternoon's accident beginning to wane. Nothing like a multicar pileup along Interstate 10 to keep things tense and focused. Luckily, there'd been no fatalities. There had been, however, a number of injuries.

He wiped his hands on a paper towel and pushed out of the staff bathroom and into the locker room.

"I don't know about you but I'm thinking a nice long shower and a tall, cold beer is in order." Terri opened her locker and pulled out her bag. "Jimmy texted to tell me the brisket he's been slow roasting should be ready for dinner. Tonight's looking good."

"I would say so." Last night, he'd gone straight

from the hospital to the stockyards arena to help out with the high school rodeo team. His plans for this evening were low-key. Check in on his father, go home, play catch with Clifford, and go to bed early. "I'm tempted to invite myself over."

"You don't need an invitation, Mike." Terri's snort was dismissive. "You're basically family. Our door is always open. But, knowing Jimmy, he might be stingy with his brisket."

"I understand. The man's a legend." Mike appreciated how proud Terri was of her longtime boyfriend's barbecue awards. He'd won several local competitions and had even placed at the state rodeo barbecue competition two years back. "Anything he cooks is a work of art."

"I won't tell him you said that." Terri shot him a look. "The man's ego is already two sizes too big." She slung her duffel bag over her shoulder.

"Next time, I'll be there." Brisket sounded good but he was too bone-tired to enjoy it.

"Sounds good. See you next week."

"Yep." He nodded as she walked out, then stowed his personal stethoscope and supplies in his locker, and stopped by the nurses' station long enough to sign out.

He was halfway down the hall before he realized where he was going. To the elevator—to Archie's room. Dr. Rowe assured him the boy was responding to antibiotics but Mike wanted to check on him all the same. Besides, his dad would want a report.

He got in the elevator and pressed the button.

"Hold the elevator, please," a man called out, the large balloon bouquet and cellophane-wrapped gift basket in his arms covering most of his chest and face.

"Got it," Mike answered, not wanting the man to trip over the dozen or more ribbons trailing on the ground. "You need a hand?"

"No, no, but thank you." The man entered the elevator.

"Going to see someone special?" He eyed the balloons and the basket. It was a lot.

"I am." The man set the basket on the floor. "My son. I haven't seen him in a while."

"Oh." Mike tried not to stare but… Were his eyes playing a trick on him or was this Eloise's ex-husband? Ted Barnes was here?

"I feel like a kid on Christmas morning." He ran a hand over his pressed shirt, then his hair. "But also like a man who's facing the most important job interview of his life."

"Is that so?" It was a good thing Mike was so tired or he'd have a hard time keeping his temper in check. There were so many things he wanted to say to this man and not one of them was nice. *Not that Ted Barnes is any of my business.*

"It is." He nodded. "You have kids?"

Mike shook his head. But if he did, he'd do everything in his power to be there for them. Things like not breaking the law so he didn't go to jail and that sort of thing.

"It's the best thing I ever did with my life." Ted shook his head. "Believe me, I have a lot of things to make up for. But today is a fresh start and, from here on out, I want to be that dad, you know? The one that embarrasses his kids because he's always there? Making them pancakes for breakfast or cheering them on at a school event. That's going to be me."

Mike nodded but didn't say a word. Hopefully, Ted Barnes meant everything he was saying. Archie and Kirby deserved a reliable, loving father—every child did.

The elevator arrived on the third floor and they both stepped out.

"Time to go surprise them." Ted picked up the basket and headed out of the elevator.

Surprise them? They didn't know he was coming? Mike was torn. Should he head back downstairs and let Ted surprise his family? Or should he be there, in case the surprise didn't go as well as Ted was counting on. Eloise was in for a shock.

He couldn't leave. With a sigh, he headed down the hall, a few steps behind Ted.

Ted was practically jogging, and the balloons bounced and the ribbons swerved back and forth along the linoleum floor.

There was no denying the man was excited. But

would the kids—and Eloise—feel the same way? Mike's discomfort grew the closer they got to Archie's room. He was overstepping—again. But when they reached room 319, it was empty. Good news for Archie. Not so good for Ted Barnes.

"Mike?" Dr. Rowe came out of one of the other rooms. "Are you looking for Archie?"

Mike and Ted exchanged a quick look.

"I am." He nodded. "Guess those antibiotics took care of the infection."

"They did. He went home about an hour ago." Dr. Rowe nodded. "Sweet kid. Sweet family." She glanced at Ted.

"Dr. Rowe, I'm Archie's father. Ted Barnes." Ted was all smiles as he shook the doctor's hand. He turned to Mike and raised an eyebrow.

"Mike Woodard." He shook the man's hand.

Ted's grip was unnecessarily strong. "I just arrived in town and was hoping to surprise him."

"It's nice to meet you. I'm sure he'll be happy to see you." Dr. Rowe glanced back and forth between the two of them. "I should get back to checking on my patients."

"Thanks, Dr. Rowe."

"Yes, thank you for taking care of my son." Ted Barnes waited until the doctor had walked away before saying, "This is awkward. Are you the Mr. Mike I've heard so much about?"

Mike couldn't have been more surprised. "I guess so."

"Mr. Mike and Clifford?" Ted gave him an assessing once-over. "Eloise's childhood friend? It seems like you've made an impression on my children."

More like, they've made an impression on me. Eloise and her kids mattered to him—more than that, they'd taken up residence in his heart. And this man showing up had Mike's defenses on the rise.

"Maybe you can help me." The man was dead serious.

For a minute, Mike was too stunned to say a word. "I'm not sure how."

"You've been friends with Eloise for a long time, so you know she's not big on second chances. Once you mess up, that's it." He gave Mike a long, narrow-eyed look.

"Is that so?" What was the man fishing for exactly?

"I don't know what she has told you about us. Or me." Ted cleared his throat.

Us? Mike shook his head. "We don't talk much about the past."

"No?" He didn't seem too pleased by that. "Why would she? I messed everything up." He looked Mike in the eye, his posture slightly defensive. "I've got a lot to make up for. A lot. But that's what I'm going to do. They are all that matter to me. My family." The muscle in his jaw clenched. "That's why I'm here to stay."

The sinking feeling in Mike's stomach was hard and fast. More like the floor falling out from under him. "You're moving here? To Garrison?" Archie and Kirby might be happy about it, but would Eloise? Quincy? For a man who wanted to fix things, this seemed like an awfully bold first move.

"The kids miss me. I miss them. I'm hoping, maybe, Eloise misses me, too." He paused, almost like he was waiting for some sort of reaction. "We were a happy family not too long ago. I want to be part of their lives again."

He couldn't stop himself from asking, "Have you talked to Eloise about this?"

"I know what her answer would be. No. She's… It'll take time to win back her trust but, lucky for me, I've got nothing but time." He went on, an edge to his voice. "I want a second chance. I'll do whatever I have to in order to get my family back."

If he was trying to intimidate Mike, it wasn't working. Irritate, yes. He was ready to wrap this up. Should he try to give Eloise a heads-up or mind his own business—something he'd had a hard time doing when it came to Eloise and her kids. "There's nothing I can do to help with that."

"That's not what I need help with. I was hoping you could give me the inside scoop on Earl Ellis. I'm going to be working for him."

Mike ran a hand along the back of his neck. He

didn't want to talk about Earl with Ted. He didn't want Ted anywhere near Earl Ellis. Earl was a friend of his father's—Tyson's father. "Good man. Hard worker. Expects his employees to do the same."

"I'm a hard worker. He won't find anyone more motivated than I am." Ted tugged at the collar of his shirt. "Anything else I should know?"

He didn't want to stand in the hospital hallway and help Ted Barnes figure out a way to make a living in Garrison. Selfishly, he didn't want Ted Barnes living here. Especially since Mike was leaving. "He's a good man."

"My parole officer, Wilson Newcomb, said as much. I'm staying in his garage apartment until I can get my own place."

"Wilson Newcomb?" As far as Mike knew, Wilson was the only parole officer in the county.

Ted nodded. "You know him?"

"Small town. You know pretty much everyone." He eyed the balloons and gift basket, his frustration welling up until there was no holding back what he had to say. "You don't know me from Adam but I need to speak my piece." He took a deep breath. "You have every right to a relationship with your kids. It's good you're here for *them*." Now came the tricky part. "I've known El since she was about Archie's age. We were close growing up. She's special—she always has been. I…care about her." *I always have and*

I always will. "I wasn't around when things got tough for her, but I'm here now. She's been let down a lot. Too much. If you're here to win her back, you better mean it."

Ted seemed to be contemplating what Mike had said. "Or what?"

"Or you'll jeopardize the relationship you want with your kids. Don't put them in a situation where they have to pick sides." He ran his fingers through his hair.

"You're saying all this because you're worried about my kids?" His brows rose. "Not because you *care* about Eloise?" He didn't sound angry so much as curious.

Mike didn't answer. He didn't owe Ted Barnes any explanations.

"I respect what you said. And that you care about the kids and Eloise." Ted shifted the gift basket. "It's certainly been interesting meeting you, Mike Woodard. I have a feeling we'll be seeing more of each other. Like you said, it's a small town."

Mike watched the man walk down the hall and get back into the elevator. Ted Barnes wasn't the out-and-out villain he'd imagined—but he still didn't like him. How could he? He'd shaken up Eloise's world. And he was about to do it again. Mike sighed. Soon, Ted would be showing up on Quincy's front porch for his big surprise.

It wasn't right. Eloise deserved a heads-up.

He pulled his phone from his pocket and called Quincy.

"Mike?" Quincy answered right away. "Everything okay with your dad?"

"He's fine." He stared into Archie's now empty hospital room. "But... I figured I should call and let you know that Ted Barnes is here."

"He what now?" Quincy barked out.

"He showed up at the hospital with balloons and presents for Archie. Almost talked my ear off, too." He ran a hand along the back of his neck. "I didn't think you and Eloise would appreciate him surprising you—I figured you'd want some time to prepare."

"You figured right." Quincy grumbled. "That would have been some surprise. And not a good one, either."

Which was exactly what Mike had been thinking. "Can I do anything?"

"Well, now, that's a good question." The older man sighed. "How about I call you in a bit. A visit from Clifford might be just the distraction the kids will need—once he's gone." He muttered an expletive. "Might help El, too. She's going to be fit to be tied."

"I'll wait for you to call." It'd be one of the hardest things he'd ever done, but he'd wait.

"I can't thank you enough for calling, son." Quincy's voice was thick. "You know, I always thought the two of you would end up together.

You'd never pull anything like this, that's for sure."
Another sigh. "I'll let you know how it goes." And
he disconnected.

He left the hospital and headed straight for his
father's house. At this rate, he might be spending another night on his dad's lumpy couch. That
way, if Quincy called, it wouldn't take long to get
to Eloise and the kids.

CHAPTER ELEVEN

ELOISE LAUGHED. "Don't let it fall." They were all gathered around the coffee table, watching the wooden block Jenga stack wobbling just a smidge as Archie slowly pulled a piece free.

"Whew." Archie sat the piece down. "That was close."

"You're good at this, Archie." Kirby sat on the edge of the couch. She didn't want to play Jenga because it scared her when the tower toppled over, but she didn't mind watching and cheering them on. She was a very good cheerleader.

Today had been a good day. Archie was healing and home. Gretta and Levi had come over after school with a stack of age-appropriate comic books. Kirby and Grandpa Quincy had made cupcakes that they were all enjoying. Brooke had dropped off a pizza for dinner that was devoured in minutes. It'd be bedtime soon and then she might enjoy a glass of the wine Brooke had brought over with the pizza. It was the first time in a long time she felt relaxed.

"Eloise." Her grandfather stood in the hallway. "Give me a hand?"

"Sure." She stood and followed her grandfather down the hall and into the kitchen. "What can I do?"

"I got a call from Mike." He sat, heavily, in one of the kitchen chairs. "We're going to have a visitor."

"Mike's coming over?" It shouldn't make her this happy. "Is he bringing Clifford? Archie will be happy to see them both."

"No." He glanced down the hall. "Not Mike. Ted."

Eloise blinked, staring at her grandfather. "What?" She sat in the opposite chair.

"He turned up at the hospital—wanting to surprise everyone, Mike said." He shrugged. "Talk about a surprise."

"But he…" She swallowed. "It's too early for parole?" Wasn't it? "Wouldn't he have known about this for a while?" He had to have known. Why hadn't he told her? What was he up to? In seconds, her muscles were tense and knotted and a dull ache settled at the base of her neck.

"I'm grateful Mike called." He reached across the table and took her hand.

Eloise was, too. If Ted had shown up out of the blue, shock was more likely than surprise. She couldn't wrap her mind around how that would have gone.

Grandpa Quincy gave her hand a squeeze, then let it go. "Now, what do you want to do about this?"

Throw up? She swallowed. "What can I do? He is their father."

"I have a few other choice words to describe the man." He stood, hands on his hips, and stared down the hallway. "I'm not all that happy to have him under my roof."

"I'm sorry, Grandpa." She rested her elbows on the table and covered her face.

"You have nothing to apologize for." He rested a hand on her shoulder. "He's the disrespectful one—springing this on you and the kids. I'm not sure how he thinks showing up like this is a good idea."

"I hate seeing you upset." Eloise stood and went to hug him.

"Well, now…" He sighed, patting her back. "I'll stop my blustering. No point to it, anyway, is there? Might as well make the best of it."

The best of it? "The kids will be so happy." Until he left. Was he leaving? What was his plan?

"Momma, it's your turn," Kirby called down the hallway.

"You good, Sassy?" Her grandfather held her by the shoulders.

She had to be—for the kids. "I'm good." She pinned on a smile. "It's my turn." She took a deep breath and headed back to the family room. "My turn?" Her hands were shaking so when she went to pull out her piece, the whole tower came tumbling down.

"Poor Momma." Kirby hugged her. "It's okay."

"Wanna try again?" Archie asked, propped on his side with his hug pillow tucked under his arm. "Or play something else?"

"Let's play again." Levi sat up on his knees.

Kirby crawled around on the floor, picking up pieces and gave them to Gretta. Gretta handed them to Levi, who was stacking up the tower.

"Excellent teamwork." Grandpa Quincy sat in his recliner, his gaze turning to the front window every few seconds.

Every creak of the floorboard or old-house noise made Eloise startle. The kids didn't notice the new tension flooding the room, but Gretta did. There was no preventing the stretching of Eloise's nerves—and patience. Being reunited after a year was bound to be emotional. And after the reunion? Then what?

They made it three rounds before the inevitable knock on the door.

"I'll get it." She stood, rubbed her hands together, and took a deep breath. She grabbed the doorknob and yanked the door open.

There he was. Ted. With balloons and a huge gift basket full of who knows what. It didn't matter really. Because it *was* Ted.

He smiled. "Hi." His smile wavered. "I… Um, surprise."

"Hi." She swallowed. "Yes. You're…*here*." And he looked exactly the same way he had the last time she'd seen him.

There was an awkward pause as he took inventory of her appearance.

She pulled at her T-shirt. She did not look the same. She'd let her hair go back to its natural color, sold off all of her couture and name-brand clothing, and there was the extra weight.

"I…I was hoping to see the kids. I've got something for Archie." He shifted from foot to foot. "And Kirby. Are they here? Can I see them?"

If she sent him away, the kids would never forgive her. That's all that mattered right now. The kids. "Sure." She stepped inside, then whispered, "Just remember, Archie needs to be pretty still for now."

"Of course." He took a deep breath and followed her into the house.

Everything seemed to move in slow motion. Ted set the basket and balloons down, then hurried to Archie's side. Archie was ecstatic. His happy smile tore at her heart—right before it was replaced by a flood of tears.

"Oh, Archie." Ted cupped his son's face. "Don't cry. Please, don't." He was at a loss, looking to her.

Eloise stepped forward, sat at the foot of the

couch, and squeezed Archie's foot. "He's here to see how you're feeling. Don't cry, sweetie. You don't want to irritate your stomach,"

"Hug your pillow," Levi said, looking mighty suspicious of Ted. "Who are you, mister?"

"That's my daddy," Kirby whispered but didn't move. She stared at Ted with saucer-like eyes, frozen in place. "Mommy and Daddy are divorced and Daddy has to travel lots and lots."

Eloise was having a hard time not crying herself.

"Hi, Freckles." Ted held out a hand for her.

Kirby blinked, glanced at Archie, then back at Ted. Her chin crumpled and her lower lip wobbled. "Daddy?"

"I'm here." Ted's struggle was real. Archie had a grip on one hand but Kirby wouldn't get close enough for him to reach her. "I've missed you two so much."

Kirby nodded, took one step, then another—until she took his hand.

Eloise watched the whole thing with a knot in her throat and her lungs fighting for air. When he pulled them both in for a hug, it was easier to breathe. She blinked rapidly, staring at the ceiling overhead until the threat of tears had passed.

"You're here?" Kirby leaned back and rested a hand along the side of his face. "You're real."

"I am." He pressed a kiss to her temple. "I

couldn't wait to see you. Hug you. See your smile—and your freckles, too."

Kirby pointed at her face. "They are still there."

"I'm glad." He chuckled and pulled her in for another hug.

"Are you done traveling?" Archie asked. "Can you stay with us for a while?"

"I'm done, Archie." Ted smoothed his son's hair from his forehead.

That answered that. If Ted was on parole, what was his plan? She might not want to know, but she needed to know. For the kids.

"Really?" Archie hugged his pillow. "You're staying here?"

Ted nodded. "I am." He glanced at her. "We'll talk about all that later. Now, tell me what you've been up to."

"Lots." Archie paused. "This is my friend, Levi. And his mom."

"Nice to meet you." Ted always had a charming smile.

"Gretta Williams." But Gretta's smile was cautious and her posture was standoffish.

"You remember my grandfather, Quincy Green? From our wedding." Which felt like another life.

Grandpa Quincy didn't bother with a smile. Disapproval was written all over his face. "Oh, I remember. You can call me Mr. Green." He didn't stand or extend a hand. "Quite a bit has happened since the last time I saw you, Mr. Barnes."

"Yes, sir." The muscle in Ted's jaw tightened, but he nodded. "I appreciate you taking care of the kids and Eloise—"

"That's what family does," her grandfather interrupted. "No thanks needed."

Eloise managed to catch her grandpa's attention. She shot him a long, pointed look. He was upset, she got that. But being angry at Ted wouldn't change this new reality. If anything, the kids might get upset with their great-grandfather for not being nice to their newly returned father.

Luckily, her grandfather seemed to get the message. He took a deep breath and tried to relax his hold on the arms of his recliner.

"Did you go anywhere exciting when you were traveling, Dad?" Archie was all wide-eyed and curious. "What was it like?"

"Did you go to Paris?" Kirby asked. "I don't know where that is. Is it far? My friend Samantha's mom and dad are going there after they get married."

"Are they? That's a good place for a honeymoon." Gretta smiled at Kirby. "It is very far away. So far, you have to ride in an airplane for hours."

"That far?" Kirby appeared impressed.

"Did you go there, Dad?" Archie wasn't going to let up. "Africa with the lions or Egypt and the pyramids?"

Ted looked extremely uncomfortable—and unsure of what to do or say.

"Why don't you see what your dad brought you." Eloise pushed the large gift basket forward. "Afterward, we'll need to start getting ready for bed."

"But, Momma." Archie's mouth dropped open. "I'm not going to school tomorrow. Do I *have* to go to bed?"

"You do." She nodded. "I'll be getting your schoolwork from your teacher. You're not going to be watching TV all day."

Archie sighed heavily and crossed his arms over his chest.

"I can come back tomorrow." Ted pulled the gift closer. "If that's okay?" He glanced at Eloise, then Grandpa Quincy.

Her grandfather snorted.

"After school," Kirby asserted. "I don't want to miss anything."

"That sounds fair." Eloise faced Ted. "Does that work for you? Around four."

"That's perfect." Ted directed their attention to the contents of the basket.

The kids "oohed" and "aahed" over every item as if they'd never seen anything so amazing. Crayons, action figures, a dog puzzle, coloring books, and more. Ted didn't seem to realize the gift wasn't what was in the basket, it was him— being here.

Every few minutes, Gretta would send a sympathetic smile her way, but Eloise was okay. All things considered, everything was going well. She didn't relish the one-on-one conversation she and Ted were going to have to have, but it wasn't going to happen tonight.

When the basket was empty, Gretta made a big production out of stretching and yawning. "We should get home, Levi. You do have to go to school tomorrow."

"Aw, Mom." Levi huffed. "I can stay home and keep Archie company. He's going to be bored. *So* bored."

"That's a kind offer, Levi. You're a good friend." After seeing the two boys together, it was clear they were fast friends. Eloise might have a few concerns about Levi being older and prone to more aggressive storytelling, but she could work with that.

"But you're going to school." Gretta stood and held out her hand. "Come on."

Levi huffed and groaned and made sure everyone knew he wasn't happy.

"Thank you for coming." Eloise accepted Gretta's hug. "And for staying," she whispered for her ears alone.

Gretta's hold tightened. "I'll call you later."

"I guess I'll head out, too." Ted ruffled Archie's hair and gave Kirby a wink. "But I need more hugs, first."

"But you'll be back tomorrow?" Archie asked. "You promise? You're not going away?"

"I promise." Ted gave him a gentle hug. "I'll be here at four."

"Okay." Archie toyed with one of the action figures Ted had brought. "I'm glad."

"Me, too." Kirby gave him a big hug. "I'm going to tell everyone in my class that you're here. I bet Samantha will be so, so happy for me."

Ted accepted a second hug from Kirby and stood. "Night, Eloise. Good night, Mr. Green."

"Night." Eloise opened the front door for everyone. "Thank you for coming." As soon as she closed the door, Kirby and Archie started talking. They were both thrilled that their father was here and staying and coming back tomorrow. Eloise only nodded, unwilling to say too much until she knew what, exactly, Ted's plans were. "It's been a good evening. Let's get you ready for bed and tucked in so tomorrow can get here even faster, okay?" And once they were tucked in, she'd take three cupcakes to the Woodard house. Mike's phone call was the only reason the evening hadn't turned into a nightmare and she wanted him to know how very grateful she was.

MIKE SAT ON the front steps of his father's porch. He'd been sitting there for an hour or more—long enough for the sky to go from blue to violet to the deep purple it was now. At some point, his father had turned on the porch light so he wasn't sitting in the dark. The solar lights lining the flower beds glowed warmly, giving enough light for Clifford to sniff out and snap at a moth or cricket.

"You tired?" he asked when Clifford climbed the steps and slid flat beside him, his big head in Mike's lap.

Clifford yawned.

Mike chuckled and gave the dog a thorough head and neck scratch.

Clifford went from relaxed and sprawling to sitting up with his ears perked up. The dog stared down the street, head turning one way, then the other.

"What's up?" Mike looked in the same direction but didn't see anything. "A raccoon or something?" Hopefully it wasn't another skunk. Clifford's attempt to befriend the varmint hadn't ended well. After two tomato baths and a haircut, the poor dog was allowed back into the house—but not on the furniture.

Clifford trotted down the steps and across the yard. He barked once, his fluffy tail swaying slowly, then faster.

"Hey, Clifford." It was Eloise.

Mike pushed off the porch. "El?" It was almost like he'd willed her here with his worrying. But she was here and his chest was the slightest bit lighter.

"Hi." She raised one hand in a little salute and held a tinfoil-covered plate in the other. "I wanted to stop by. I hope it's not too late."

"No, it's not too late." He was so relieved to see her. The last couple of hours had been all stressing and pacing and hoping she and the kids were okay. He opened the front gate. "Come on in."

She did, laughing when Clifford circled her several times. "Are you saying hello, too? I'm sorry I didn't bring anything for you, Clifford. I don't know what I was thinking."

He loved that laugh more than any other. "Oh, believe me, he's been spoiled plenty today. Dad's a little too generous with the treats." He glanced at her as they walked, slowly, to the front porch. "You want something to drink? A lemonade or tea or something?"

"No, thank you. If it's okay, can I sit? It's so peaceful." She followed him up the steps of the porch.

She wanted to stay? He drew in an easy breath. "Anytime." He took the plate she held out to him. "What's this?"

"Cupcakes. 'Thank you' cupcakes."

"Thank you? For what?"

She shot him a disbelieving look and sat in one of the wicker rockers. "Calling Grandpa. If you hadn't, he probably would have had a heart attack and I…well, I don't know what I'd have done." She glanced up at him. "Thanks to you, it went smoothly. As smoothly as one could expect, all things considered."

He sat in the other rocking chair, placing the

plate on the small circular table between the chairs. As much as he wanted to know more, he wasn't going to push. She seemed okay, that was enough.

"It's a nice night. Cool. It's almost fall-like." She leaned back in the chair.

"A rarity." Made better by the fact that he was enjoying it with her.

She sat for a while, one leg tucked beneath her, the other kept the rocking chair rocking. "The kids are thrilled he's here." She turned her head and met his gaze.

"He is their father. It's good they're happy." He paused. "Isn't it?"

She took a deep breath. "I think so... Yes." She shook her head. "I don't know, honestly. I'm still processing *everything*." She stopped rocking. "I should be mad, Grandpa Quincy sure is, but I can't be. I have to..." She stopped talking and shook her head again.

"Go on. Let it out." He leaned forward, resting his knees on his elbows.

The way she was studying him—she seemed to be searching for something.

His gaze held hers. "I mean it. I honestly can't imagine what you're thinking or feeling. It's probably all over the place. I'm on the outside looking in and I'm hot one minute, cold the next."

There was a hint of sadness to her smile. "I'm... I'm so tired of being mature and keeping it together." She pushed out of the chair. "I haven't had a choice in so long." She paced the length of the porch, then came back, turning to him. "It's not just Ted. It started years before Ted." She leaned against the wooden porch railing. "My mind is sort of spinning and spinning, you know? I'm trying to sort it out."

He sat back. "You talk. I'll listen."

"Why, Mike?" She swallowed. "I know you're a great guy. I know you've always been here for me... I just don't understand why."

Because, fool that I am, I still love you. He cocked an eyebrow, doing his best to keep his tone light. "Too nice, remember? Go on."

She swallowed again. "When Mom died, Dad sort of...broke. He'd been drinking, you know that, but I wanted to stay close to Mom after that first heart attack. Then he got *really* drunk and he hit me. I think it shocked him as much as it shocked me—that's why I wound up here that Christmas. That one thing changed my whole life." She shrugged.

He ran a hand over his face, his heart twisting and a huge lump in his throat. Her own father had struck her? Not hugged her or comforted her or given her the love she needed. No, he'd hurt her mentally and physically.

And then she'd come to him—to find him fall-down drunk... No wonder she'd been so upset. If he could go back, leave that bottle of whiskey untouched, and hold her, he would.

"Dad's drinking stole the security I needed." Her gaze locked with his. "And everything good and stable was buried with my mother. Dad couldn't talk about her—wouldn't talk about her—or he'd drink. Obviously, I stopped talking about her. I never got a chance to really grieve her."

He hadn't let her grieve? For her own mother? He swallowed against the knot in his throat.

"We moved a lot, Dad got married and divorced a lot, and I felt more trapped with each passing day. Once I was accepted to university, I left and severed all ties with my father." She ran a hand over her hair. "College was the first time I was on my own. It was pretty great. And I met Ted. He was this life force. So...so kind and funny. He didn't drink." She shook her head. "I'd talk and he'd listen. Fast-forward a couple of years to graduation, the kids, I got a little flower and tea shop and his business was taking off." She laughed. "You should have seen some of the big dinner parties and events I'd organize to help grow his business." She shuddered. "I didn't know what he was doing." She glanced at him. "I didn't know a lot of things until after we divorced. Like his mistress."

Mike was stunned. "I thought the man couldn't be a total fool since he married you..."

She was smiling. She'd just told him all she'd told him and she was smiling?

"Why are you smiling?"

She stood. "Because… You're *you*." Her cheeks flushed.

What did that mean?

"The memories I have of here, growing up… It's one of the reasons I brought the kids here." She laughed. "Well, and because I had no place else to go."

He could study her face for hours. "Most of our memories together were…special to me."

"Me, too." Her hand rested on his arm. "Thank you for today."

All he could do was stare at her. If he spoke, he'd say something that he'd regret.

"I'm sorry if I hurt you. Then and now." She squeezed his arm, then rested her hand on the railing between them. "Time has passed and things change and here we are. I'm trying to start over and you will be soon, too."

He blinked. "How's that?"

"Your job." She pushed off the railing and sat in the rocking chair once again. "When do you go?"

"After Founder's Day." He ran a hand along the back of his neck. "I don't trust Dad to take it easy." Not that that would change after he left. And that worried him.

"You're a good son." She smiled. "And you're a good friend, too. I'd really like to be your friend again, Mike."

There were so many things he wanted to say

but all he managed was, "Done." She'd just shared years of upheaval and hurt with him.

"Tell me about this job?" She sat forward as Clifford sat at her knees, waiting. "I hear you'll be traveling?" She scratched behind Clifford's ear.

"It's with the National Rodeo League. Doing what I do here, only there." He smiled. "Pick-up man and EMT."

"Always the protector." She said this in a baby voice, totally besotted by Clifford's floppy-tongued smile. "Isn't he? Your daddy is taking care of everyone."

Clifford's tail thumped against the wooden-planked deck.

"I don't know about that." He chuckled. "But it's what I'm trained to do."

"More like what you're wired to do." She sat back, smiling when Clifford rested his head in her lap. "Even when we were younger, you were that way."

"I was?" He sat back in the rocker. "Do tell."

"Okay. One example?" She peered at him.

"You have more than one?" It felt good to be sharing stories with her. There were so many happy ones.

"Oh, Mike. I have so many." She shook her head. "How about Easter. I'd just reached for a golden egg—which, if I recall correctly, was a big deal—and that boy tripped me, took the golden egg, and started picking up all the eggs that had spilled out of my basket." She paused. "What was his name? RJ something?"

"Malloy." Mike chuckled. "RJ Malloy. He's still causing trouble."

"You know what they say, if you love what you do, you'll never work a day in your life. He did love getting into mischief."

Mike laughed—and so did she. "He did and he does."

"Anyway, you came over and told him to make it right or else." She glanced at him. "What would the 'or else' scenario have looked like?"

"I never found out. I was always just that much bigger than everyone else that no one tried to test me." He grinned. "It's a good thing, too, because I don't have much of a stomach for fighting."

She was doing that thing again—like she was looking for something. "RJ not only handed over all the eggs I'd dropped but the golden egg, too."

He nodded. "I *do* remember that."

"Fourth of July. I was really young." She kept rubbing Clifford's head. "I'd never been that close to fireworks before and it was so loud. It felt like the ground was shaking, too. You told Rusty to stay with me and you ran off. When you came back, you had those safety headphones for me to wear. So, I sat there, wearing those too-big earphones, watching the fireworks." She smiled at him. "It wasn't just me, though. You took care of all your friends."

He listened as she regaled him with tales of bandaging up Rusty's leg after he'd fallen out of a tree—into a cactus. Another time, he'd crawled under Brooke's grandma's house to get an entire litter of kittens out before the impending flash-flooding put the little felines in danger.

"I was covered in mud." He chuckled. "I remember my mother's face when I stood on the front porch. She made Rusty hose me off in the back-yard, while it was pouring rain, before she let me into the mudroom."

Eloise laughed, too. "Rusty probably loved that."

"He did. My little brother never passed up a chance to torment me. Come to think of it, that hasn't changed all that much." He shook his head.

"He idolized you."

"That part has changed." He laughed, loving that she was laughing along with him.

"When I first met you two, I was so jealous. You were so close and, being an only child, I'd never had that sort of connection. But you included me, in everything, and I felt like part of the family." She sighed. "Coming to Garrison was always…special."

He nodded. "It's a good little town."

There was another stretch of silence.

"Won't you miss it?" she asked, her voice soft.

"I'm not leaving, not really. I'll be on the road part of the year, is all." But the more he thought about it, the less enthusiastic he became.

"So really, the best of both worlds?" She doubled her pats at Clifford's grumble-moan.

"I guess." His mind wandered, circling back around to where this all started. "You and the kids are going to be okay? With Ted here, I mean?"

She nodded. "I think so. I want to believe it will be. We have some details to work through but we will. If he's going to stay in Garrison, I'm going to be the one to set the terms."

"Good." He liked hearing the resolve in her voice. "That's as it should be, El."

"I'll have to stay vigilant until Ted accepts that." She shook her head, her jaw tightening. "I hate giving the man any more of my time, but it's what I have to do until I know he's on the same page as I am. Right? It's worth it for the kids?"

Ted Barnes didn't deserve the thought and consideration she was giving him. He'd hurt her and disappointed her and the kids over and over. Yet, here she was, figuring out how to fit him back into their lives. If the man hurt them…

Mike gripped the arms of the rocking chair and took a slow, deep breath. She was smart and tough and he trusted she could handle this. It was Ted he didn't trust. El needed his support, not to be burdened with his concerns. "For the kids." He nodded.

"I'm their mom. They come first. And they're counting on me to protect them." She glanced at him. "You know all about that."

"You're a good mother, El-Bell. They don't know how lucky they are to have you as their mom." He swallowed the lump in his throat. "Just remember you've got a whole team of folk here that will support you—and be on standby for you and the kids. I know what you've been through but things are different now. You're not alone, you hear me? People care." *I care*. He cleared his throat, the warmth in her eyes pressing in on him. "And if good ol' Ted gets out of line, let me know and I'll come 'or else' him."

She was laughing again, her whole beautiful face alive and happy. This was how she should always be. El-Bell deserved nothing less than a life of laughter and love—surrounded by people who'd offer her nothing but the same. Now that he had her friendship again, he'd be one of them. She was his first and only true love and he'd always love her. That was fact. But that didn't mean he had to act on it. She'd come to him as a friend. His fool heart would just have to accept that her friendship was more than enough.

CHAPTER TWELVE

AFTER A SOLID night's sleep, Eloise had woken with the sun. Her talk with Mike had given her a sense of calm and purpose. She could do this. She would do this. And she didn't have to do it alone. Her morning walk had only confirmed what Mike had told her. People did care. Not only had the sweet couple from Old Towne Books and Coffee come out with a box of freshly baked blueberry muffins and to ask after Archie, she'd come home to find Miss Patsy Monahan—with her fire-engine red hair—waiting on the front porch with two casseroles and a coloring book.

"How is sweet Archie?" she asked.

"He's doing well." Eloise opened the front door. "Would you like to come in?"

"Oh, no, I wouldn't want to intrude." She hesitated. "But, well, we heard about your unexpected visitor last night and we, the Ladies Guild, wanted you to know that we are one phone call away." She handed an envelope to her. "We girls have to stick together. This is *your* home now, Eloise Green, you and those kids."

Eloise wasn't sure how to respond.

"My own late husband was a no-count excuse of a man that spent more of our marriage in jail than out. When he dropped dead in his cell, it was a relief. I'm not saying the same is true for your ex-husband, I'm simply saying we'll be keeping an eye on him." She patted Eloise on the cheek. "I'm sure we won't be the only ones."

She wasn't about to feel sorry for Ted but... things were certainly going to be interesting.

"That's all I wanted to say." She offered over the two casserole trays and the coloring book. "We'll stop by in a day or two to see what we can do to lend a hand around the house. Your grandfather relies on you at the shop. We might not be able to work magic with flowers like you can, but there's not a one of us in the guild that hasn't raised at least one child." And with that, she spun on her heel and left.

She wasn't going to ignore her grandfather's warning about the guild, but she couldn't help but be touched by Patsy Monahan's confession.

Miss Patsy wasn't the only one who had left care packages. Her grandfather had said it was all part of small-town living but it touched Eloise deeply. She was smiling as she packed Kirby's lunch box, kissed her cheek, and said good-bye to her little girl and her grandfather.

"What are we going to do today?" Archie asked, walking oh so slowly from his bedroom to the couch. He sat, his pillow pressed to his abdomen.

"Rest, rest, and more rest. Doctor's orders. With a little bit more walking each day. How are you feeling?" She sat beside him. "How's your tummy?"

"Better than yesterday." He gave her a thumbs-up.

"That's great news." She smoothed his curls from his forehead. "Make sure you tell me if that changes, okay?"

He nodded. "I'm really hungry."

"I just happen to have some breakfast for you." She smiled. "Blueberry muffins or donuts from Mr. Woodard. Lucille from the café sent a breakfast pizza."

"What's breakfast pizza?"

"Lots of sugar." She chuckled. From the looks of it, it was all cinnamon sugar and a cream-cheese topping.

"Can I have some of that?" He rubbed his hands together.

"A sliver." She nodded. "But you have to eat an egg, too."

"Yes ma'am." He grinned.

"This is for you." She handed him the activity workbooks Miss Patsy had brought with her. "Crosswords and word searches, hidden object pictures, all that sort of stuff. Good exercise for your brain." She helped him get comfortable against the pillows and placed his hugging pillow along his side.

"I don't want my brain to get bored." He opened the book.

"Me neither." She handed him a pencil. "I'll get breakfast going."

"Thanks, Momma." He was already working on the first page.

Eloise turned on the radio, then pulled the eggs from the refrigerator. Her son was recovering from surgery and her ex-husband had showed up in town, but she was surprisingly upbeat. She put a skillet on the stovetop, turned on the gas burner, and added a touch of butter to the skillet.

The house phone rang so she reached for it. "Hello?"

"Eloise? It's Nolan Woodard. I wanted to check in on you and the boy."

"Archie's doing really well, thank you. I'm doing well, too. And thank you for the donuts, too." She cracked an egg into the ceramic mixing bowl.

"Mike said Miss Kirby liked donuts so I was hoping Archie did, too." He chuckled. "You think Clifford and I could come over and visit for a spell later on this afternoon? I was thinking around two or so?"

Would Mike come, too? No, he had a job. Jobs.

"Oh, Mr. Woodard, that sounds wonderful." She added another egg.

"Well, you let me know if you need anything before then. I know you've got your hands full. You have a good morning."

"You, too, Mr. Woodard." She hung up and reached for a whisk—when the phone rang again. He must have forgotten something. "Mr. Woodard?"

"No. Mr. Barnes." Ted chuckled. "Good morning."

Great. Okay. We're doing this already. "Morning."

"I thought you'd like to get together and talk things through." He paused, waiting.

She let him wait.

"Now that I'm here, we can set up some sort of visitation schedule that accommodates your work and *social* life." There was a smile in his voice.

What did that mean? She whisked the eggs before dumping them into the skillet. "It's best if we take it a day at a time."

"Eloise—"

"I'm happy for you to arrange visits here, for now." She wasn't going to budge on this.

"Fair enough." He sighed. "I have a garage apartment at my parole officer's place a few blocks from you."

"Your plan is to stay here?" she asked. He'd yet to say that outright.

"Yes. You and the kids are here. This is where home is." He paused. "I've got a job lined up at Ellis's Feed Store or something or other."

"Oh?" It was Garrison. From what Grandpa said last night, Ted was going to have a hard time finding a job without a local vouching for him.

"Parole officer set it up. Your friend Mike said Earl Ellis was a good man."

Eloise frowned. Mike and Ted had talked? How had that gone? "If Mike says he's a good man, then he is."

"Mike's a decent guy."

Decent? That was almost offensive. Mike was so much more than that. Not only had he listened to her long-winded rant last night but he'd talked to Ted about his new job and reassured Ted about his new boss? Decent didn't do him justice.

"He's very fond of you and the kids." He cleared his throat. "Sounds like he's been a good friend to you for a while so… I guess I need to find a way to like the guy."

She frowned, grabbed a spatula and flipped the eggs. She was not going to talk about Mike with Ted.

"You hold the keys to the kingdom here, Eloise. I just want to be part of your lives again."

"The kids want that, too." She turned off the burner.

"What about us?" He cleared his throat. "No chance—"

"No." She closed her eyes and pinched the bridge of her nose. "No chance. If that's part of your master plan here, this isn't going to work. I need you to understand that. I'm not playing hard to get. I mean it. There is *no* chance of the two of us *ever* getting back together."

"Message received."

"I hope you'll respect my decision." She pulled two plates from the cabinet and divided the eggs between the two. "Can you?"

"I can and I will, Eloise. You can't blame me for asking, though. Once upon a time, we had a good thing."

"I'm going to hold you to that. Respecting what I say, that is. The rest doesn't matter. That part of our lives is over." Ted having a mistress was a deal-breaker for her. There was no recovering or coming back from that. "We will see you at four?"

"I'll be there." He hung up the phone.

She added a piece of dessert pizza to Archie's plate and carried it into the family room. "Breakfast is served."

Archie didn't look up from his workbook. "Almost done."

She smiled and sat the plate on the table. "It's right here waiting, when you're ready."

The day consisted of reviewing the online queries for the Garrison Gardens website—a project she'd taken on when she'd first arrived in Garrison.

The Carmichael-Briscoe wedding had caused all sorts of chatter. There were three serious inquiries. She had to look up where, exactly, Jasperton and Holsom were in relation to Garrison but it might be worth the drive. She'd have to discuss that with Grandpa Quincy.

And, possibly, bringing on some part-time help. Her grandfather had happily been working shorter days since they'd moved. He was seventy-six, so he'd earned it. While she hoped there wouldn't be a lot of days like this in her future, it would be nice to have someone that could cover for both of them so he could rest and she could be with the kids—as needed.

When Mr. Woodard and Clifford showed up, Archie was ecstatic. Clifford happily laid alongside Archie on the couch while Mr. Woodard read to them about King Arthur, Lancelot, and Merlin. Eloise listened in while making raspberry thumbprint cookies for later.

Gretta showed up a little after three with Kirby, homework for Archie, and Levi. Her grandfather walking in ten minutes later was a surprise.

"It was a slow day," he explained, standing in the middle of the kitchen. "I put a sign on the door. It's not like people don't know how to reach me." He sighed. "Besides, I wanted to check in on Archie."

"Aww, that's so sweet." Gretta nodded. "He's

right, Eloise. Everyone knows what happened with Archie."

Eloise poured out four glasses of tea. "You being here early doesn't have anything to do with Ted coming for a visit?"

He shrugged.

"I love you." She smiled at him. "You go sit with Mr. Woodard. I'll bring you some refreshments."

"Will do." He grabbed a cookie and popped it into his mouth. "Mmm-mmm."

"He is precious." Gretta stacked cookies onto a plate.

"He is. But don't let him fool you. He and Mr. Woodard are here for Archie—*and* Ted. You just watch." She eyed the cookie plate. "How about I chop up some apples for the kids, too?"

At three thirty, Mabel and Samantha arrived. At three forty-five, Brooke and Audy showed up with a set of miniature cowboys and horses—that all four kids immediately started to play with.

When Ted knocked at four, conversation came to a stop and all eyes turned his way.

"Hello?" He stepped inside the front door Eloise held open for him, shifting from foot to foot. "Ted Barnes."

"He's our daddy." Kirby jumped up and gave him a quick hug. "We're playing cowboys, Daddy." She sat on the floor, holding up the cowboy and his horse for him to see.

"Hi, Dad." Archie patted the couch beside him. "Come meet Clifford. And everyone."

Introductions were awkward, but Ted managed not to shy away from Audy's very direct eye contact and Mr. Woodard's rather tight-jawed nod of acknowledgment. Once he'd settled on the floor with the kids, Eloise decided it was safe to clean up the mess she'd made in the kitchen.

"Goodness. Did you use every bowl and pan in the house?" Brooke sat in one of the kitchen chairs at the table.

"Almost." Eloise smiled. "Here." She slid another chair around. "For your feet. I don't know about you, but my ankles got lost toward the end of my pregnancies."

"Same." Brooke pointed at her ankles.

Mabel tied on one of the aprons. "I can't wait to have babies."

"Babies?" Gretta laughed. "How many babies are you and Jensen planning to have?"

"Oh, I don't know. Lots, I hope." Mabel grinned.

"You do not have to help clean up, but you can keep me company." Eloise filled the sink with soap and water and got to work.

"How is *this* going?" Mabel pointed at the hallway. "When Gretta told me he'd just showed up, I couldn't believe it."

"Me, neither." Brooke shook her head. "Rusty told Audy. He also said Mike was pretty upset last night."

Eloise stopped scrubbing long enough to look at her pregnant friend. "He seemed okay when I saw him." If she could rewind the last ten seconds, she wouldn't have said those words.

But she had and all three of the women in the kitchen were studying her.

"You saw Mike last night?" Brooke asked, her brows high.

Gretta and Mabel seemed equally expectant.

"I...I wanted to thank him for warning us so I took him some cupcakes." She finished scrubbing the pan. "That's all."

"That was nice of you, Eloise." Mabel took the wet pan and dried it with a clean kitchen towel.

"He's still sweet on you." Brooke said it so matter-of-factly that Eloise turned to face her. "What's that look for?"

"We're friends. That's all." Eloise's chest was heavy.

"I think he wants more than that." Brooke pushed.

"But...he's leaving." Eloise went back to washing the bowl.

"Maybe." Brooke shrugged. "Audy says Mike took this job to fill some sort of hole in his life. Now that you're back, I don't think that applies."

It took her a moment to digest this. She liked Audy's take on things—a little too much. The only way to know how Mike truly felt was to talk to him herself. "I thought you weren't going to do the whole matchmaking thing. Now you sound worse than Mabel. No offense." She smiled Mabel's way.

"None taken." Mabel smiled back. "You really think he's still in love with her, Brooke?"

"It's Mike," Brooke said, as if that explained everything. "Loyal to the end. He was devastated when you stopped visiting, Eloise. And by the fight you two had. He looked for you every holiday for the next two years, at least, hoping you'd show up."

Her heart bounced off her ribcage before twisting one way, then the other. He'd looked for her? Missed her? Then. A long time ago. "That was fifteen years ago," Eloise interjected, refusing to buy into Brooke's romantic notion.

"Fine, don't believe me. He didn't sit in some corner, pining for you. He dated and all, but it wasn't the same." Brooke's sigh was all impatience. "But he is interested now. We've all seen the way he looks at you, Eloise. If you gave him the slightest hint you were interested, Mike would jump at the chance to be with you."

"STICK HORSES?" Mike repeated. Was Tyson pulling his leg? "How many?" He helped Tyson wiggle the ten-foot bleacher board free from its bracket.

"Oh, at least fifty." Tyson ran a handkerchief over his face. "Probably twice that when it's all said and done."

"They want kids to ride stick horses down Main Street?"

"One of the Ladies Guild members saw something about some world record of the largest group of people riding stick horses and thought it sounded like something we needed to add to the Founder's Day Festival." Tyson squinted as he peered up at the sun overhead. "Why'd it get so warm all of a sudden?"

"It's Texas." Mike shook his head. "Stick horses. That'll be something."

"Yep." He looked his way. "You ready?"

"Yeah." On the count of three, the two of them hefted the ten-foot wooden board onto their shoulders, navigated their way down the stands, and stacked it on top of the pile they'd already removed. "Remind me why I'm helping you with this, again?"

"RJ bailed on me, as usual. It's hard finding people to do physical work. And you're a good friend." Tyson rolled his neck. "And you've been laying low for the last few days and this helps out with that."

Mike glared at his friend.

"Sometimes the truth hurts." Tyson chuckled. "No updates?"

"Plenty," Mike grumbled before giving Tyson the news. His father had been dutifully visiting with Archie for the last week. Every time Mike had planned to visit himself, something had stopped him. From Clifford having tummy trouble to taking his father in for a check-up to having to cover two extra shifts at the hospital, he'd had to make do with his father's updates or whatever he heard around town.

From what he'd heard, Ted Barnes was visiting his kids every day after school, doing good work at the feedstore, and on his best behavior in general. It was good news—as long as Eloise kept her eyes open. She would. He didn't need to be there or to protect her, she was smart and more than capable of handling things. But that didn't stop him from worrying anyway.

"Is that what's eating at you?" Tyson opened his water bottle and gulped down the contents.

Yes, it was eating at him. After Eloise's visit, his heart and his head had been in two very different places. His heart wanted Eloise to be his. His head told him friendship was better than nothing. "You're seeing things." He ran a handkerchief along the back of his neck.

"You want to try that again?" Tyson waved as Audy opened the arena gates. "Before Audy and the high school rodeo team gets here and sees you all riled up like this."

"I'm not riled up," he snapped.

Tyson tried not to laugh, but it didn't work. When he stopped, he said, "I'm sorry, man. I've never seen you this way. Ever. I know it's not funny but…it sort of is."

"I'm going to saddle Chuck." Mike was officially out of patience and energy.

"Hold up." Tyson caught up to him, keeping stride. "Why don't you ask her out? On a date. Her ex can watch the kids, can't he? He must be good for something?"

Mike wasn't sure if Tyson's suggestion was genius or ludicrous. Friends didn't go on dates.

"I'd think, before you leave, you'd want to at least try?" He held up his hands. "I'll stop now, before your face gets any redder."

But Tyson's words caught up with him and Mike stopped walking. "You could hire him."

"Hire who?" Tyson's brow creased in confusion.

"Ted Barnes." He shook his head. "The man said he was looking to find a place of his own. Might help him do that."

"You want me to hire your... Eloise's ex-husband? It's weird enough that he's working for Dad." He scratched the back of his head. "You want him to work here, where you'll see him on a regular basis? Are you feeling all right? Dehydrated, maybe?"

"You need help. He needs a job." Though it was hard imagining Ted out here, sweating and doing physical labor. "And I'm leaving. Soon." Probably. Maybe.

"I guess it might work. I don't need someone full-time." Tyson still looked confused. "But Dad's working him pretty hard. Just remind me why you want to help this man?"

"It's not about him, it's about—"

"Eloise."

"No. His kids." Mike hung his head. "If he's trying to be a better man for his kids, I don't see the harm in helping him. If I'm being honest, I kinda like the idea of him doing physical work—sore muscles, calloused hands, sweating, and being miserable." He grinned.

"When you put it that way." Tyson chuckled. "I can get on board with that. Tell him to stop 'round the store and ask for Dad."

He wasn't going to go looking for Ted Barnes, but he'd find a way to relay the information to him. "I appreciate that."

"Does it make us even?" Tyson nodded at the stack of rotted boards.

"No. Not even close." He put his hands on his hips. "You owe me."

"I figured as much."

"Mike," Rusty called out, his horse trotting across the arena. "Hey, Tyson. You look like you've been up to something."

"Work." Mike stretched. "I'll go get Chuck ready."

"You look worn out." Rusty's horse, Briar, followed the fence line. "You up for this?"

"Not really. He's in a temper, too," Tyson answered for him.

"What's going on?" Rusty asked.

"Are you asking him or me?" Mike glared up at his brother.

"Oh." Rusty frowned. "Tonight'll be fun."

Mike muttered all the way to the corral where Chuck was waiting. He saddled the horse, grumbling the entire time. "Sorry." He ran a hand along the horse's neck. "You're not the problem here." He patted the horse, put his boot in the stirrup, and swung up and into the saddle. "Let's go." With a gentle squeeze, he and Chuck cantered from the corral, between the holding pens, and up and around the arena to the side entrance and paused. The Garrison Ladies Guild was here? From the looks of it, *all* of them.

"What's all this?" Mike asked as he and Chuck pulled alongside Rusty.

"You got me. They wanted to talk to Tyson." Rusty tipped his cowboy hat back on his head. "I'm going to mosey to the other side of the arena."

Mike let Chuck trail after his brother's horse, Nugget, until the expanse of the arena separated the Woodard brothers from the group of women. Staying out of their line of sight wouldn't guarantee they'd escape without notice, but it couldn't hurt.

"How's Dad doing?" Mike drew Chuck to a stop.

"I think hanging out with those kids is good for him. I mean, I'm not happy poor Archie had to have surgery but Dad sure has enjoyed reading to him." Rusty glanced his way. "King Arthur."

Mike chuckled. "His favorite."

"Don't look now, but I think Martha Zeigler is… Yep, she's heading this way." Rusty sighed in exasperation. "Should we make a break for it?"

Mike chuckled again. "She'd only hunt us down later."

Martha Zeigler waved and waved until the two of them had no choice but to ride halfway across the arena to meet her. "Boys."

"Miss Zeigler," they said in unison.

"You know Hattie is off on her honeymoon for another week and there's been a little problem with Career Day, over at the elementary school."

"What sort of problem?" Mike already felt the hair along his arm pricking up. She was about to ask him for something.

"We had a couple of speakers back out." She pointed at Mike. "You, being an EMT, would make an excellent speaker."

Yep, he'd called it. "I appreciate that, Miss Martha—"

"Good. You can thank Eloise Green for the idea." Miss Martha almost smiled. "She was the one who suggested you—after she agreed to come and participate herself."

Mike's objections faded away.

"I can count on you?" Miss Martha's steely gaze was fixed on his face.

"Yes, ma'am." There was a chance he was going to regret this.

"Good." She gave Mike the date and time and headed off without another word.

"You know she just manipulated the tar out of you, don't you?" Rusty shook his head.

"I do." There was no point denying it. Miss Martha had played the Eloise Green card and he'd gone all in.

"There are probably easier ways to spend time with the woman." Rusty's hands rested on the pommel of his saddle.

"Eloise or Miss Martha?" He glanced at Rusty, then laughed.

Practice went off without any worrisome incidents. Alice Schneider got her pinkie finger caught in the saddle cinch lacing but, after icing it, it turned out to be a sprain and not a fracture.

After practice wrapped up, he loaded Chuck into the horse trailer. Tonight, he wanted his own bed—not the lumpy couch in his father's parlor. He swung by his father's place for Clifford and to give his dad a quick hug before making the drive out of town to his little homestead.

Garrison wasn't a noisy town, but there was quiet in the country that couldn't compare. When he'd found this piece of property, it'd just clicked. Yes, the place was a bit of a drive the two times a day he came by to check on the horses, and the house had a heap of work that needed to be done but, little by little, it was coming together. The barn had been his first priority. His horses, Chuck, Goliath, and Mars, needed shelter from the Texas elements. If it wasn't the brutal heat, it was a flash flood, a tornado—even an occasional ice storm.

The walk from the barn to the house wasn't long, but it was plenty long enough for Clifford to run circles around him until the dog was panting.

They were headed inside when the crunch of gravel signaled someone arriving.

It was the Garrison Gardens van. Once the van was parked and the driver door opened—it was Eloise.

"I come with apology cookies this time." She carried the foil-covered plate up the path to where he stood.

"What did you do?" He smiled. "Did it already happen? Or is it going to happen?"

"Oh, well, I'm not sure." She winced. "I don't supposed Martha Zeigler has reached out?"

"She has." Mike took the plate. "She showed up at the stockyards during the high school rodeo team practice. I was trapped."

She smiled. "I'm sorry."

"It's fine. If Hattie were here, she wouldn't have asked—she'd have told me I was doing it." He shrugged. "Come to think of it, I'm not sure Miss Martha asked, either." He lifted the plate.

"You didn't have to drive all the way out here. You could've called."

"Right." Her smile dimmed. "Of course. I should have called." She patted Clifford's head. "I'll get out of your hair—"

"I wasn't trying to chase you off, El." His hand clasped hers. "You're welcome anytime—for as long as you like."

She was staring at their hands. "You're sure?"

He nodded. There was that lump again—making it impossible for him to say a thing. Now was the perfect time to say something.

Her eyes met his. "Are you sure I'm not intruding?"

He nodded.

"Okay. I didn't know you lived out here." She slid her hand from his and turned, inspecting the uneven porch they stood on. "I guess I assumed you lived with your dad. I'm not sure why? Maybe because I live with my grandfather?"

"I needed a place for the horses." He nodded in the direction of the barn. "Dad's yard was too small."

She laughed. "Horses? I'll have to tell Kirby— she'll be so impressed. Samantha Crawley has her becoming quite the horse fanatic."

"You should bring her out and let her go for a ride. Goliath is a gentle giant."

"Goliath, huh? We'll have to see." She tucked a strand of hair behind her ear.

"You want to come in? Have an apology cookie or two? The place isn't much to look at but it's got good bones."

"No, I can't stay. The kids aren't even in bed yet. I left Grandpa alone with them." She glanced at the van, hesitating. "Mike...the apology cookies aren't the only reason I'm here."

"No?"

"I...I..." She swallowed, her gaze bouncing between him and the van. "Did I say or do something to make you upset? You sort of disappeared after I dumped everything on you—it was too much—"

"El, no. I wanted you to talk to me. I still do." He understood then. "I'm not going to shut down on you. It guts me that that's what you thought."

"I used to tell you everything and... Well, old habits die hard." She stared at the ground. "You don't have to be my friend because of everything I dumped on you... Out of guilt, you know? I really am okay. I was just having a...moment." She shook her head. "I was a bit of a mess." Her attempt at a laugh was forced.

"We all are, El." He stepped closer. "This week got away from me—work, mostly. But I'll be honest with you and say I wasn't sure I should come by."

She stared up at him, a V between her brows. "Why?"

Every time he looked into her eyes, he saw something new. The shades of gray and gold and green were mesmerizing. "Like you said, old habits are hard to break. I've always been protective of you, El, even though I know you don't need protecting. This whole thing with Ted is something you have to do without me trying to get in the middle of it. I figured giving you space was the best way to do that."

"Okay." Her eyes swept over his face as she smiled. "But this is too much space. For me, anyway. I...the kids like having you around." Her cheeks were a dark red as she patted Clifford on the head and took a few steps down the path toward the van. "I'll see you later."

He nodded, watching as she drove away. "I can't be sure, Clifford, but I think El-Bell just said she was missing me?" And he, his heart, was oh so happy.

CHAPTER THIRTEEN

"AT THIS RATE, you'll be able to go back to school next week." Eloise reached into the back seat and patted Archie's knee. "Isn't that great news?"

"I guess." Archie pushed up his glasses. "I like hanging out with you, though."

She smiled at him. "You know, it's been nice having special time with you."

He beamed up at her.

"How about an early lunch date? Just me and you?" They were passing the Buttermilk Pie Café and it was almost eleven o'clock.

"I am getting hungry." Archie's enthusiasm for food was impressive. He'd inhaled bacon, eggs, a blueberry muffin, and a piece of toast not three hours ago.

She pulled into one of the spaces, parked, and turned off the ignition. "You're sure you're up for it?"

He nodded. "Dr. Rowe said the only thing I can't do is pick anything heavy up. She did say to add more steps."

The doctor had said that, but Eloise wasn't sure walking from the car to a table and back again was what the good doctor had in mind. She came around to help Archie out of the car. He was healing, yes, but he was still tender around the spot where they'd gone in for the laparoscopic procedure.

"Well, if it isn't the one and only Archie Barnes and his lovely momma," Miss Lucille greeted them. "How are you feeling?"

"Better." He smiled up at the older woman. "That breakfast pizza you made was yummy. I had to hide it from Kirby so she didn't eat it all."

Miss Lucille cackled at this. "I'm glad to know you enjoyed it—your little sis, too. You find a table you like and we'll see what we can whip up for you this morning."

"Yes, ma'am." He pointed. "Look, Momma, there's a booth."

"A booth it is." Eloise loved that he still held her hand. It wouldn't be too long before he'd be too old for such things.

"Hey, Archie. How'd your doctor appointment go?" It was Nolan Woodard.

"Dr. Rowe says I'm on the mend." He smiled. "How are you feeling, Mr. Woodard?"

"Doc Johnston told me the same. I figured I'd have some lunch to celebrate. You're welcome to join me, if you like?" Mr. Woodard indicated the empty chairs. "My boys are supposed to be joining me soon but I'm sure they won't mind."

"No, thank you, sir." Archie looked up at her. "Mom and me are on a date. We don't get to do lots without Kirby, so we're doing this."

"Is that so?" Mr. Woodard's smile was huge. "You go on and enjoy yourselves then."

"Thank you for the invitation." Eloise nodded his way and let Archie lead her to the booth he'd spotted. "That's very sweet of you, Archie."

He nodded. "Yeah."

Which made her laugh.

"What are you going to eat?" Archie started reading over the menu. "I am hungry."

"You said that before." Eloise was still smiling.

"Let's see." It was the softest whisper, but Eloise could make out what was being said.

"Yes, that's the woman." A woman whispering. "And that's the boy. He just had surgery."

"We should go check on him, poor dear." Another woman, also whispering.

Eloise didn't have time to prepare herself for the arrival of two older women. They stood at the end of the booth, wearing looks of equal parts sympathy and curiosity. One, she recognized as Dorris Kaye. The other was tall and thin, with a piled-up white bun on the top of her head. It looked more like a beehive, really.

"Good morning," the tall woman said. "We were

on our way out but wanted to see how the young patient is doing. Archie, isn't it?"

"I'm doing real good." Archie smiled.

"I'm happy to hear it. Miss Patsy, a dear friend of ours, was telling us what happened. You've had quite the time of it. Surgery. Hospital stays. Your daddy getting out of jail and coming to see you." Dorris Kaye breezed through her speech as if she was talking about the weather or her favorite kind of ice cream. Not that she'd pulled the pin on a grenade and was standing back to watch.

"You poor thing." The tall woman directed this at Eloise. "It must be hard, your little boy hurting and the talk about your ex-husband being a criminal."

Eloise was so flabbergasted she couldn't come up with a thing to say. But one look at Archie changed that.

"And your grandfather. All this scandal." The first woman kept going. "He's always been such a proud sort."

"Quincy Green is proud as punch of his family," Dorris argued. "Besides, it's not their fault."

Archie's knuckles were white as he held the menu—but his little face was whiter. "Momma, what are they talking about?"

It was painfully quiet then.

"Hey." Archie slid from the booth and stared up at the women.

Both women looked like they had bitten into

something sour—their lips puckered, their brows shot up, and acute looks of discomfort covered their faces.

"You're being rude." Archie was upset. "Making up stuff about people is even worse."

"Archie, come on." Eloise reached for his hand.

"No, Momma. They need to apologize." Archie stood his ground. "You said to use nice words, not mean ones. So, you two should say you're sorry."

"Well, I never." The tall woman clutched her beaded purse to her chest. "And where are your manners, young man?"

"Why should I use them on you? You don't have any." Archie was red-faced. "Are you going to apologize? If you do, I might forgive you."

Dorris Kaye's mouth opened and closed but no words came out.

"Eloise?" It was Mr. Woodard. "Can I help with something?"

"Mr. Woodard." Archie pointed at the women. "They came over and started lying and saying mean things about me and Momma and my dad, too."

"Is that so?" Mr. Woodard straightened, his gaze unyielding and frigid. "Don't you two have something useful to do today? You've done more than enough here."

"And…" Archie shook his head. "Lying is bad."

"I do not lie." The woman sniffed. "But your father does, young man. It looks like your mother does, too." With that, she brushed past Nolan Woodard and out the front door.

"Oh dear," Dorris Kaye murmured, giving them all a panicked look before hurrying after the other woman.

Eloise steered Archie back to his seat. "Archie?" She dipped the corner of a napkin into the water glass and patted his forehead and cheeks.

"Don't let those old crones get to you, Archie. My father used to say that people who gossip have nothing in their own lives to talk about so we should feel sorry for them." Mr. Nolan's voice was low and gentle.

She glanced up, to thank him, only to find Mike and Rusty standing close by. How long had they been there? Mike's nod was answer enough.

"Momma." Archie's voice was soft. "Was that lady right? Was Daddy in jail?"

"Archie." Mike crouched by the seat. "Let's go home. Clifford's in the truck and he's been missing you. How about you, me, and your mom go home and we'll figure out food later?" Mike ruffled her son's hair. "Sound good?"

Archie nodded.

Eloise wasn't certain how Mike managed to get them out of there without further incident but she was grateful he did. Archie was too dazed to react as she buckled him into his booster seat in the van. He barely responded when Clifford jumped up on the bench seat beside him. Eloise's hands were shaking so much that she handed Mike the keys and climbed into the passenger seat.

Not a word was said all the way home.

There was a vise on her chest—squeezing the air from her lungs and compressing her heart. As much as she hurt, it couldn't compare to what her son was feeling.

There was only one thing she could do. Call Ted. He needed to be here for his son—to help him understand. If he could.

"We're here." Mike jolted her from her thoughts.

Sure enough, they were sitting in front of her grandfather's house.

"I'll get him?" Mike offered.

"Yes, please." She unbuckled her seatbelt. "I need to make a phone call."

Mike's jaw clenched but he nodded.

It felt like she was moving in slow motion. Every step from the van to the telephone inside weighed a ton. Her brain bounced back and forth through all the "if only" situations that could have prevented this from happening.

She gripped the house phone, one ring. Then two. "Ted?"

"What's wrong?"

"Archie." She sucked in a deep breath. "People…he knows. About jail. He's upset. You need to come and explain this to him. Now. I'm going to call his old therapist—see if she has any helpful tips."

"Okay." The line went dead.

She hung up the phone and headed back into the family room.

Mike sat on the couch with Archie cradled against his chest. He was so small, so young... She'd wanted to do what was best for them. Instead, she'd wounded them.

She was too anxious to sit and too unsteady to pace so she leaned against the doorframe. She shot a quick text to Archie's old therapist and shoved her phone into her pocket.

The thump-thump of Clifford's tail on the floor was the only sound. The big dog was leaning against Mike's knees so Archie could give him long, slow strokes down the neck.

The way Mike was looking at her didn't help. He was disappointed in her, too. She hadn't just lied to her children, she'd been lying to everyone.

She couldn't cry. She couldn't fall apart. She couldn't.

When Ted opened the door, Eloise didn't know how to feel. She was relieved he'd actually come and he was stepping up. And yet, the fear and uncertainty on his face reminded her there was no easy fix to this.

"Hey, bud." Ted sat beside Mike, ignoring the giant man and focusing only on his son. "Archie. Talk to me, okay?"

Archie shook his head.

"Okay." Ted sat back against the couch, pressing his hands to his thighs. "We can sit. Whenever you're ready—"

"Did you lie?" Archie leaned forward, his little face twisted with anger. His voice wobbled then broke. "*Why* did you lie, Dad?"

Clifford whimpered, putting his paw on Archie's leg.

Eloise pressed a hand to her chest, pain rising from inside. She'd give anything to make this better.

"I did. I lied to you and your sister and I'm sorry, Archie." Ted met Archie's gaze. "I was wrong. I was so wrong, son."

"It's bad to lie." Archie sniffed.

"It is. I was ashamed of what I'd done. I didn't want you and Kirby to be ashamed of me, too. I didn't want you two worrying about me, either." He took a deep breath. "But that doesn't make my lie okay. Nothing does. I know that. I've never been so sorry."

Archie stared at him for a long time.

Eloise waited. Archie had every reason to be angry and reject Ted—reject her. Instead, her sweet, loving boy reached for his father.

As soon as Ted had Archie in his lap, Mike slowly pushed off the couch—Clifford hopped up to take his place. The dog leaned against Archie and scooted down until he'd rested his head in her son's lap.

Mike was watching the exchange, a curve tugging up one corner of his mouth. This big man with broad shoulders and a protective spirit had no reason to stay... Why would he? This was a nightmare—hers, not his. She couldn't leave, but he could. He would. Now. And she had no right to ask him to stay—

Mike crossed to her. His warm eyes swept over her face. "Breathe." He took her hand and gently pulled her down on the loveseat beside him.

"But you..." she whispered. "You don't have to stay. I understand—"

"I'm here for you, El." He slid an arm around her waist. "And for Archie."

She nodded, so grateful for him.

"I know it's hard to understand, Archie." Ted took a deep breath. "Adults mess up and make mistakes, too. I lied to you and I made your mom keep it a secret. She didn't want to, she told me to tell you, but I was too scared."

Archie peered at her.

"I'm so sorry, Archie. More than you'll ever know." She could barely breathe.

"You and Kirby are the most important things in my life." Ted's voice was unsteady now. "I was afraid to lose you."

"You can't lose us. We are your kids." Archie's irritation was oddly comforting.

"I know." Ted nodded. "I know that sounds silly. It is silly. I made a stupid mistake. A big one. A bad one. And I am so sorry."

Archie took a deep breath. "I wanted that mean old lady to be wrong."

"What mean old lady?" Ted glanced at Eloise for clarification.

"The one that came over and talked to me and Momma at the restaurant." Archie shook his head. "I didn't want her to be right."

"I know. And you can be mad at me for putting you in that position. You should be." He smoothed Archie's hair back. "But I'm not going anywhere. When you want to talk or stop being mad at me, I'll be here."

"You're not leaving?" Archie's expression was far too grave for someone so young. "You won't go traveling or go back to jail?"

"I won't go anywhere." Ted winced. "I promise."

Eloise gripped Mike's hand. As much as she wanted to believe Ted, she had her reservations. Yes, he was saying the right things, but there was no guarantee that would last. And if it didn't and Ted left, Archie would learn how it felt to have a promise broken. It was horrible. *This* was horrible.

She concentrated on the feel of Mike's hand running up and down her back. She could fall apart later—not now.

"Can you go now?" Archie asked. "And come back after school? Later, maybe."

It took a minute for Ted to mask his hurt. "If that's what you want."

Archie nodded and eased himself onto the couch beside Clifford. Clifford waited for Archie to get settled, then lay beside him.

"Okay." Ted sniffed. "I'll come back." Eloise could see how shattered he was when he glanced her way. "Eloise. Mike." He walked out, gently closing the front door behind him.

"Oh, baby." Eloise couldn't bear it. Mike helped her up and steadied her before she hurried to Archie. "What can I do?"

"Can Clifford stay for a while?" Archie rolled onto his side and draped his arm across the dog. "He makes me feel better."

"Yes, of course." She adjusted the pillows and spread a light fleece throw over him. "Do you need anything else?"

He closed his eyes and shook his head. "Stay close, Momma?"

Eloise sat on the floor beside the couch and smoothed her fingers through Archie's hair. She didn't know what would happen next or if there was anything she could say to make this easier. But this, staying close, wasn't just for him—it was for her, too. There was nothing and no one that needed her more than Archie did, right now.

"Want some tea?" Mike asked. "Coffee?"

"No." She couldn't stop herself from adding, "Stay close? Please."

"That's the plan." He smiled.

This was hard and messy, all of it. Ted, the

lie, the talk around town, and being in love with Mike—who was leaving soon. All she could do was take things day by day. Today wasn't the day to worry over her potential heartbreak. Today was the day to be strong for her son and grateful to Mike. So, that's what she'd do.

MIKE PEERED OUT the front window of Quincy Green's house and bit back a curse. A car was pulling up in front of the house. Even from this distance, Patsy Monahan's fire-engine-red hair stuck out like a sore thumb.

Archie and Clifford were piled up on the couch, sound asleep. Eloise had finally dozed off in Quincy's recliner. This is what they needed. Rest. Peace and quiet.

He slipped out the front door and down the front path to see Patsy wasn't alone. Martha Zeigler was with her. He never thought he'd have to face off against Martha Zeigler but today might just be the day. *This day just keeps getting better and better.*

"Don't you scowl at me, Mike Woodard," Miss Martha huffed as soon as she'd stepped out of the car. "I get that you're standing guard but we come in peace."

Mike didn't budge or relax.

"Like you, I'm furious. Furious, you hear? And I will never call either of those women my friend again." Martha's voice was all indignance. "Not ever. Dorris can't keep her mouth shut but she's harmless. I can't say the same for Pearl Johnston. She's got a mean streak in her. As you saw yourself." She cleared her throat and pulled herself upright. "Patsy and I are here representing the Ladies Guild. Is there anything we can do for Eloise or to help with damage control?"

"Eloise is a good girl—she and her boy didn't deserve all that. How are they holding up?" Patsy Monahan peered around his shoulder.

"They're both sleeping." No matter what the two women were saying, he wasn't going to invite them in. Eloise didn't need more negativity and neither did Archie. "It's been a real humdinger of a morning for them both and they need some peace and quiet."

"Of course they do." Patsy stepped forward. "Is there anything we can do? Anything they need?"

He'd been asking himself that very thing for the last couple of hours. "Clifford's taking the edge off all this for Archie—that boy loves the dog. But Eloise?" He chose his words with care. "She can't seem to catch a break and she needs one."

"Don't you go underestimating that woman." Martha shook her head. "She's weathered fiercer storms than any of us."

"I know she's capable. I'm saying she shouldn't have to go through this." He paused then, looking Martha Zeigler in the eye. "There is something you can do. You can stop the talk. All of it.

Nothing about Eloise, her kids, or her ex. At least, nothing *juicy*—or gossipy."

One of Martha's eyebrows rose. "And just how do you propose I go about that?"

"I don't know, Miss Martha. But if there's anyone that *can* do it, it's you." He sighed. "Eloise came here for a fresh start. I don't think that's too much to ask."

"No, it's not." Martha Zeigler glanced at Patsy. "We'll see what we can do, won't we?"

Patsy nodded.

"Before we go, I have one question for *you*." Martha was frowning. "Have you come to your senses yet? About this job? About leaving your home and family?" She nodded pointedly at the Green house.

Mike chuckled. "I've always admired how upfront you are, Miss Martha."

"There is no point in wasting time." She wagged a finger at him. "Are you going to answer me?"

He took a deep breath. "I'm considering my options."

Martha Zeigler smiled. "Fine. Just know the best options are here in Garrison." She patted his arm and nodded at Quincy's house. "Like I said, no point in wasting time. Neither of you are getting any younger." She sniffed. "Now, I promised Dwight I'd make him an apple pie for dessert and it's not going to bake itself." With a wave, she headed back to Patsy Monahan's car. "Come on, Patsy."

Mike managed to slip inside without waking Archie, but the recliner was empty. No Eloise. He tiptoed into the kitchen to find her making coffee. She'd turned the radio on low, the mournful strains of an eighties rock ballad filling the room.

"I can do that, El."

She jumped, dropping the canister of ground coffee and spilling its contents all over the floor. "Oh, no." She stared down at the mess.

"I'm sorry. I didn't mean to scare you."

"You're scary quiet." She glanced at him, slightly accusatory. "I didn't hear a thing."

"I didn't want to wake Archie." He scanned the room. "Broom?"

"In the pantry." She pointed behind him. "I was making us some coffee but…"

He smiled at her. "I appreciate the thought."

Her answering smile was fragile. She gripped the kitchen counter behind her. Tension rolled off her in waves. "I can't relax. I need to *do* something."

He forgot about the broom. "How about a dance?"

"Dance? Here? In the kitchen?"

She didn't argue when he took her hand in his. "Yep." He placed his other hand against her back. "I don't see why not." He started dancing, guiding her effortlessly across the coffee-sprinkled floor.

He liked the way she fit in his arms, the way they moved together with such ease.

"There's coffee all over the floor." She glanced down. "And we're in my grandfather's kitchen."

"First, a lot of dance halls put down sawdust so people don't slip. Coffee could do the same? Second, you can dance anywhere if the mood strikes you." He steered her across the room, then circled back around. "We'll clean it up. But this is a good song for dancing." It was a cheesy song—the sort of song that would instantly make him change the station. But, somehow, he knew every word to it.

"It is?" She stared up at him. "I wasn't listening."

He spun her. Her startled laugh was all the encouragement he needed to keep right on dancing. "How's the song go?" He stumbled over the lyrics, but he did try.

"Faithfully." Eloise grinned. "You like this song? *You* listen to Journey?"

"I didn't say I liked it." He shook his head. "I said it was a good dancing song. It's one of those songs everyone knows. An earworm."

"True." She nodded. "My mother loved Journey. She had all their albums. Vinyl records."

Mike chuckled and spun her again.

When she laughed, her whole face lit up.

"You're beautiful, El-Bell." The words slipped out as a whisper but, holding her close this way, there was no chance she hadn't heard. He was okay with it, though. She should know she's beautiful.

She sighed. "You need to get your eyes checked, Mike Woodard."

"I have twenty-twenty vision, Miss Green." He shook his head. "That means my vision is perfect. If I say you're beautiful, you are beautiful."

"Maybe the coffee fumes are getting to you?" But she was smiling and there was a pink hue on her cheeks.

He'd made her blush? And it looked good on her. "Is that a thing?" He cocked his head to one side. "Pretty sure it's not."

"Whatever." She grinned as he spun her twice. "Are you trying to make me dizzy?"

"No. I'm trying to make you smile. It's good for you. When you smile, your brain releases endorphins and serotonin that make you feel good." Where that random tidbit of knowledge had come from, he didn't know. But it was true.

"You're saying this is a medical treatment?" Her brows rose.

"Kirby did say I'm a doctor cowboy." He shrugged. "So, as an official doctor cowboy, I'm prescribing at least one *real* smile a day. All you have to do is find something that makes you happy. Today, it's dancing in the kitchen. Easy."

"You know the song is over, don't you?" But she didn't stop swaying along with him or let him go.

He didn't care about the music. At the moment, Eloise was in his arms and smiling up at him. She was right where she belonged. And, from the way her gaze dipped to his lips and she swayed into him, he thought—maybe—she was feeling the same way.

She stepped closer, her hands sliding up his chest to go around his neck.

He drew in a ragged breath and bent his head. Her lips were so soft, so warm, and clinging to his.

"Momma?" Archie stood in the kitchen door with Clifford sitting at his side. "What are you doing?"

"Archie." She slipped out of his hold. "I—I dropped the coffee and…it spilled."

Clifford's nose was working overtime.

"Stay, Clifford." Mike held out his hand for the dog. "The last thing you need is a bunch of caffeine in your system."

Clifford groaned but lay down on the floor, sniffing the air.

Archie pushed up his glasses and looked back and forth between the two of them. "What were you and Mr. Mike doing?" He wasn't upset so much as curious.

She shook her head but she was smiling. "Mike was trying to cheer me up with a dance."

"Oh." Archie sat in one of the kitchen chairs,

staring at Mike with a stern frown. "It didn't look like dancing."

"I'll clean this up," Mike said, pulling the broom from the pantry.

"That's nice. Can we take Clifford for a walk, Mr. Mike? Dr. Rowe said I should walk more and you said Clifford likes to take walks."

"I think that's a great idea," Eloise answered. "I'll find my shoes—"

"Just me and Mr. Mike and Clifford." Archie rested his elbows on the table. "For man-to-man talk time."

Mike stopped sweeping and looked at the boy. It made sense that Archie had some things to discuss; he just hoped he was the right one the boy should talk to. He wasn't a father. He didn't have experience at this sort of thing. But, if Archie wanted him, he'd try. He could only hope he'd figure out the right things to say.

Eloise turned to him. "Do you mind?"

"Nope." Mike finished sweeping the coffee grounds into the dustbin. "I think some man-to-man time is just what the doctor cowboy ordered." He emptied the dustbin into the trash.

Eloise rolled her eyes. "Okay, then. Take it slowly, please. You're still recovering, Archie. When you get back, I'll make us some lunch."

"Okay." Archie climbed out of the chair. "Let's go, Clifford."

Clifford trotted after Archie, his tail wagging.

"Thank you," she whispered. The smile she gave him had his heart tripping over itself.

They were halfway down the block before Archie said anything. And what he said wasn't what Mike had been expecting.

"Mr. Mike, are you my mom's boyfriend? Levi says you are and that I'm the man of the family and I'm supposed to decide whether you are a good boyfriend or not." Archie frowned up at him.

Mike had nothing. He was speechless.

"Kirby thinks you'd be a good new daddy." The boy shrugged. "And Clifford would be ours, too, and I'd like that." The dog heard his name and trotted back to Archie's side. "I think Clifford would like that. Wouldn't you?"

Clifford wagged his tail.

"I think that means yes." Archie smiled.

Mike was still pondering the whole "new daddy" comment.

"Grandpa Quincy says you're moving. Does that mean we have to move, too? I like it here. Mostly." He glanced up at him. "Dad's here, too. I know he was in jail but he's not a bad guy..." Archie stopped walking and looked up at him. "*Is* he a bad guy, Mr. Mike? Bad guys go to jail, don't they? Not good guys."

Mike was scrambling to keep up. He wasn't going to speak for Ted or address Ted's incarceration, but he respected Archie's questions. Hopefully, Ted would, too. "I bet your father will tell you what you need to know." He paused, then added, "It's important to trust your instincts, too, Archie. You'll know what's best."

"Okay. I know I'm supposed to be mad at Dad, but do I have to be mad at my mom, too? She was just keeping a promise to my dad. She didn't want to lie." Archie started walking, a little slower this time. "I don't want to be mad at either of them."

"Archie." Mike rested a hand on the boy's shoulder. "That's up to you. You don't have to be mad. But if you are, that's okay, too. Today has been a lot. It's okay to feel a lot. It's okay to feel numb, too. Sometimes it takes time for our feelings to catch up."

Archie nodded. "You know a lot about feeling things, Mr. Mike."

"I do?" Mike chuckled. "More like I don't mind talking about feeling things. It's not easy, is it? To share what's going on inside. Sometimes, it's hard to find the right words to say how you're feeling."

Archie nodded again.

"When you find the words or want to talk, you've got me and your mom and dad and Grandpa Quincy to share with."

He smiled up at Mike. "That's a lot of people."

"Yep. A lot of people love you." He loved Archie. He loved Kirby. And he loved Eloise. If he had it his way, they'd be a family. All he had to do was get up the nerve to say as much to El-Bell.

Miss Martha was right. Everything he wanted or needed was here. Eloise was at the top of his list.

"Clifford, too?" Archie patted the dog. "He loves me?"

"Clifford, too."

"Can we go back, now?" He rested a hand on his stomach. "My tummy's growling."

Mike chuckled. "Well then, let's go." More importantly, he wanted to talk to Eloise. If she didn't care for him the way he cared for her, he'd take the job. But if she did... If she did, he'd be the happiest man in Garrison, Texas.

"Mr. Mike." He paused before they reached the front steps. When he spoke, there was an edge to his words. Fragile and desperate and even a little scared. "Levi said I'm supposed to decide about you and Momma... And I have. Dad broke Momma's heart and they got divorced. Grandpa said you broke Momma's heart so you can't be her boyfriend. She should be with someone who won't break her heart." He frowned as he shook his head. "I know she's pretty and nice and cuddles good, but you can't have her. My instinct says no and you said to listen to that. I am. No more kissing and stuff." He walked up the porch steps. "That's my man-to-man talk." He shrugged. "But you can be her friend. Ours, too. Okay?"

Mike stood there for a second, his happiness fading. Archie didn't want him with Eloise. After everything that little boy had been through, how could Mike put his wants above Archie's? Maybe, in time, Archie would come to see things differently? Maybe he wouldn't. The only thing he knew was his heart was hurting something fierce when they stepped inside.

CHAPTER FOURTEEN

"STICK HORSE PRACTICE." Eloise read over the flier Kirby had given her. *They needed to have a practice for this?*

"Yep. Samantha said there would be stick horses for all the kids—one for me and Archie, too. And we get to ride them down the street and wear a cowboy hat and say 'yeehaw.' That's what real cowboys say." Kirby took a deep breath. "Samantha said she's going to do a dance, too. Can we go see her dance, Momma? Did you know Miss Gretta is a dance teacher?"

Eloise nodded. "I did." She stuck the flier to the front of the refrigerator and went back to stirring the pasta on the stovetop.

"I want to go to dance school like I used to." Kirby spun in the kitchen. "I like dancing."

"Then you should go to Miss Gretta's," Grandpa Quincy said, helping Archie set the table. "I think that's a fine idea."

"Do I have to ride a stick horse?" Archie was not in the least enthused. "I'm too old."

"You don't have to do anything you don't want to do." Eloise smiled. "Besides, it might not be a good idea to jostle your stomach around."

Archie stepped back, looked at the table, and counted the plates. "Yep. That's five."

"Me and Grandpa and Momma and you and Dad." Kirby nodded. "When is Daddy going to be here?"

"Any time now." Eloise checked the clock. If anyone had told her Ted would be sitting down to dinner with them, she'd have laughed. Now, it was happening.

Considering how rough the morning had gone, there'd been surprisingly little drama since Archie and Mike had returned from their walk. Mike had seemed a little distracted, but Archie had been in a great mood. Mike had been unexpectedly called in to the hospital, but he'd left Clifford to "watch over Archie" for him. Clifford was taking his duty seriously, trailing after Archie or Kirby wherever they went.

"Can Clifford have pasta?" Kirby asked, sitting in the middle of the kitchen floor beside the dog.

"I'm not so sure about that, Freckles. But Mr. Woodard is dropping by some food for him so he won't be hungry." Grandpa Quincy pulled the pitcher of iced tea from the fridge.

"I can't believe we get to have a sleepover with Clifford," Kirby squealed, then lowered her voice. "I can put bows in your hair tonight."

The knock on the door sent Kirby running. "I'll get it."

Grandpa Quincy stood in the kitchen doorway to watch.

"Daddy." Kirby's voice carried down the hallway. "You're here. Guess what. Mom's making chicken fettucine 'cuz it's my favorite. Guess what else? Clifford is having a sleepover 'cuz Mr. Mike had to go to the hospital so we get to babysit."

"All that, huh?" There was a smile in Ted's voice. "He must trust you and Archie a lot to put you in charge of his dog."

"He does." Kirby came skipping back down the hall. "It's Daddy."

"Eloise. Mr. Green." He gave them both a warm smile. "Hey, Archie."

Eloise held her breath as Archie turned to greet Ted.

"Hey, Dad." Archie hugged him. "You look dressed up."

"I came from work." Ted gave him a big hug. "It was a good day."

"A job?" Kirby frowned. "Here or far away somewhere?"

"Here." Ted smiled. "I'm staying right here."

"Oh goody." Kirby went back to Clifford. "Did you hear that, Clifford?"

Clifford wagged his tail.

"Dad wasn't gone because of work, Kirby." Archie sat on the other side of Clifford. "He was in jail."

Kirby frowned at Archie. "Are you sure?"

"Yep." Archie nodded.

"Is he right?" Kirby asked Ted.

"Well…" Ted cleared his throat. "Yes, he is."

"Oh." Kirby kept on frowning but didn't say anything else.

"Are you a bad guy, Dad?" Archie's question flooded the room with tension. "I was talking to Mr. Mike and he said you'd tell me what I needed to know. He said I should trust my…instincts. He also said it was okay if I wasn't mad at you or to be mad and sad. He said I could feel all of it."

Ted smiled. "He's right."

"He knows lots about feelings and emotions and stuff." Archie shrugged. "Are you a bad guy, though?"

For a minute, Eloise thought he'd run. There was a look of total panic on his face. Then, he took a deep breath.

"I did some bad things," he managed.

"Did you wear a mask and have a gun?" Kirby's frown grew. "Did you hurt people?"

An odd strangled sound escaped Ted. "No, Freckles. I've never held a gun in my life. The only masks I've worn have been on Halloween."

Eloise couldn't blame him for avoiding the last question. It was the most complicated of them all. Had he physically hurt anyone? Hopefully, no.

But by taking away people's retirement or education funds, he'd taken people's choices and plans away. Eloise knew firsthand how much that hurt.

"Where are you working?" Grandpa Quincy asked. "What's the position?"

"Office manager for Ellis Family Feed & Ranch Supply." He nodded. "Mr. Ellis wants me to update his software and filing system."

"Earl Ellis is a good man. Hardworking but fair." Her grandfather rubbed his jaw.

Her worlds were colliding, and she wasn't sure how to feel about it. Ted. In Garrison. Working for Mike's best friend's father? It was beyond weird that Ted and Mike had run into each other—that they'd had a conversation.

"Eloise?" Ted interrupted her thoughts. "What's this about a stick horse parade?"

Dinner was an overall pleasant event. Archie and Kirby seemed to have put aside the whole jail thing—for now, at least. After Eloise explained how horrible their morning had been, Grandpa Quincy was on his best behavior. Ted even stuck around to take care of the kids' bedtime routine.

"Need a hand?" Ted came into the kitchen.

She was elbow deep in soapy water. "I'm almost done."

"Perfect timing on my part." He grinned. "It could have gone worse. Telling the kids the truth."

"It was pretty bad." She took a deep breath. "But you're right. It could have been worse." She finished washing the pan and placed it on the drying rack. "I'm glad it's out. No more secrets."

"Deal." His blue eyes met hers. "While I'm handing out apologies, I'm sorry for putting all of this on you."

"Thank you." She wiped her hands on the kitchen towel. "I'd offer you some coffee but we're out."

"Yeah, Archie mentioned something about you and Mike Woodard dancing in here—with coffee all over the floor?" He crossed his arms over his chest. "Sounds like a real party to me."

She laughed. "It was…something." Something special. But then, Mike made everything better.

"That's a look." He sighed.

"What look?" She glanced around the kitchen to make sure she hadn't missed anything.

"That one. The one you get when Mike Woodard's name comes up." He pushed off the counter.

"Oh, please." She led him from the kitchen and into the family room. Grandpa Quincy was snoring in the recliner.

"I'll go," he whispered. "Can I borrow you for a couple of minutes first?"

Eloise turned on the porch light and followed him out. "What's up?"

"I'm not sure how to say this." He walked slowly along the path to the gate. "I just… I want you to be happy, Eloise." This far from the porch, it was too dark to see his face and know what he was after.

"I do, too." She wasn't sure she wanted to know where he was going with this.

"What's the deal with you and Mike Woodard?" He cleared his throat. "Are you two—"

"Friends?" She couldn't keep the irritation out of her voice. "Yes. We are friends. That is all. He's leaving Garrison." She took another deep breath, forcing the words out in the hopes that she'd believe them. "Poor guy keeps getting sucked into my drama. It's not fair. Once he leaves, he can get on with his life and I can get on with mine, and the whole town can find some other pair to match up. One that makes sense. Not one that hinges on some tween romance from fifteen years ago." It didn't make sense, not one little bit. But that didn't matter. She loved Mike Woodard and his leaving would destroy her still-fragile heart.

Ted was staring at her, shocked. "I didn't mean to get you upset, Eloise."

She'd overreacted. Ted hadn't meant to send her on some tirade. How could he have known? No one knew how she really felt and that was the way it was going to stay. "I... It's been a long day." She sniffed.

"I know." He opened the gate, then stopped. "The thing is, it's okay if you do care about him."

"Ted." Her eyes were burning—she was going

to cry. *No.* She was *not* going to cry over her first love to her ex-husband.

"If he makes you happy, then go for it. The kids love him. He seems like a genuinely good man. And the way he looks at you makes me think he'd treat you the way you deserve to be treated. The way I should have treated you."

She shook her head, her voice higher than she'd intended when she spoke. "Even if I do love him, I'd never ask him to stay. I couldn't do that. If this is something he wants, then I should want it for him. Not ask him to give it up for…this." She gestured at herself. "I couldn't live with myself."

"This—" he gestured to her "—might be what he wants most. You're right about giving the people you love what they want, but how can they know what they want if they don't have all the information?" He shook his head. "You should tell him how you feel, Eloise. If you don't, you'll regret it." He sighed. "Goodnight. I'll stop by tomorrow after school? If that's okay?"

"Sounds good." She closed the gate and lingered there until the chill in the air had her walking back to the house. When she slowly opened the front door, it was to find Grandpa standing inside the door. "You heard?"

He nodded. "You okay, Sassy?"

She shook her head and sat on the couch. "I will be."

"You want to talk about it?" He sat forward.

She shook her head.

"Are you sure?" He sighed. "I hate to agree with that Ted but, on this, I do. You gotta tell Mike how you feel."

"I'm scared." She wiped at the tears sliding down her cheeks. "I'm scared he'll reject me. Or… or what if he stays and winds up resenting me for losing out on this opportunity? It will hurt to lose him, but it's the least painful option."

"Oh, Sassy. Don't you let fear win. Not now. What if none of that happens and you're just happy? You and Mike and the kids—happy together?"

Archie stepped out of the dark hallway. "Do you love him, Momma? Mr. Mike?"

"Oh, sweetie, I'm so sorry I woke you up." She wiped away her tears, hurrying to calm Archie.

"Momma, do you love Mr. Mike?" Archie grabbed her arm and tugged.

Eloise couldn't read the expression on her son's face.

"I told him he couldn't be your boyfriend because he was mean to you before. I told him you can be friends only." He took a deep breath. "But I didn't know that you wanted him to be your boyfriend or I would have told him it was okay. I like him. I don't know if I want him to be our new daddy like Kirby does, but maybe. And I do like Clifford."

Eloise hugged him close, smiling. "Oh, Archie. I love you."

He nodded. "I want you to be happy. I don't want you to be stressed and needing a spa day all the time."

"I don't want you to worry about all of this." She eased her arms from Archie and smoothed his hair from his forehead. "Everything will be okay, I promise. You don't need to worry about me or Mike or your dad anymore. You need to sleep and get better." She stood and took his hand. "Come on, let's get you back to bed."

She sat by his bed long after he'd fallen asleep. Her sweet, tender boy—too burdened with worry at such a young age. She needed to be more careful around him, so he wouldn't take on problems that weren't his to carry.

Like me and Mike. She couldn't imagine how the conversation between Mike and Archie had played out, but she'd find out. And, maybe, she'd find a way to tell him how she really felt. If he loved her, she'd never have to protect herself from him. She could love him with her whole heart and he'd keep her, and her heart, safe forever.

HE HADN'T SLEPT in days. He couldn't. His dreams were disjointed. From proposing to Eloise to Archie running away to losing El and her kids in a dark fog. Others had him holding Eloise close, and in the next he heard Archie's determined little voice telling him to leave his mother alone.

He'd been avoiding Eloise ever since Archie had put him in his place. He didn't know how to face her without telling her he loved her. He did. So much. He'd been planning to spill his heart to her as soon as they'd come back from their walk… But, after Archie's heartfelt objections, he'd swallowed his declaration and left with a heavy heart. There was no way, no way, he could go against Archie's wishes. He'd never willingly hurt that little boy.

"How's it look? Everything secure?" Rusty was wearing that expression again. He was worried but smart enough to leave well enough alone.

"Yep." He double checked the team harness, making sure both horses were secure and comfortable. "You're good to go. Have fun." He tipped his cowboy hat at his brother.

"Be safe." Rusty called out, releasing the brake on the wagon and clicking his tongue. The horses responded, keeping a slow and steady pace to the other side of the square and the children and families waiting for the hayride.

Mike smothered a yawn as he strode across the street to where he and Terri had parked the ambulance.

Somehow it was Founder's Day. Sure, the last week or so had been a blur, but he couldn't believe it was almost over. Now that his father had been cleared to return to normal activity, Mike was clear to leave. In two days, Garrison would be a speck in his rearview mirror and he wasn't too torn up over it.

"You can go do whatever it is that you…do." Terri waved her plastic spoon at him. "You've got your radio. I can call you if something comes up."

"I'm good." He leaned against the side of the vehicle.

"If you say so." Terri went back to eating her yogurt. "Did you know there are about a million videos of cats doing things on here?" She held out her phone. "Cats knocking stuff off of things. Cats giving hugs. Cats riding dogs. Cats' meows that sound like a person talking." She shook her head.

"I didn't know that." Mike yawned.

"People have too much time on their hands." Terri kept scrolling. "I have an extra yogurt in my lunch bag, if you want it."

"I'm good." He stared across the courthouse lawn.

"Mike." Terri put her phone down. "Don't take this the wrong way, but you've been about to fly off the handle for the last week. I know I didn't do a thing to get you this riled up, so who did? I feel the need to give them a piece of my mind."

Mike shook his head. "I don't know what you're talking about."

"Yes, you do. I'm not going to pussyfoot around,

either. And you know it." Terri jumped out of the ambulance and stood beside him. "Last week, you were smiling and happy and thinking about staying put and now you're all grouchy and spitting nails and ready to leave town tomorrow."

Mike sighed.

"Did you tell her?" Terri offered him a piece of gum. "Did you tell Eloise she was the bread to your butter?"

Mike waved the gum away. "I'm going to take a walk."

"Good. That's what I said." She waved him away. "Turn on your radio."

"Yeah," he called back, then adjusted his radio. Terri might be a pain in the rear but she was a good medic. He'd miss working with her.

He sat on one of the wrought-iron benches that skirted the courthouse lawn. He didn't want to get close enough for anyone to think he was looking for company. But he was out of luck.

"Mike." Forrest Briscoe was all smiles as he shook his hand.

"How was the honeymoon?" He held up his hand. "Forget that. I don't want to know. When did you get home?"

Forrest sat beside him. "About a week ago? Give or take a day. Hattie jumped right back into work and, well, you know, things had gotten sloppy around the ranch since I left. For all their complaining about how controlling I am, they can't seem to manage without me reminding them of what needs to get done."

Mike chuckled. "Nice to know you're needed."

"I guess." He slumped back against the bench. "Your dad looks good. Saw him in his frontier settler getup serving cider to folk in front of the shop."

"According to Doc Johnston, he's as fit as a fiddle." Which meant there was no reason for Mike to stay. His father had a clean bill of health and Rusty was up to speed on helping the high school rodeo team—he'd made sure he'd covered his responsibilities.

"You look a little rough around the edges." Forrest was giving him a hard look.

"Yeah, well, I'm feeling a little rough around the edges, so let's not talk about it." Mike leaned forward.

"Okay." Forrest didn't say a word. The longer he didn't say a word, the more wound up Mike felt.

"Ever feel like things are closing in on you?" He sat back.

"A time or two." Forrest grinned. "Mostly it was me putting off something I didn't want to do. Once I did it, things went back to normal."

"Or maybe I'm just ready to get out of Garrison." He shrugged.

"Maybe." Forrest adjusted his cowboy hat. "I wouldn't know about that. I did hear from Webb, though. He's doing well. Hasn't blown off anyone's fingers or toes yet—or his own, for that matter."

Webb was one of Forrest's younger brothers. When he'd enlisted, the rest of the Briscoes had taken it hard. They were a tight-knit family, after all.

"Glad he's doing well." Mike meant it. "Any plans to visit soon?"

"It'll probably be a year or so." Forrest sighed. "Not soon enough, that's for sure. Missing out on Audy and Brooke's baby being born and, likely, Mabel and Jensen's wedding. The sort of things you don't want to miss out on, you know?"

Mike nodded. He'd miss out on those things, too.

"Forrest." Hattie was waving at him. "There they are. Mike." Hattie kept on waving. "Get over here, you two."

"The wife calls." Forrest chuckled. "You might as well come or she'll march over here after you."

Mike pushed off the bench and followed Forrest. There were too many voices and smiles and people he'd rather avoid than talk to.

"Mike. You're just the man I was looking for. Someone has been trying to find you." Hattie stepped aside. "Said something about having her first hayride with you?"

"Mr. Mike." And just like that, Kirby was hugging him around the knees like her life depended on it. "Where have you been? I looked all over for you. You didn't come."

Her words were like little pinpricks on his heart. He'd missed Kirby's hugs and her sweet smiles—like the one she was giving him now. "I've been working nonstop, Freckles." It was a flimsy excuse, but it was the only one he had.

"You've been working for a long time." She took his hand and started pulling him through the crowd. "Mr. Woodard brings Clifford over to visit, but it's not the same as when you visit. I miss you, Mr. Mike. And Archie misses you, too."

That was the thing about Kirby, she had no guile. She said it like she saw it and he'd missed that. So much. He squeezed her hand, too many words clogging his throat. He knew people were watching them but chose to ignore it.

"Are you being a doctor cowboy tonight?" she asked, inspecting his uniform.

"I am." He chuckled.

"Archie, Archie!" Kirby yelled. "I found him. Look!"

Archie had no right to look so happy to see him.

"Mr. Mike." He came running. "Momma thought maybe you'd already moved, but I told her you'd say goodbye first. I was right. You're here."

"Should you be running like that, Archie?" He didn't want the boy hurting himself.

"Oh, I'm all better. Back at school, too." His smile faded. "You look kinda sad."

"I'm fine." He was sad. He'd been so determined to keep distance from El, he hadn't thought about how that would make the kids feel. It'd been selfish—and cruel.

"He's been working lots and lots and lots," Kirby explained.

"That's about right." Mike managed a smile. "Maybe even more."

"Grandpa said you need to take better care of yourself." Archie was frowning. "You have an important job and you need to get plenty of sleep and drink lots of water—"

"And eat healthy food. Yep. You do. My teacher says so, too," Kirby finished. "Momma said you took her on her first hayride, so you have to take me on my first hayride." Kirby was still holding his hand. "Samantha says I don't have to be scared of the horses but they're really big. Will you go with me, please, Mr. Mike? Please?"

How was he supposed to say no to that? He couldn't. "I'd like that, Kirby."

"Yay." She tugged him along behind her until they were standing at the end of the line. "I found him so I can go." Kirby hopped up and down. "See?"

Samantha clapped, just as excited. "Hurray."

Mike was beginning to think he might actually enjoy himself. The line waiting for the next ride wasn't that long so the wagon wouldn't be too crowded. Samantha and Mabel were fine. For Archie's sake, he'd put up with Levi Williams and his loud grandfather, Buck. His gaze shifted to the first person in line and his chest caved in. Eloise? He'd hoped she was working at Garrison Gardens or…anywhere else.

"Mike." Eloise sounded downright happy to see him.

"Evening," he murmured, refusing to meet her gaze.

"This should be fun." Buck Williams chuckled. "This is a festival. We're supposed to be festive and celebrate. You know, laugh and smile and all that."

Mike was having serious second thoughts about this hayride.

"I'm having fun. Mr. Mike is having fun." Kirby was swinging his arm with hers. "Are you having fun?"

"I am." Samantha nodded.

The girls started listing off all the treats they'd enjoyed during the day's festivities so far. Mike would be popping antacids if he'd eaten half the stuff they had. Archie and Levi were far more interested in what would happen if one of the horses pooped while they were on their hayride. Since Mike had nothing to add to either conversation, he got to stand by awkwardly and wait.

"Audy said you've been working extra shifts."

Mabel sighed. "You're no use to anyone if you're dead on your feet."

"What happens if someone calls 911 and there's no one answering, Mabel?" He shrugged, doing his best not to look Eloise's way. It was hard not to. She looked extra pretty in that green sweater. When she turned his way, his gaze fell. "I'm just doing my job." But he had volunteered for the extra shifts before anyone else could.

"Time to load up for the hayride." Audy stood beside the wagon, offering a hand to anyone who needed help getting up and into the wagon. "Mike. You look like you could definitely use a hand."

Mike sighed and pulled himself into the wagon.

"I'm so excited." Kirby squealed and climbed into his lap. "Are you excited?"

He nodded. "I am." Kirby's energy was hard to resist.

"Are you ready, Kirby?" Eloise sat in the hay beside him. "Do you need to sit on Mr. Mike's lap?"

Kirby nodded.

He smiled at how quickly she answered. "It's fine." If she wanted to sit on his lap, she could sit on his lap.

"Archie, don't lean over the edge." Eloise's mom voice had Archie scooting away from the back of the open wagon. "Thank you."

"After the hayride, there's going to be a stick

horse parade around the courthouse." Kirby relaxed against him.

"Is that so? Are you riding one?"

Kirby nodded. "A pretty red one. It has long sparkly hair. Guess what I named him." She stared up at him, her eyes wide and her whole face excited.

He had a pretty good idea what the name was, but he decided to have some fun. "Red?" Mike scratched his chin. "Tomato? Beet?"

"No." Kirby giggled.

"No? Hmm, Watermelon?" He paused. "How about Ladybug?"

She kept giggling. "No. I named my horse Clifford."

"That's a good name." Mike was laughing right along with her.

Somehow, his eyes got tangled up with Eloise's and he felt like he'd been punched in the throat. She looked happy. Why shouldn't she be? His heart was the one that had been shattered, not hers. And, as hurt as he was, he didn't wish that on her. El deserved to be happy. So did her kids. Even if he wasn't a part of that.

The longer she stared at him, the harder it was to hold on to all the things she'd said.

"Here we go." Kirby clutched at his shirtfront and held on tight. "We're moving."

"Rusty's driving. My brother. He's a good driver. You don't need to worry." He patted her back.

"Oh, I'm not worried." Kirby smiled up at him. "Momma said you always kept her safe so you'll keep me safe, won't you?"

He forced himself to smile. "Count on it, Freckles." A quick glance assured him Eloise was watching the two of them. She'd said that? He glanced at Archie, strengthening his resolve.

Kirby giggled over each bump in the road. When Rusty turned a corner, she and Samantha squealed in unison. About halfway around the courtyard, Levi got upset that neither of the horses had pooped but Archie said it could still happen. Mike had no choice but to relax and find the whole thing amusing. Yes, he was aware of every little thing Eloise said or did, but he could enjoy everything anyway.

When the wagon came to a stop, the sighs and groans of disapproval made him smile. This was what these festivals were all about. New experiences, laughter, and having fun. There was no denying Kirby had had all three. Archie might be disappointed no horse poop appeared, but he'd still had a good time.

He scooped Kirby out of the wagon, then Samantha, too. He offered his hand to Mabel and, gritting his teeth, did the same for Eloise. He wished her touch didn't get to him. He wished he could ignore the jolt that raced up his arm and settled in his chest, but it was impossible. Even after he'd let go, he could feel her hand in his and the pull that tied him to her.

"I've got to get back to work." He crouched by Kirby. "But I had fun, Freckles."

"Will you watch me in the stick horse parade?" She stared up at him.

"Of course." He pointed. "I'll be right over there. Make sure to wave as you ride by and I'll be looking for you and your red horse."

"Okay." She threw her arms around his neck and gave him a tight hug. "Thank you for protecting me from the big horses, Mr. Mike."

"My pleasure." He was smiling as he stood.

"Mike." Eloise tucked a strand of hair behind her ear. "Do you have a minute? I know you're working, but I need to talk to you."

What more could she possibly have to say? He'd had a good time with the kids, and he'd rather leave on a high note. "Now's not a good time." He turned and bumped into Ted Barnes.

"Mike." Ted's ready smile disappeared when he saw his face.

"Ted." He tipped his hat and brushed past the man. He'd played nice long enough. Now, he was done. He quickened his pace as he headed back to the ambulance.

"Have fun?" Terri asked, glancing up from her phone long enough to see his face, sigh, and go back to scrolling. "I'm telling you, Mike, you gotta fight for what you want."

He didn't bother looking at her. "Wake me when the stick horse parade starts, will you?" He tilted the passenger seat back and covered his face with his hat. A nap wouldn't stop his heartache but, maybe, it'd make his world feel a little less bleak.

CHAPTER FIFTEEN

AFTER A NIGHT of tossing and turning, Eloise woke up with a splitting headache. She made pancakes, drank coffee, and tried to keep up with the kids' giddy recount of the festival the night before. They'd had a wonderful time. She, on the other hand, had not.

All night long, she'd tried to make sense of how Mike had treated her. It was obvious he didn't want to talk to her—let alone look at her. Something had to have happened. But what? The last time she'd seen him, he'd seemed happy. Or maybe that's what she wanted to see? Knowing today was Mike's surprise going-away party only compounded the headache—and heartache.

"What's burning?" Kirby asked.

Eloise stared down at the blackening pancake. "Oops, this one got a little overdone." She scooped the scorched pancake aside and poured out a fresh one.

"Want me to take over?" her grandfather offered.

"No." She forced a smile. "Got a little distracted."

She waited for the last pancake to brown, added it to the serving platter and carried it to the table.

"Are you distracted because today is Mr. Mike's party?" Kirby set about cutting her pancake into bite-size pieces. "Is he really leaving, Momma? Why?"

"He's got a very exciting new job." She used as much enthusiasm as she could muster.

"A real job?" Kirby's voice lowered. "Not jail?"

"Yes, a real job." Eloise tapped her daughter on the nose. "Mr. Mike has a real, good job that lets him take care of lots more people. And that is what makes him happy so we should be happy for him."

"We get to go to the party, too?" Archie asked, swirling his bite of pancake in syrup.

"Yes." Grandpa Quincy added another dollop of syrup to Archie's plate. "Once the party is underway. You don't want to show up the same time as the guest—it'll ruin the surprise."

"Oh no," Kirby moaned. "I don't want to ruin Mr. Mike's surprise."

"Remind me to pick up a new O-ring for the bathroom sink." Grandpa Quincy served himself another pancake. "The thing was dripping all night. Waste of water."

"Mr. Woodard's bringing over Clifford soon, isn't he? I can go if you tell me exactly what to get." Eloise poked at her food, then sat back. "I'm not really all that hungry so I can go whenever."

"You need to eat, Momma." Kirby pointed at her with her fork. "Or you'll get a tummy ache."

Eloise obediently ate half of her pancake—it felt like lead in her stomach. While she left them to tidy up the kitchen, she walked down Main Street to Old Towne Hardware and Appliances. Grandpa Quincy had called ahead so Mr. Woodard could have the part ready and waiting for her.

But it wasn't Mr. Woodard inside, it was Rusty.

"Eloise." He nodded. "Dad said you were stopping by." He handed her a brown paper bag. "There's a washer in there, too." He opened his mouth, then closed it.

"Thanks."

"Yep." He nodded, barely glancing her way.

"Rusty…" She swallowed. At this point, she had nothing to lose. "Can I ask you something else?"

He nodded.

"About Mike?" She held her breath. "Please."

Rusty ran a hand over his face. "I guess it depends on the question."

"What happened? Did I do something?" She shrugged. "I tried to talk to him last night but he…he practically looked right through me. Now he's leaving and I just… I don't want things to go left unsaid."

He went from wary to sympathetic. "Ah, Eloise, I wish I knew. He's been in a real bad mood ever since the other night. I figured you two had a fight or something. All he said was he didn't want to talk about it. So we didn't talk about it—and he's been in a snit ever since." Rusty adjusted the stapler and pen canister by the register. "I can't say for sure what upset him, but I'm pretty sure it has something to do with you."

"If I don't know what I did, how can I fix it?" She shook her head, more frustrated than ever. Surely, this wasn't over what Archie had said? "He's not leaving until I know what happened. Is he working?"

"Yes, ma'am. Last shift with the hospital."

As tempting as it was to search him out now, barging into the hospital or chasing down his ambulance was wrong. "Then I'll have to wait until this afternoon. At his farewell party."

Rusty chuckled. "I can't wait to see how that goes."

She grabbed the plumbing supplies and walked out of the shop. The whole way home, she tried to make sense of what Rusty had told her. How could he be upset with her when she hadn't done or said a thing to him? He wouldn't invest in gossip. And even if he'd heard something, he'd have come to her to sort it out. If he wouldn't come to her, she'd go to him.

That left Archie. Mike, being the big-hearted wonderful man that he was, was keeping his distance because that's what Archie told him to do. She couldn't decide if she adored him all the more for taking her son's words to heart or irritated that he hadn't come to her to talk himself.

Her mind kept spinning. If she dared give in to the over-the-top romantic idea that was taking shape as she walked, she might be able to sort out what the problem was and tell him what was in her heart all at the same time.

By the time she reached her grandfather's house, she was resolved. She wasn't going to let last night throw her off. Yes, Mike had been a bit cold—and distant. He'd seemed hurt. Maybe even a little angry. And it was up to her to set the record straight and, hopefully, fix it.

She could do this. She should do this. If she did, he'd know how serious she was. Besides, if she started second-guessing things, she'd never get the words out. As soon as she got home, she called Brooke.

"I need your help with Mike." She took a deep breath. "Audy's, too?"

"You've got it. What do you need us to do?" Brooke laughed. "It had better be something sweet and romantic because I'm feeling huge and miserable and need some cheering up."

"I'm hoping it will be both." She swallowed. "There's a chance Mike won't want any part of it but…" She was not going to go there.

"Audy, honey, you owe me five dollars." There was a smile in Brooke's voice. "So, what's the plan?"

Three hours later, Eloise stood under the massive canopy of erste Baum's branches having serious second thoughts. "This is dumb."

"This is sweet," Gretta argued, stooping to adjust a teddy bear.

"I look dumb." Eloise reached up. "I have a clip in my hair."

"You look exactly like you did in the pictures." Mabel held up one of the old photographs. "This is the most romantic thing I think I've ever seen."

Eloise wasn't sure if this was genius or pathetic. "It's too late now."

"Breathe." Brooke sat, fanning herself. "Seriously, Eloise, you're stressing me out."

Eloise took a deep breath. "Sorry. No stress."

"It's okay." Mabel tapped one of the long ribbons that hung all around them. "This is beautiful. All of it."

The idea had been one thing. Yards of ribbon hung from the branches overhead. Each of the ribbons had dozens of photos of her and Mike pinned to them. She'd added lights and flowers, too. Mabel and Gretta had gone above and beyond to find props that fit some of the photos. A teddy bear in a tuxedo. A large, light-up Santa. Some Easter eggs scattered around in the grass. She'd even done her hair to match their *wedding* photo.

"It's too much." She sank into the chair. "You were there last night, Mabel. I've never seen him so…so…upset." Upset with *her*. He could barely look at her.

Mabel sat beside her. "Maybe he was so over-come by your beauty and, knowing he couldn't pull you into his arms and declare his love for you, he was…mad."

"I'm sure that was it." A nervous giggle slipped out. "I'm sorry I commandeered your good-bye party, Mabel."

"Are you kidding me? This is the most roman-tic thing to happen in Garrison—"

"Since my wedding?" Hattie joined them, hold-ing a large baker's box.

"That's exactly what I was going to say, Hat-tie." Mabel winked. "This is the most romantic thing to happen since your wedding."

"I can't take any credit for that either." Hattie's laugh-snort had them all relaxing. "That was all Eloise, too. Just like this." She shook her head. "If the man can't see the love and thought you've put into this, good riddance." She smiled at Elo-ise. "But it's Mike so he will see it."

Eloise had to hold on to her hope, not her fear. If there was anyone worth risking her heart on, it was Mike Woodard.

"You're right." Brooke nodded. "I, for one, can't wait to see him get all moony-eyed over this."

"I hope so." Eloise's gaze swept over the photos and ribbons again. "Or he's going to think there's something wrong with me."

That had them all laughing again.

Eloise smoothed every tablecloth, checked every extension cord, straightened each bouquet, and tried not to check the time every five minutes. The closer it got to Mike's arrival time, the more people arrived—and the more absurd her decorations appeared. She'd committed and there was no going back. After she'd told Mike her hopes and dreams for the two of them, it was up to him. All she could do was hope that once Mike knew how much she loved him, it wouldn't be a going-away party after all. Just a party.

"WHAT ARE WE doing here?" Mike was having a hard time keeping his eyes open. His last shift hadn't been quiet. From a semitruck accident on the interstate to a kid getting his head stuck between the stair railings, they'd been on the go for a solid ten hours. He'd showered before he left the hospital so he could fall face down into bed as soon as he got home. Unfortunately, his father needed something done before that.

"He said they borrowed that old wheelbarrow for the festival yesterday. We just need to pick it up." Rusty parked the truck on the far side of erste Baum Park.

"You got this." Mike rested his head against the seat and tipped his cowboy hat over his eyes.

"The thing weighs a ton, Mike." He slammed

the driver's door closed and, seconds later, opened the passenger door. "I need a hand."

Mike glared at him. "Hurry up then." He stepped out of the truck, rubbed his eyes, and followed Rusty down the path and around erste Baum.

"Surprise!" The cry was so loud and unexpected, Mike jumped back.

"What in the Sam Hill?" He frowned, beyond bewildered. All the faces. The balloons and streamers. A banner that read, Good Luck & We Will Miss You was strung up over some tables. He glared at his brother.

"It wasn't my idea." Rusty held up his hands. "But, you know, maybe try to be nice since all these people are here for you."

Mike tried, he did. He couldn't have been more surprised… Until he was standing face-to-face with Eloise.

"Come with me for a second?" She took his hand and led him to the other side of the tree.

"El—" He pulled his hand from hers but the damage was done. "What is all this?" All around him were pictures of him and Eloise. "What…" He broke off, marveling over the stuffed bear and the Easter eggs and a hundred other tiny things that cut so deep. He drew in a deep breath and faced her. "What is all this?"

"This is us." She cleared her throat. "This is me, trying to tell you how I feel… And, maybe—

possibly—going overboard." She fidgeted with the clip in her hair.

He stared at the clip, his jaw muscle working. She looked a lot like she did when he'd "married" her here all those years ago. "I don't understand."

"I…I love you." She swallowed. "I love you more than anything, Mike."

"You what?" He couldn't have heard that right. "But…"

She stepped forward, taking his hands in hers. "I made a mess of things, I know. I was… I am so scared." She rested a hand against his cheek. "I'm sorry I fought so hard to hold on to my heart. It's yours. I want you to have it—if you want it?"

"Am I dreaming?" That's the only way this made sense.

Her sweet smile sent his heart into overdrive.

"No." She cradled his face in her hands. "I love you, Mike."

Her touch was real. "But…" He shook his head. "We can't, El. I can't." And it was tearing his heart to bits.

"Because of Archie?" She slipped her arms around his waist. "He said he wasn't so sure about you being his new daddy but, if I wanted you to be my boyfriend, he was okay with that because he wanted me to be happy."

Mike swallowed. "He said that?"

She nodded.

"And you love me?" When he drew her into his arms, she was soft and warm and alive.

"I don't want you giving anything up, though. We can make it work with your new job… If that's what you want—"

"What I want is right here, El-Bell. In my arms." He shook his head. "It might not have made sense to love you as much as I did when we were younger, but I did. And the truth is, I never stopped loving you."

Her breath hitched and she leaned into him. "You do love me?" she whispered.

"I do." Mike kissed her then. A soft kiss—that turned into something more. He held on to her with everything he had, breathed her in until he was wide awake. This was no dream. This was real. This was everything he could ever want and more. He broke off to whisper, "I'm glad Archie changed his mind."

"You'd leave?" She shook her head. "Because of Archie?"

"I didn't want to. I avoided you for fear I'd break my word to him." He shook his head. "But, El, we had a man-to-man talk. I don't think I've ever had a more serious man-to-man talk in my entire life. That boy was speaking from the heart. Who am I to break it?"

"Oh, Mike." She smiled up at him. "You are too good to be true. Loving and kind and supportive and…well, you're you. And I love you. I can't lose you."

"El-Bell, you won't." His arms tightened around her. "I'm in this all the way. I breathe easier when you're with me, don't you know that?"

"That you make everything better?" She smiled. "I know that." She stood on tiptoe and pressed a kiss to one cheek. "I know I love you." She kissed his other cheek. "So much."

"That's all that matters." He rested his forehead against hers. "I'm so glad you came back, El-Bell."

"I'm so glad I came home to you, Mike." She ran her fingers along his jaw. "And since Archie is okay with you being my boyfriend and Kirby is okay with you being her new daddy, there's nothing to worry about."

"Not a thing." He kissed her again. "We've got this, El-Bell."

"We do." She tilted her head back. "But, before we go tell everyone you're staying, I'd love another kiss. Or two."

* * * * *